A White Bird Flying

By Bess Streeter Aldrich

NATAL PUBLISHING LLC

ARS LONGA, VITA BREVIS

CHAPTER 1

It was the first Tuesday in August. The Nebraska heat rolled in upon one like the engulfing waves of a dry sea,--a thick material substance against which one seemed to push when moving about. Two women, standing by the back porch of a house in the north end of Cedartown, commented wearily.

"Hot."

"Awful."

The one, gingerly holding between her thumb and forefinger an egg which she had borrowed from the other, made feeble attempts to pull herself away.

"Too hot to bake. . . ."

"I'll say."

After an interim of dull silence, she effected the threatened withdrawal, and started down the path toward her home. But she had not gone a dozen feet until she stopped, turned back, and called to the other in the low mysterious tones of the chronic tale-bearer: "For the land sakes! Look there. There goes Laura Deal. I do believe she's goin' over to her grandmother's house the same as she always did."

And the other, in equally semi-excited voice (it takes little to bring on an animated conversation in the north ends of the Cedartowns of the country): "Yes, sir! She is. Did you ever! And her grandmother just buried day before yesterday."

For a time the two stood watching the young girl pass by and down the elm-shaded road, but when she approached the gate of the house to the north and turned toward it, they were looking discreetly at a petunia bed. Their conversation, however, was not of those funnel-shaped blossoms.

"She's turnin' in the little gate and goin' up the path between the cedars. Do you suppose she's goin' *in* the house?"

"On my word, I believe she is. And they ain't a soul there . . . not a soul. Christine Reinmueller even took the cat home with her when she come over to feed the chickens."

"That twelve-year-old girl . . ."

". . . is the oddest."

"You'd think she'd kind of . . ."

". . . at her age."

"Just day before yesterday . . ."

". . . *buried.*"

Neither one made a complete sentence nor waited for the other to speak. Their conversation was rather a duet, the parts similar and in perfect rhythm.

"She's got the key . . ."

". . . all by herself."

"Well, on my soul!"

". . . kind of spooky."

Laura Deal, having unlocked the side door of the old house behind the cedars and disappeared from view, the two loitered expectantly for a time; but when she did not reappear, they reluctantly returned to their labors, with special attention to the sweeping of east porches.

Laura softly opened the side door of her dead grandmother's house, stepped in, closed the door gently, and stood with her back to it.

The hot afternoon sunshine lay in long streaks across the floor of the sitting-room with the cross shadows of the window-casings in them. There was a faint odor of flowers in the air--roses and tube-roses and the cinnamon-like odor of carnations. It was deathly still. A fly bumbling against the pane with little bumping noises was the only sound in the house. The clock was not even ticking. Everything was just as Grandma Deal had left it. The old chintz-covered couch in one corner had Grandma's shawl folded neatly over the back. The rocking-chairs were in their places. A little square stand with a red spread on it held the church papers and seed catalogues and an old song book, and on the mantel shelf were the two flowered vases and the turkey-feather fan. Not a thing looked different. Everything seemed just as it had the week before when Grandma was going in and out, putting away the eggs and washing her dishes and sorting poppy seed into paper folders. On Friday morning she had done all her work and called them up on the telephone. In the afternoon she had visited with the grocery boy and called to Mrs. Johnson to come over and get some turnips any time she wanted them. Mrs. Curtis had seen her reading the newspaper on the screened porch--and then when old Christine Reinmueller had come over about supper time, she was gone. *Gone. Gone where?*

Heaven, of course, for Grandma was the best person that ever lived. But where was Heaven? And how could you go? Miss Bliss, her Sunday School teacher, said it was beyond all the worlds. She couldn't comprehend that distance. Miss Sherwin, a friend of her mother's, said it was here and now within one. That was still harder to believe. Grandma wasn't *here,* so why did they try to tell you that?

But in one way Grandma didn't seem to have gone away at all. That was the queerest thing. She could summon Grandma into her mind just as clearly as though she were standing over there by the table,--small, shrunken, shoulders rounded, a little white knot of hair at the nape of her neck, wrinkled face, bright brown eyes, slender hands, veined and trembling, with queer brown spots on them, and long tapering fingers twisted a little with rheumatism. Just last week Grandma had stood right by that table and laughed about a funny thing Christine Reinmueller had said--Grandma could laugh so heartily. It almost seemed that if she would call her now, Grandma would just walk in from the kitchen and--

"Grandma," she called softly, scarcely above a whisper. Her heart beat rapidly at the sound of her own voice in the stillness.

There was only a great silence, deep and unfathomable--the same vast quiet that has confronted all humanity--that always will confront it, until one by one each hears a voice in the silence.

For a few moments longer Laura stood rigidly with her back to the door. Then she moved quietly over to the bedroom and looked in. This was the room where old Christine Reinmueller had found her--over there lying across the foot of the bed. She had been all alone. Every one of Grandma's children had felt so troubled that she died alone. They all talked about it a great deal--her own father, and Uncle Mack, Aunt Margaret and Aunt Isabelle and Aunt Grace. It worried them all the time as though the being alone was the sad thing. That wasn't the sad part. Why did they think so? To die with no one else looking on at you--that was the best way. Just doing it yourself. You had to do it by yourself anyway. Nobody could help you do it. You'd *rather* do it by yourself maybe.

She went into the bedroom, looked about her a moment, then carefully opened the wardrobe doors. Grandpa Deal had made the heavy old piece of furniture for Grandma years and years before. It was walnut, and the two had planted the trees from which the lumber was sawed. Grandma's things were hanging limply on the hooks,--the black silk and the second best silk and the house dresses. It gave her a queer feeling to see them. The new lavender silk wasn't there. Grandma had it on the other day when-- when she was taken to the church and cemetery. Aunt Emma Deal had brought it down from Omaha two weeks before for Grandma to wear to Cousin Katherine's wedding,--the dress and a lace cape collar from Vienna. Did you wear the things that people put on you right up to Heaven? If you did, Grandma wouldn't feel very comfortable in the presence of God,-- Grandma would have felt more like herself in the second best with a plain white fichu. She could scarcely remember how Grandma looked in the strange lavender and lace, but she could see her just as plain as day in the second best and the white fichu with her cameo pinning it.

She was half enjoying herself in an emotional way. There was sort of a gruesome ecstasy in making herself sad with memories. She would like to write about it. "The girl moved about from room to room, touching the things lovingly" went through her mind. She was in one of those familiar moods when she looked upon life in a detached way as though she herself were not a part of it. She could never talk to any one about it, but in some vague way she felt withdrawn from the world. She lived with people, but she was not one of them.

There was the old sewing-machine and the little red pincushion on it, bristling with black and white pins like a variegated porcupine. Queer, how things lasted longer than people. To-morrow the house was to be dismantled. Tomorrow Aunt Margaret and Aunt Isabelle and Aunt Grace were all coming to divide the things. It seemed a horrible plan,--to talk of separating the old things. They ought to be left together. She wondered if they would miss each other after nearly sixty years of standing side by side. How could the sewing-machine get along without the little red pincushion? Or the blue flowered vases without the turkey fan?

Aunt Isabelle had said she wanted this tallow lamp. It was a queer old thing, with the wick hanging out like a tongue. Grandma had told her it once hung in *her* Grandmother's house, an Irish peasant's hut among the whins and silver hazels of Bally-poreen. She loved the musical sound of those words, and said them over: "the whins and silver hazels of Bally-poreen."

From under the bed she drew out a little calf-skin-covered box with the initials M.O.C. on it in brass nail heads. This was the one thing she wanted,--this and Grandma's scrap-book. To-morrow when they divided the things, she was going to say right out at the start that Grandma had promised those to her. She sat down on the floor and pulled the little trunk into her lap and thought of all that Grandma had told her about it; how Grandma's mother, Maggie O'Conner, an Irish peasant girl, had taken it with her to the big estate in Scotland when she married Basil Mackenzie. Basil's mother, a grand lady, Isabelle Anders-Mackenzie, had given her little Irish daughter-in-law a white silk shawl and a jeweled fan and a breastpin and a string of pearls, and she had brought them all to America in this very box. When she had given the things away to her daughters, the pearls had come to Grandma. And now only two weeks ago, when Cousin

Katherine Deal was married, Grandma had given Kathie the pearls. She felt no jealousy about Katherine owning the pearls. She did not care for jewelry and wanted only the funny little hairy trunk.

She shoved the box back under the bed and went out to the kitchen. It was clean and neat and very quiet out there. The old Seth Thomas clock stood silently there with its little brown church painted on the glass. She had heard them talking about it,--how strange it was that it had happened. Several old ladies said it often happened. There it was, showing fourteen minutes of six. And Christine Reinmueller had found her about half-past six. The doctor said she had been dead less than an hour. So it must be true- -*clocks stopped when people died.* How did they know to stop? Grandma had brought the clock into Nebraska in the covered wagon--sixty years before--and to-morrow the house would be dismantled, and the clock and all the other things that had lived together so long would be divided. The house would be empty, for Herman Rinemiller's hired man was going to move here.

She ought to be going now for she had been here for quite a while. The sun was lower and it was almost supper time. She walked over to the door and turned back to the rooms. She could imagine how this would be in writing: "The girl hesitated at the door, at a loss to know how to proceed." She said aloud, "Good-by, little house." She threw out her hands in dramatic gesture. "Good-by to all the days that have gone by, and all the Christmases here and all the birthdays . . ." She loved the sad emotion which she was feeling. She would write a poem about it as soon as she got home. It would begin:

"The little house held its memories . . ."

She would enjoy doing it. And when it was finished she would read it to--

Why, no,--how terrible--there was no Grandma to read it to. She had completely forgotten for a minute and was planning to bring it here and read it to Grandma. Oh, no, no! For the first time the tears broke,--wild, uncontrollable little-girl tears. She could not stand it,--not to have Grandma here to talk things over with and read things to. Nobody else cared about her writing,--no one in the world understood it but Grandma and herself. She always read everything to Grandma. And Grandma would never listen again. There was no one, then. She was shaken with grief and threw herself down on the old chintz-covered couch. Great engulfing sobs tore at her sturdy little body and she moaned aloud. This was her real self,--the real Laura Deal,--not that other queer person who dominated her, who felt emotions play about her as a swimmer feels the waves. This was the first time Grandma's death seemed really to have happened. She had witnessed the sorrow of all the relatives but she herself hadn't seemed to comprehend it before. And now she did. Grandma was gone--*forever.* There was no one to take her place. No one else to turn to. No one else understood.

She sobbed and cried again in the loneliness she had just realized was hers. She wished she could talk to some one about it. But no one would understand. Only Grandma herself would understand. She wished she could talk to Grandma herself about it. How queer! To want to talk to Grandma herself about Grandma's own death. But it wasn't just the fact that Grandma had died that made her feel so terrible. She could even imagine having a good time without Grandma. It was something else,--something strange that only they two knew about,--some great desire in life that just they two had,--some vision,--some longing that none of the other Deals had,--*to write lovely things.* Only Grandma understood it and now Grandma was gone. If Grandma could only come back to talk to her about it,--Grandma always knew such comforting things to say. Suddenly she sat up. She wiped her swollen eyes, and when vision was clear again, went over to the square stand, pulled out the scrapbook, took it back to the couch and began turning the pages.

Grandma had always cut out everything she especially liked and pasted it in this big catalogue. She turned the familiar pages. The first of the old articles were brown with age, cut from newspapers of the past. A conglomerate collection of things they made,--poems and obituaries, news items of the Deal clan and bits of sermons. Grandma had pasted them all in neatly with home-made flour paste. There was the death of Grandma's mother,--Mrs. Maggie O'Conner Mackenzie, who "died far from her native land,"--patriotic verses, letters from Laura's father when he was in Alaska and printed at Grandma's prideful request in the local newspaper, an account of the death of Grandma's husband with a crude water-colored border of everlastings around it in neat cramped design, and more verses from newspapers and magazines. But these were not what she wanted. She was wondering what things Grandma had recently pasted in the old book, so she hurried over the pages and came immediately to the last work that had been done. There was no mistaking it, for the verse stood out clear and clean on a new page, the wrinkled clipping scarcely dry from its pasting.

It said:

Pain has been and grief enough and bitterness and crying,
Sharp ways and stony ways I think it was she trod,
But all there is to see now is a white bird flying.
Whose blood-stained wings go circling high,--circling up to God.*
   * Margaret Widdemer.

She read it through twice, her heart beating fast in response to the attractiveness of it. She and Grandma always liked the same things. Grandma had found it in a magazine, loved it, and evidently saved it for her to read.

As always, the rhythm and exquisite loveliness of the thought caught and held her emotions. She thrilled to the lilting symmetry of it and the sadness of its beauty. Nimble in committing verse, already she could say it without looking. The line that captured and held her fancy the most was the third one:

But all there is to see is a white bird flying.

A white bird flying! That was like Grandma's death. Nothing was left to her now of Grandma,--nothing remained of Grandma's love and sympathy, of the dreams and desires Grandma held for her,--nothing but the memory. No one else had understood her so thoroughly, had liked the same things so well, had talked to her as Grandma had,--not her own mother, nor her father, nor a single one of the Deal relatives.

The subjects she and Grandma had talked about together,--the dreams they had for her future, the desires that life would give her some of the things Grandma had missed,--could never be talked over again. For Grandma was gone. And all there was to see now was a white bird flying.

It was as though Grandma had left her a message,--as though Grandma, in going away, had not taken the lovely strange desire with her. She felt a vague sensation of relief and comfort. Grief no longer seemed tearing at her very soul and body. She would never tell any one about it,--no one would understand,--but in some unexplainable way everything was just as it had been before Grandma died,--all the dreams and desires were still there, all the vague yearnings for something fine and big in life. *A white bird flying.* That was what Grandma had left her. Well, she would always see it--always keep her eyes on the sheen of its silver wings.

She put the book back under the little stand, slipped quietly out of the side door, locked it and put the key in her pocket. She walked quickly down the path between the cedars, turned west on the grassy path toward the setting sun, averting her head when she passed Mrs. Johnson and Mrs.

Curtis so they would not see her red eyes, and came then to the paved street that led south and toward home.

When she went into the house, her father and mother, her brothers, Wentworth and Millard, and her visiting Aunt Grace were all getting up from the supper table.

"Laura Deal, *where* have you been?" It was Eloise Deal, her mother, exasperated and worried. "I phoned Kathie's and two or three other places, and even ran over to old Oscar Lutz's. You ought to be more thoughtful than to worry us after all we've been through with Grandma's death. She ought not to do a thoughtless thing like that to worry me, had she, John?" Eloise always picked a subject to pieces, squeezed the parts dry and then put them together again. "I always tried to teach you children to be considerate of me and your father and of each other. And it isn't considerate just to disappear at supper time. The worry itself of where you are is bad enough, to say nothing of your not helping. First, I was afraid you were at Katherine's bothering just when she's beginning to settle her new house, and when I found you weren't there, I hardly knew where to think you were, now that Grandma's gone." Having practically exhausted the various ramifications of the subject, Eloise fell back on the initial question: *"Where were you?"*

John Deal stood by the chair he had just vacated, silently regarding his young daughter. Wentworth frowned with the critical displeasure of twenty-one for errant twelve. Millard grinned with the malicious satisfied glee of eight that temporarily he was not as other men. Aunt Grace looked on accusingly with her most austere expression.

Laura averted her head. The painful flush of embarrassment flooded her face, so that her eyes, already swollen, felt hot and bursting.

How could she tell them? How could they understand? How could she explain that she had been on a long emotional journey and back again? How could this energetic, efficient mother without imagination, this grim, silent father with the burdens of the whole community on his shoulders, and this stern uncompromising teacher-aunt, comprehend or sympathize? How could they know that a little girl, with a head full of fancies and a heart full of longing, had climbed a ladder reaching from the depths of a grave to the top of high heaven?

She turned to them all:

"I went for a long walk . . . out by Grandma's old house."

How could they see *a white bird flying?*

CHAPTER 2

Grandmother Deal's old home behind the cedars was dismantled, with every one hot and hurried and uncertain what to do with things. Margaret Deal Baker, wife of Dr. Frederick Baker of Lincoln, and Isabelle Deal Rhodes, the singer from Chicago, were there. Grace Deal, the University teacher, was there. Eloise, Laura and Millard went out to the house in the morning. Mackenzie Deal, the Omaha banker, and Emma, his wife, drove down in the late afternoon. John Deal, Laura's father, came when he had closed his law office. Katherine Deal Buchanan, Mack's and Emma's daughter, a bride of two weeks, drove over in her sport roadster, although there was practically nothing she wanted, the old things giving no promise of fitting in the smart new English cottage with any degree of artistry.

In the beginning, the daughters and daughters-in-law were a bit red-eyed and tearful. At the first sight of her mother's clothes in the old walnut wardrobe, Margaret Baker thought she could not go on with her sorrowful task. Isabelle Rhodes had a bad moment or two as she took down the recipe books and saw her mother's cramped handwriting. The rather austere Grace broke down when she took the glasses off the old Bible in the bedroom and put them in the case. It was almost as hard for Emma and Eloise, the daughters-in-law. Mother Deal had been good to them. Mack and John tramped around out doors, taking down tools that had been their father's and, uncertain what to do, with masculine helplessness, put them all back again. Katherine sat on the kitchen table with the declivity in one corner in which old Doc Matthews had rolled pills in Civil War times, swung her chic-looking feet and, to keep the tears back, made snappy remarks about the dismantling. Millard ran in and out, with Eloise calling: "Millard Deal, do stay *in* or *out*."

It was all very confusing, and very strange, with the familiar things in a queer rearrangement, clustered together in piles on the floor. Laura went in and out of the rooms with something tearing a little at her heart every time an article was taken from its old place. Once she took the red pincushion from a pile and placed it back on the sewing-machine, and once she surreptitiously slipped the turkey-feather fan into a blue flowered vase. She could think of nothing but that Grandma was looking on and saying: "You'd better let Annie Johnson have the cape. She could make it over for Dottie." Or, "Tell Mrs. Curtis she can have the geraniums." Yes, that was just what Grandma would have said. It seemed queer to think she could almost hear her. How could it be? Because all the Deals were there together, it seemed that Grandma was there, too. How could some one who was dead live on and move among them just as she had always done?

Everything seemed as natural as though nothing had happened. After the first few attempts to stop the tears and keep from breaking down, the whole clan grew brisk and talkative. In the stress of sorting and making disposition of things the conversation became practical and cheerful. After awhile they even began the old joking way of the Deals. Katherine laughed gayly and made extravagant statements about the old-fashioned clothes which her mother was unearthing in bundles from a closet shelf. Aunt Margaret and Aunt Isabelle even staged a well-bred but intensive argument over which one could have the old tallow lamp with the wick hanging over the side like a dog's tongue hanging out of his mouth. Life always closes over the vacancy and goes on.

Christine Reinmueller, Grandma's neighbor and friend for sixty years, came over, her blue calico dress gathered on full at the place where her waistline should have been, her colorless hair braided in moist flat strands and wound from ear to ear, like a miniature braided rug that had been pinned on the back of her head.

"*Ach . . . solch ein aufbrechen . . .* such a splitting . . . breaking up . . ." She wrung her hard old hands.

They gave her countless things,--clothes and dishes and garden seeds tied up in rags, and fruit jars. And although she still owned three eighties of land after giving away eight other quarter sections to her children, she was glad to get the things; said they would help her out through the hard winter. Old Christine always thought she was poverty-stricken, on the verge of entering the county home.

While every one was sorting, warm and hurried, old Oscar Lutz came tap-tapping with his cane around to the door. The remarks on the side concerning his arrival were more frank than polite: "Good-night! . . . old Uncle Oscar."

"Of all days!"

"He *would.*"

Old Oscar Lutz came tap-tapping smilingly into the confusion of the dismantling. He had string beans in an old pail with a rope for the handle. He had brought them as a gift for any one who wanted them, but no one seemed overjoyed at the donation.

Old Oscar Lutz was Cedartown's oldest inhabitant. In every town and village west of Iowa there is still some old man who has seen the beginning and the growth of the community, who has watched little saplings grow to ancient trees, and the boys of three generations slip into manhood. Even east of the Missouri River they are gone. But west of the Missouri you will still find them, a few old men who have seen everything from the beginning, who once climbed down from covered wagons into the waving prairie grass, to turn the first furrows in the virgin soil. Some of them are still active. Some mill around like restless old buffaloes. And some sit on their porches watching the stream of life go by.

There are old men of the sea and old men of the mountains,--but here in the midwest live the old men of the prairie. The old salt tells of the mightiness and fascination of the sea, the hillman of the majesty and the lure of the mountains, but the old man of the prairie lives over his days on the plains. One recalls strong ships scuttled on far shores, one the rockribbed fastness of the hills, but the other remembers the wave of the grass on the prairie. To one there is no memory so lovely as the moonlight on the sea, to one the dawn breaking over the mountains, but to the old man of the prairie it is the sudden hush of the winds at twilight.

Old Oscar Lutz was Cedartown's last old man of the prairie. Tall, gaunt, as gnarled as the cottonwoods he had planted, he looked akin to the elements with which he had once wrestled. Furrows in the virgin soil, and furrows in the red-brown face! Eyes the color of the gray-blue ice on Stove Creek. Hair and beard like tangled wheat stalks under the snow. Hands hard and calloused as old buffalo hide. He wore two buttons in the lapel of his shiny old coat,--a G.A.R. token, and a little button with the number "68," the year he had settled in the state. He was as proud of one as the other; a war record on one, and the record of an equally harsh war on the other,--the tussle with nature to make a home on the prairie.

Old Oscar Lutz spent his winters in California, but about the time that countless tiny maltese kittens scrambled over the branches of the willows down by Stove Creek, old Oscar would arrive from the Far West. These were the things in Cedartown's calendar of events which proved that spring had come: a robin or two suddenly swooping down onto some one's leaf-covered lawn, an intermingled odor of bonfires and subsoil from over the meadows, pussy-willows at the creek bend, and old Oscar Lutz's cane tap-tapping on the sidewalk.

There was scarcely any one but old Christine Reinmueller left now in the community who had been his friend of the early days. But he came back to his old haunts every spring, spent a day each with the Mackenzie Deals of Omaha, the John Deals of Cedartown, the Bakers of Lincoln, and a day with a son or two of some old companion of his plainsman's days, regaling them with accounts of their ancestors' uprisings and downswings and his own first early experiences; tap-tapping through the town with his cane ("yes, sir, whittled from a young elm branch down by the creek") to his own old closed and musty dwelling. Sturdy as an old hickory limb, he would go through the house, open up doors and windows, beat some of the ancient rugs and hang his dead Marthy's quilts out on the line. There they would swing all day in the fresh spring wind and the sunshine,--the Rose of Sharon and the Dutch Puzzle, the Log Cabin and the Rising Sun. His rather superficial house-cleaning done, he was ready for the garden. The bursting of the first wild plum blossoms, and the bumbling of the first honey-bee always found him in his garden behind the fussy old house.

There were those he bored with his constant talk of the early days. Because time hung heavily on his hands, his greatest delight was to have a listener. The ratio of his happiness in declaiming his experiences rose in proportion to his audience. One person was a pleasure, two a greater satisfaction, three or more standing about listening to his tales, taking in attentively all he had to say, lifted him to a heaven of rare delight.

And now he was here to-day, tap-tapping up the cement walk to the side door. And the Deals in unison groaned.

"Well, well," he tapped in smilingly, unaware of his lack of welcome, "and so you're getting the old household things divided up?"

"Hello, Uncle Oscar." He was Mrs. Mackenzie Deal's uncle (she had been Henry Lutz's daughter), but he was "Uncle" to the others in name only. Emma pushed forward a chair. He lowered his gaunt frame into it heavily.

"Well--well--the time goes by and one by one we all pass on. . . ."

"And out," Katherine whispered to Laura. Kathie's recent honeymoon had in no way mellowed her flippancy.

"Well--well--it seems like only yesterday. I mind as how--"

"Old-Mind-As-How is all wound up ready to go," Katherine muttered.

". . . we all come across the prairie from Plattsmouth,--Marthy and me and the three little tads . . . my brother Henry and Sarah, his bride, and Will and Abbie Deal, your folks, . . . and you and Gus, Christine. I mind as how, Christine, you and Gus had a boat for a wagon-box, the stern next to the oxen's hind quarters."

"Nein . . . no." Christine spoke up. "De bow . . . he vas next."

"No, I think it was the stern, Christine."

Christine was adamant. *"Nein* . . . de bow he vas next."

"My money is on Christine," Katherine whispered. "She'll never give up. She'll die saying 'De bow he vas next' if old Mind-As-How doesn't give in."

Old Oscar went on unperturbed. "We met at the Weeping Water and traveled all day against the sun. We could see a faint fringe of trees outlinin' the horizon and we knew it was Stove Creek. We camped by the creek bed . . . made a campfire . . . the stars come out . . . and the Injuns come . . ."

Every one went on about his work. Margaret sorted clothes, Grace packed dishes, Isabelle, books. They all went in and out unheeding the old man's tale.

It made Laura feel sorry for him. People were always that way with old Oscar. Something about the disinterest they seemed to show brought out her sympathy. She wondered how it would feel to be old and to bore people. Of course, he didn't realize he bored them,--that was one good thing.

"I mind as how when Henry and I first come we got a house nigh about where Plattsmouth stands . . ." He was going on and on with no one giving him any special heed. "Stayed all night with some folks by the name of . . . wait a minute . . . name slips . . . tell you in a minute . . . A B C D E F G . . . Gunwall . . . always run down the alphabet if you can't locate a name . . . works every time . . . stayed with a family by the name of . . . what's I say a minute ago?" he asked Laura. "Gunwall . . . that's it. Slept on the floor, had a latch . . . a wooden latch you run a leather thong through to hook the door . . . like this. . . ." With his cane and fingers he showed definitely the form of the latch. "Toward daylight . . . come clear daylight, mebbe, I should say . . . saw the leather thong on the latch keep moving . . . somebody workin' away on the latch . . . pretty soon the leather pulled outwards, and the door opened 'n' in come four o' the biggest Injuns y' ever saw . . . feathers 'n' moccasins 'n' tommyhawks 'n' all. For two cents I'd crawled out 'n' drowned myself in the Platte. Come to think . . . don't know's I could a drowned . . . water was lower 'n' git out. This man . . . what'd I say? . . . A B C D E F G . . . Gunwall . . . this man Gunwall met 'em 'n' talked to 'em. They grunted 'n' stepped around over the beds on the floor . . . made known they wanted something to eat . . . ate a handout . . . laughed a bit. You always think of Injuns serious I bet, don't you? T'ain't so . . . full of jokes . . . if you don't mind the kind they sometimes perpetrated."

He stopped and fell into an absent-minded mood as though he were actually seeing the scenes of which he talked so fluently. The Deals moved all around him, back and forth, sorting, packing. Soon he came to the present with "Goin' to take a flower down to lay on Gunwall's grave some of these days; think I can locate it . . . it'll be som'ers on the north side of a bunch of cottonwoods at the old Prairie Home cemetery."

Out in the kitchen Isabelle Rhodes was saying: "I could scream to have to listen to him. He doesn't live in the present . . . just inhabits another world."

Eloise said stiffly: "He's like house-cleaning and taxes and being fooled the first of April,--you just have to have them all whether you want to or not."

"If he starts visiting me," Katherine, the bride, made her definite pronouncement, "I'll simply disappear when he arrives. Great-uncle or not, life is too short to be bored by the old pest."

It made Laura feel sorry for the old man. "I kind of like him," she admitted. "He sort of fascinates me, now that Grandma's gone. When he's gone, too . . . did you ever stop to think, Katherine, that when your old Uncle Oscar Lutz and old Christine Reinmueller are gone, there won't be any one . . . not a soul left that came here in wagons, and started the community. Just think, we'll lose connection forever with the pioneer days."

"You can sever the connection any time, Lolly, as far as I'm concerned," was Katherine's rejoinder. "Nothing bores me to a state of coma quicker than a rehash of this native-sons-and-daughters, heroic-lives, corn-bread-in-a-sod-house stuff."

It was getting late and the Deal clan stopped work for the day. Old Christine took her things and waddled down the lane toward home, her blue calico dress switching the tall grass at the roadside. When the Deals all left, the old man was still mulling over his recollections, and no one had taken the string beans.

There were a half-dozen cars in the lane road. Every one offered to take him home.

"No," he said, "I'll walk. Don't stop walking and you'll never get rusty in the joints."

When the John Deal car turned out of the lane road, Laura looked back. The old man was leaning on his cane and looking across the fields and meadows to the sun slipping low in the west. A sudden mist came to her eyes. She wished the others liked him better. Poor old man. When she got home she would write about him:

Poor old man, looking toward the sun,
What do you remember, now that life's done?

CHAPTER 3

The Deal clan worked three days before they had finished dismantling their mother's home and getting it ready for occupancy by Herman Rinemiller's hired man.

"I never saw so many things in my life," each one insisted. "Loads and loads of the accumulations of years. Every magazine, every paper, every string and button that ever came into that house Mother had hoarded."

And so the old things, once so precious, each one representing sacrifice for the purchase, were scattered to the four winds,--to children, grandchildren, neighbors, friends, church organizations, Salvation Army, the junk pile down by Stove Creek,--like leaves from some sturdy old oak blown hither and yon in the dead of the year. Margaret took the clock with the little brown church painted on the glass, Isabelle the tallow lamp, Mack the thumbed-over Shakespeare,--"Mother used to make me read it when I didn't know what it was all about," he explained,--and John the blue plush album, with Eloise deeply annoyed at his absurd choice. Katherine deigned to admit into the lovely new home of English architecture, the newest looking of the pieced quilts,--of Jacob's Ladder design. Grace, choosing the scrapbook, was surprised beyond measure when Laura, usually quiet and shy as a little brown quail, pounced upon it with an almost tearful ferocity: "Oh, no, Aunt Grace, not the scrapbook. It's mine . . . please. Grandma always read them all to me . . . she *said* I could have it. . . ."

Eloise was upset beyond measure and was ready to insist upon Laura's turning it over to her Aunt Grace with apologies, but Aunt Margaret intervened, and Laura bore home her two possessions in peace,--the little hairy calf-skin trunk with the nailhead initials on it, and the thick old scrapbook with all the lovely verses.

Eloise did not understand Laura. Mother and daughter, they seemed not even remotely related. Brisk, practical, efficient and humorless, Eloise, by some strange joke of nature had given birth to a child of emotions, of fancies and dreams. And no barnyard hen on the river's brink was ever more worried and exasperated over her swimming duckling than was Eloise over Laura's disinclination to show any characteristics of her own (the Wentworth) side of the house.

Toward the last of that month, when all seemed normal again after Grandma's death,--so soon does Life slip back to its regular routine--in the privacy of her upstairs blue and white room, Laura began writing a long story. It took her several days, and Eloise went many times to the stairway with: "Laura, whatever are you doing? Do get at some work. We all have to work,--people in our circumstances, at least. If we were better off maybe you could sit around that way, but we might as well face facts that we never will be wealthy and able to enjoy life." There are those who would have taken exception to Eloise's statement. But that was Eloise's philosophy: great wealth brought comfort and happiness. And having no great wealth, she resigned herself, perforce, to a state of no great comfort and no deep happiness.

Laura would dutifully get up, stir things around a bit in her room and then settle down to the absorbing story. It was entitled "A Love That Never Came to Pass" or "The Professor's Life Tragedy." It involved the unrequited love of a college professor for a fellow member of the faculty. To be sure, no obstacle seemed to stand in the way of a happy culmination of the affair, excepting the advice against marriage freely given by a villainous unmarried roommate of the wooed-but-not-won lady, the former resembling Aunt Grace so thoroughly in Laura's mind that she felt a little guilty over the accurate description.

On the third day of the composition period, the embryonic author grew so upset over the tragic affair that she cried too copiously to see the pages clearly. It was in this state that her mother found her. Exasperated mother and embarrassed daughter took part in a dialogue which got them nowhere; indeed, which only seemed to push them farther apart in their understanding of each other.

"That child worries me so," Eloise told John that evening.

"Do you suppose anything could be"--Eloise was pale in her earnestness--*"wrong* with her?"

"Of course not. She's a smart kid."

"But where did she get it . . . that foolish emotion? Not from *my* side of the house, that's certain."

"Oh, we'll assume responsibility . . . the Deals." John grinned.

"The Wentworths are all so practical. Look at Uncle Harry Wentworth--worth a half *million,* if a dollar."

"I thought that money originally came from his wife." John could not resist. At which Eloise closed her mouth with the unspoken eloquence she sometimes assumed, and John went silently back to his office.

When Laura had carried the sad life story of the professor to a close which ended in a grave under a weeping-willow tree with the erstwhile juggler of his happiness planting bleeding-heart bushes on the grave, she washed the visible liquid form of her emotion from her eyes, and went down to cousin Katherine's.

Katherine's and Jimmie Buchanan's new home was lovely and modern and smart, just as Katherine herself was lovely and modern and smart. Its lawn was only beginning to emerge, pretty and green, from the recent dirt of the excavation. But the house itself was a finished affair from the beveled glass of the front door to the green and white incinerator.

Laura opened the immaculate white front door and stepped into the hall with a little, "Hoo-hoo!" She reveled in the sight of the lovely rooms with the gay wedding gifts all about, the inner doors with their sparkling glass and filmy lace, the mahogany and white stairway winding to the upper rooms, the long lovely sitting-room with the one end taken up by the fireplace and the open bookcases. No one was in sight, but immediately she heard a door open, and Katherine's head appeared around the corner of the upstairs hall to be followed by the rest of Katherine in an orchid-colored underslip.

"Oh, it's you, Lolly." That was Katherine's pet name for her cousin. Millard, she had long ago dubbed "The Tribulation," shortening it later to Trib, a nickname which half the town called him now.

"Come on in and make yourself homely, Lolly," she called down.

Laura giggled appreciatively. Kathie was always so funny. She wished Kathie liked her better. No, that was not quite the right thing to think. Katherine liked her, but she took no pains to conceal the fact that she thought her odd. "You're the queerest little duck," she would say whenever Laura ventured one of her mature opinions on any subject.

"I'm going out, Lolly." Kathie looked down at her as she dropped a lovely orchid afternoon gown over her head. "Bridge at Mrs. A. R. Brown's,--that's short for Ashes of Rose, I suppose." Laura giggled. "My word, Laura, this little burg has as much going on as Omaha,--that is, providing you count every church supper and every study club and every female tea. Jimmie wants me to toddle to everything . . . good business, he says . . . the old diplomat in international relations . . . so I run around to them all . . . blue blood, red blood, Catholic, Protestant, Republican, Democrat, wet, dry, our bank's customers, t'other bank's customers. . . ."

She was downstairs now, lovely and slim and sparkling. Laura thought she had never seen any one so gay and pretty. And she smelled like the violets at the foot of the old trees by the creek bed. She threw her arms around Laura now and gave her a swift caress. Laura was surprised and embarrassed beyond measure. So seldom did Katherine notice her except to tease. "How old are you, Lolly? Twelve?"

"Thirteen last week."

"Imagine! Bless your little kid heart. Well, all I can ask for you, Laura," she was suddenly sweet and serious, "is that seven or eight years from now, you'll be as gloriously happy as I am."

"If you mean getting married," Laura said, with the crimson creeping under the olive of her skin, "I'm never going to. I'm going to do something else." She loved watching Jimmie and Katherine--they were a handsome couple. She liked the thrill it gave her to look at them together, but she could not imagine herself under the same circumstances. She shrank from the thought of placing herself in the picture--wanted only to look at others.

Katherine laughed, "You're a queer little duck." She threw her arm around Laura again. "Well, I must go, honey. There isn't anybody here. My butler, maid and chef have all gone. They're all one person, you know,--I call her my 'unholy trinity.'"

"Do you care if I stay and read?"

"Of course not. But . . ." Katherine paused in slipping on a white coat. "What makes you read so much, Lolly? Why don't you get out and *do* more?"

There it was again,--the thing her mother always said. "Oh, I don't know. I guess I like people in books better than the ones outside," she admitted.

There was the sudden sound of tap-tapping on the cement walk running around to the rear of the house, and Katherine looked out to say: "Oh, darn! There's old man Whiskery-Whee-Come-Wheeze. Stay here, Lolly, and don't squeak, or we'll have to march with Sherman to the sea all afternoon."

Katherine slipped out to the back door, accepted with thanks the beets all washed and clean, took them gingerly out of the old bucket with a rope for the handle, kept surreptitiously closing the door a little more while the old man was talking and finally escaped back to Laura.

"It wasn't Sherman. It was eatables. 'Knew some families further out on the prairie had a worse time than us.'" Katherine imitated the old man's high husky voice to perfection. "'Didn't have nothin' to eat . . . no money . . . last resource was to go out on the prairie 'n' gather up the bleached bones o' the buffalo, haul 'em to town and get a dollar a load. Nature is kind under her harsh exterior. . . . Always leaves somethin' around . . . even if only bones bleachin' on the prairie.'"

Laura laughed. Katherine was so droll. But something hurt her, too. It troubled her to think of the old man trying to tell that to Kathie in her orchid-colored chiffon dress and her lovely white coat. It *was* true about the buffalo bones. Grandma had said so, too.

Then Katherine, gay and lovely, left for the bridge party. When Laura saw the car go out of the drive, she locked the front door and went into the long living-room. But she did not read.

She tiptoed down the length of the room as though even then some one might be listening. In front of the fireplace she stopped and looked up at the huge portrait which filled the entire space above the mantel.

It was the painting of a lovely lady in velvet draperies, her reddish-brown hair curling over her shoulder and a string of pearls at her neck. In her slender tapering hand she held a hat with a long drooping plume.

It was no ordinary painting,--but an heirloom that had come to Katherine on her wedding day,--the picture of lovely Isabelle Anders-Mackenzie, Katherine's and Laura's own great-great-grandmother. Standing there alone in the silent house and looking up at the lovely lady, Laura recalled all that her Grandmother had told her about it,--how the lady had been an aristocratic Scotch woman; how her only son, Basil, riding to the hounds, had met and wooed and won a little sixteen-year-old Irish peasant girl on the Scottish moors, married her and taken her home to the great estate near Aberdeen; how this lady of the picture had tried to make a grand dame of the little Maggie O'Conner, but had not succeeded, for the little bride would put on her peasant dress and shawl and run away over the moors to her own folks. Isabelle Anders-Mackenzie died, and the young Basil and his Irish wife had seen all the property slip away and revert to the crown. They had come to America then with their children, and Grandma herself had been born soon after they landed.

It was only because Grandma had told about hearing of this huge painting that used to hang on the landing of the great house in Aberdeen that Kathie knew about it. She had teased her father to find it. Uncle Mack had set agents to work and though it had cost a great deal of money--he never would tell how much--they had found the painting and shipped it to Katherine. That was just like Kathie. Kathie always got everything she wanted. She wondered if Kathie cared very much for the painting, now that she had it.

For a long time Laura stood and looked up at the lovely lady. The lovely lady looked back at Laura. But Laura was the first to speak.

"Isabelle Anders-Mackenzie," she said aloud, and the sound of her voice in the silent lovely room half startled her. "I'm an author."

Isabelle Anders-Mackenzie gazed back from heavy-lidded eyes, her cupid's-bow lips smiling mysteriously as though she possessed the concentrated wisdom of all the ages. One could not conscientiously say that she seemed pleased at the news and approving of it, but neither could one justly contend that she was annoyed and distressed. She merely smiled that puzzling smile as though, sphinx-like, she knew the secret of deep mysteries.

"I live in a little house all by myself," Laura told the lady confidentially, "no one can touch me when I am there. And no one can come in." She was enjoying herself, dramatizing the situation. She could see herself, a member of the fifth generation beyond the lady of the portrait, standing in front of the ancestor and confiding in her. "I hereby take a vow . . ." she went on. All at once it struck her that there should be some special emphasis to such a serious statement, some rite performed which would verge on the sacred. She ought to do it with human blood, but she did not quite relish the thought of puncturing her own anatomy. She wished she had something that would make a good imitation of blood. Perhaps Kathie had beet juice. She tiptoed to the icebox. There were potatoes and head lettuce, pickles and pie and cold meat, but not a single red condiment. In the medicine closet her quest ended. With the cork from a bottle of disinfectant she went back to the scene of her solemn promise. "This is a symbol," she said, touching her forehead with the scarlet-colored drug: "Laura Deal . . . I hereby plight my troth to a career. Nothing shall keep me from it. If love comes by, I shall spurn it."

She liked the sound of that statement so well that she repeated: "If love comes by I shall spurn it . . . him . . ." Of course, love had to be a *him.* She fell to wondering what he would look like, providing he did come by. In fact, it would be rather disappointing if he did not come by to be spurned. It made the tears come to her eyes to think how terrible he would feel. But she would be obdurate. *Obdurate.*--that was her new word. She mustn't forget it.

The door bell ringing suddenly and harshly threw the author into something of a panic. She hastily drew a handkerchief from her blouse pocket and wiped from her forehead all pharmaceutical manifestations of the oath of allegiance to a career. Her heart thumping rapidly, she tiptoed to the door and peeped cautiously out through the lace-covered glass. It was no one at all but Allen Rinemiller, dressed in brown corduroys and a blue shirt open at the throat. Allen had graduated that spring from High School and the captaincy of the football team. He was big and blond. There were three distinct waves in his close clipped hair; his eyes were crinkling and jolly looking and his tanned skin was smooth and firm. She opened the door.

"Hello, Allen."

"Hello, Laura. I went to the back door first where all decent tramps and peddlers go, but nobody came. You the hired girl?"

Laura laughed. She didn't know Allen Rinemiller so very well, but she had watched him lots of times at football games and heard the older girls talk about him, and sometimes when she had been at Grandma's he had plowed or used the disc or picked corn close to Grandma's yard, for his father's land joined it.

"Cousin Kathie's gone away," she volunteered. "What did you want?"

"*I* didn't want anything. *She's* the one that wanted it. Wood." And Laura noticed for the first time the truck in the driveway. "Dry elm wood for the fireplace. I want to know where to put it, but first I want to try a chunk in the fireplace if I can, to see if the size is right."

Laura told him to come right in and try the chunk and she would phone Kathie at Mrs. A. R. Brown's to see where it was to go.

So Allen Rinemiller, stepping gingerly over Kathie's oriental rugs, brought in a huge chunk, carrying it easily on his stalwart shoulder. And when Laura came back with the message that the wood was to go in the south end of the basement, he had the screen removed and the chunk in place.

"O.K. . . . if this one goes, they all go," he said and stood up, looking curiously about him.

"Gee . . . swell joint." He was evidently appreciating the lovely rooms with their soft rugs and draperies, their attractive furniture, books and pictures and bowls of flowers. "Gosh . . . I'd like a house like this." Without apology, he walked back to the hall and looked out to the diningroom. There were lavender asters on the dark polished table out there and a big bowl of white ones beyond on the bench in the green and white breakfast-nook. He could even catch a glimpse of the white enamel of the kitchen with its dainty green and white curtains over leaded windows. "Gosh," he reiterated ". . . just about perfect."

"I think it's nice, too. I like to come here." Laura was glad Allen Rinemiller liked it so well. She had been in his house with her grandmother and knew that it was scrubbed to a shining neatness but terribly plain, straight wooden chairs, shining oak table and sideboard, coarse lace curtains ruffled and starched.

When he was going back to the fireplace for the chunk, he stopped short. "Who's the dame?"

Laura almost blushed in her fear that the lovely lady in the picture might suddenly open her cupid's-bow mouth and start to tell all she knew.

"That's Kathie's and my great-great-grandmother," she told him. And for the first time she sensed a rather snobbish pride in the aristocratic ancestor. No one could say Allen's ancestors, on his father's side at least, were aristocratic. Old Christine Reinmueller, his grandmother, was "Dutchier than sauerkraut" every one admitted. She had never even learned to talk all English, but would mix her German words atrociously with the American ones. They said Gus, his grandfather, who died a few years before, had wound rags around his feet for socks.

"Her name was Isabelle Anders-Mackenzie, and she lived on a big estate in Scotland. My Uncle Mack in Omaha had this painting sent over from Scotland this summer when Kathie was married. And those pearls she has around her neck in the picture are the very pearls Grandma Deal gave Kathie for a wedding present."

"Can you beat it?"

"It was painted lots more than a hundred years ago, about a hundred and fifty, I guess, and the agent Uncle Mack hired had an awful hard time finding it." Laura was surprised at her own talkativeness. After all, it wasn't hard to talk to any one who was really interested in the same thing you were. And Allen Rinemiller acted interested.

He asked her another question or two, said "My gosh," and "Can you beat it?" and suddenly came to the present with a cheerful: "Well, this'll never buy the baby a shirt," shouldered his log lightly and started away. At the door he paused. "Did you know I'm going up to the University to school?" It was the pride of the male of the species strutting a little before the other sex, even though the female was a plain brown wren of a girl.

"Why, Allen, I'm glad. Isn't that nice?" Laura was genuinely surprised. Not many of the Reinmuellers had gone away to school. But Laura was forgetting something. Laura was forgetting that it was the Reinmuellers who seldom went away to school. And Allen, of the third generation, was a *Rinemiller*.

"Is Verna Conden going too?" She asked the question teasingly. It still seemed slightly audacious for her to be talking to the big High School football captain.

Allen grinned. "No, she's looking for a job . . . clerking or something. Say, Laura, I'll appoint you a committee of one to keep an eye on my girl when I'm gone."

Laura laughed at the frank retort.

They talked a few moments more about the University, and then Allen went singing to the truck and the piling of the wood.

For a long time she could hear the chunks whacking against the cement and a gay unmusical voice singing of a lady in a balcony in a little Spanish town.

CHAPTER 4

When Allen Rinemiller left Katherine Buchanan's home, he drove around by the Conden cottage and dated Verna to go down to Weeping Water to a show in the evening. Verna was pretty in a wind-blown fashion, with fly-away hair upon which a beret was usually perilously perched. She was gay and noisy, conscious always of her own vivacity. Her eyes were hard and bright, her generous mouth too scarlet.

"Landed a job yet?"

No, Verna had not landed a job. She guessed she'd just have to go in some one's kitchen. Maybe it ought to be her own kitchen. She believed maybe she'd advertise for a man. Her hard bright eyes laughed at Allen. Allen liked her--he liked her a lot--but whenever she talked that provocative way it made him uncomfortable.

When he left her and started home, driving the little truck fast over the graveled roads, he gave her no more thought. In fact he was thinking of the home in which he had just been. He wished their own house looked like the Buchanans'. There was something about it that you just absorbed into your system,--it was so satisfying. Several of the members of his old High School class had some homes similar,--all low-shaded lights and cushions and book-ends and rugs that were soft as Turkish towels. He believed he'd talk to his mother about getting some new things.

His drive on the highway was very short, only a half mile beyond the town limits. But there was another quarter of mile drive on their own land, for the Rinemiller house sat back so far that one approached it down a long private lane bordered by walnut trees. The house itself was plain, a white box so symmetrical that, save for the narrow porch across the front, it looked like a child's huge cubic-shaped block set down in the exact center of the Rinemillers' holdings. Old Gus Reinmueller, dead these many years, had come over sixty years before into the young state with Christine, "his woman," driving oxen hitched to a rowboat on wheels with a dingy cover over it.

They had been part of that great general movement in settling Nebraska. Bison herds, bands of Indians and wild fowl had held complete possession of the land until the first isolated settlements, clinging to the banks of the sluggish Missouri, made their advent. Indian trails then became trails for adventurers, Mormons, gold hunters, freighters. These were followed by the settlers with the homing instinct of so many birds of passage. Covered wagons jolted over the old trails and made new ones through the prairie grass. Many of these homesteaders were of the old stock of corn farmers from Illinois, Iowa, Indiana, Wisconsin. Many more were of foreign blood. These latter, because of their common language and background, tended to group themselves in the same regions. Thus, Kearney County became predominately Danish; Phelps County, Swedish. The Mennonites grouped in Fairbury, the Bohemians in Saline and Butler Counties, the Hollanders in southern Lancaster. All were highly efficient farming people. But everywhere came the Germans, equally efficient and thrifty. Of these were Gus and Christine Reinmueller, Allen's grandparents. And a far cry it now seemed from old Gus and Christine to young Allen with his finer sensitiveness, his clear-eyed modern viewpoint, his flexibility toward all the modes of the times.

In those old days Gus and Christine had built a dugout at the end of a ravine by digging into the low hillside, setting sturdy tree trunks a short way from the opening and covering the top with poles cut from the branches of the few trees growing along the creek bed, across which they packed a solid roofing of sod. Into this, with only the hard dirt floor and the one opening, they had moved from their wagon. For several years they lived there with their babies, like so many rabbits in a hutch.

Gus and Christine worked early and late; Christine in the field by the side of Gus, staying away from her man's work only when her babies were born, proud of the small number of days she took off for those events. They bought almost nothing. Clothes were handed down from child to child. They ate what they raised. They suffered with the rest of the pioneers through all the long hardships of drouth, grasshoppers, blizzards, crop failures. They suffered with the other early settlers, it is true, but with one difference,--their hardships were all physical. There was no suffering of the spirit, like that which came to the Lutzes and the Deals. They were stolid, inured to poverty, cared nothing that they were deprived of food for the mind, thought being able to write one's name on a receipt the only necessity for schooling. When money came in they hoarded it. They thought only of one thing. Land. Before Gus had quite finished paying for the first eighty acres of land he was contracting to go in debt for another. To enlarge their holdings became a fetish with them. Two eighties now.

"That's like paying for a dead horse," Will Deal, his neighbor, had once told him.

"Ya--dead horse." Gus had shrugged his shoulders. "But purty soon already . . . that dead mare she come to life. Ya?"

The dugout gave place in time to a small cheap two-roomed frame house in which they all huddled. They were up at four o'clock in the morning, routing out the children, too. The little boys husked corn with half frozen hands. Three eighties. Four eighties. Later they added two more rooms. The girls could husk now. Five eighties--six eighties.

They bought Abbie Deal's land. Seven eighties. It was across the road on this eighty that they built the white house as it now stood, large, cubic-shaped, as long as wide and as high as long, a cheap narrow porch across the front, four square rooms downstairs and four square rooms up. They bought more land of Oscar Lutz. Oscar was living in town now, merely holding his land for investment. Eight eighties. Some of the boys could work away now, the girls take places in town, and all bring home their wages. Nine eighties. There were no conveniences in the house; water was carried from the well in buckets. Small kerosene lamps made glow-worm lighting in the rooms when, indeed, lighting became necessary. It was extravagant to sit up and use kerosene. "Get to bed, all of you. To-morrow yet the husking begins."

They kept the two front rooms closed. Too much fuel to have them open. "Keep hustling . . . all of you. If you're cold already yet . . . work faster some more. Get out at that milking." Oscar Lutz still owned two eighties. Gus and Christine could not stand it to see the black loam across their barbed-wire fence; could not bear to see Oscar Lutz's tenant plowing up close to their own holdings. They made Oscar an offer. "Too much he wants. For himself he say he keep two eighties. To come back from California summers and see some of his own land yet he wants. I no more ask him," Gus had said. But Christine's mind had harried her with land gluttony; her little eyes glinted with the thought of the ownership of the mellow soil. *"Du narr* . . . Some more you ask." She had urged Gus. "A little more you offer. Go on . . . qvick."

And finally Oscar Lutz had sold. Ten eighties. Eleven eighties. No one in this end of the county owned so much. Only one boy was left at home at that time,--the youngest, Herman. For some unknown reason, Gus and Christine had been a little more lenient with Herman. There had been a bit more leisure for Herman, not quite so much "Get to work . . . you" for the youngest. Herman had gone into town almost every day to school, riding his pony and carrying rye bread and sausage in a tin pail. They had only required him to stay out at husking time and for plowing. Herman had gone clear through the eighth grade, had even gone on into High School for one year, but Gus and Christine had put an end to that foolishness. "For what good you think them Latins is?" Christine wanted to know. And Gus had laughed, "Ya, Herman . . . that Latin make you pick more corn faster and bring you in more pigs . . . huh?"

So Herman had dropped the subject of going on through High School and had cut alfalfa all that first day when his class entered as sophomores. But as time went on, there had been something in Herman that would not prostrate itself so thoroughly before the god of Work. He had labored hard enough, when he was at it. But he had done other things too. He had taken farm papers. He had put a tin bathtub in one of the empty upstairs rooms, fixed it with a plug to let the water run out even though he had to carry the water up to it, had "slicked up" and gone to all the town doings, left the church of his fathers for an English-speaking one, had begun going with gentle Lucy Steele without a drop of German blood in her veins. About this last procedure, Gus and Christine had made a great many caustic comments.

"Why don't you get yourself a German girl?" Gus had wanted to know. And "Ya!" Christine had snorted. "A *stark* . . . strong one mit some *harte muskeln*--muscles."

And then, while Herman was still going steadily with the pretty and refined Lucy Steele, old Gus had suddenly died.

Death played old Gus a mean trick by slipping up on him unawares, with no more advance notice than the scratch of a shingle nail. Herman, looking at the red wound, had wanted his father to go right over to town to the doctor. But Gus and Christine had said no, the doctors just took your money whether you needed any treatment or not and they would put plenty of fat pork on it to draw out the poison. But the drawing qualities of the butchered hog had failed to materialize, and quite suddenly old Gus was dead. "At the seedin' time, too," Christine had wailed. "Mit the calves comin' in . . . and all. How ve get along already? Mein Gott!"

Surprisingly, old Gus had made a will. John Deal had drawn it up. It had been signed by Gus and duly witnessed,--signed with a cross and a notary public's affidavit that the cross was the signature of one Gus Reinmueller. The land was left to Christine to do with as she wished. Gus had realized that Christine was the more crafty of the two.

And old Christine had land then. Old Christine had her life's desire. Lots of land. The boys were all on the various eighties. Heinie here, Fritz there, Ed on another, Emil farming two quarters, the girls' husbands on others. All had bought more land of their own. All but Herman were getting toward middle age. They were hard working, well-to-do. Their homes were beginning to have conveniences, and they were sending their children on through High School. Christine deeded over an eighty to each of six, but gave two, including the home eighty, to Herman. Three adjoining ones she kept for herself.

Then Herman married the soft-voiced Lucy who had gone through High School and taught a year, and brought her home to the cubic-block of a house, up the long road by the walnut trees.

Old Christine had said a great many things about it. She had gone over to her neighbor, Abbie Deal, many times in her grief and distress.

"Ach . . . Gott!" She had wrung her hard hands in distress. "Sale carpets on de two front rooms . . . mit green roses every t'ree or four feet already. Curtains by de vindows . . . mit ribbons tied back. *Närrish* . . . voolish."

"But, Christine, that's nice." Abbie Deal had comforted her. "You ought to be glad. You ought to be happy because Herman is happy with such a nice wife and that she is fixing it up so comfortably."

But Christine could not be comforted. She had waddled in disgust back down the lane road at the Deals', her blue calico dress gathered at the waistline, angrily switching the dusty jimson weeds. Each time she had gone over to the Deals' there was more distressing news to convey,--the advent of a piano and a piece of furniture in the dining room she thought they called a "boardside." But of them all, nothing seemed to irritate her so thoroughly as the carpet "mit de green roses every t'ree or four feet," as though the multiplicity of flowers added insult to the general prodigal expenditure.

Old Christine had lived with Herman and Lucy the greater part of a year. And then Herman, seeing that his beloved Lucy was ill and nervous, and that Christine was making her more so, quite firmly had moved his mother to a small tenant cottage across the road, and had seen her comfortably settled there in the little house where the wastefulness of fuel and the lavish squandering of money for kerosene need not distress her. That was the year--eighteen years before--that Herman and Lucy's only child had been born,--Allen.

That was also the year that Emil and Fritz and Ed and Herman and all the rest of the Reinmuellers met together and decided to drop the superfluous letters from their name. Their young folks were marrying here and there, some were changing their memberships to English churches, several going away to school. The young folks preferred the English spelling.

The Reinmuellers had become Rinemillers.

At home now, Allen put the truck under the shed and went into the house, looking about him with the eye of a critic. He saw the shining oak chairs and sideboard, the scrubbed oilcloth, the rope portieres hanging between the rooms, the axminster rugs which had long since replaced the carpet that had so distressed his grandmother. He knew nothing was right. You couldn't just get something new and put in as he had planned on the way home. It wouldn't improve things a rat-i-tat--that was a cinch, he said to himself. The only way to go about it was to ditch everything out and start new. Even then,--and he made himself imagine the square rooms divested of furnishings,--even then nothing was right; the shape of the rooms, the windows, the floors, the ceiling. Oh well,--this was kind of a silly thought, but if he ever had a home of his own,--it was going to be just right, like the Buchanans'.

His mother came in with her egg-basket: "You back, Allen?" She was sweet faced and pleasant looking--a plump little lady with neat light brown hair and wide humorous blue eyes. Allen resembled her but he had his father's physique. "Eighty-six. I think the White Wyandottes are the best breed I've ever had. Was the wood all right?"

"Yep--and gee, Mother, you ought to see the bride's house. Looks like the pictures in your women's magazines."

"Yes, I can just imagine it. I hope the Woman's Club will meet there so I--oh, Allen," she broke off with a girlish squeal of excitement. "How could I forget? Your letters! Papa brought in the mail when you were gone." She picked them up from the oak sideboard and held them out,--two square white envelopes, almost similar in size and texture.

Allen tore into one. "A University fraternity party card," he said in an awe-struck voice, "--the Xi Kappas."

He tore open the other. "Another one," his voice shook a little, "--the Pi Taus. The *Pi Taus.*" He repeated it with reverential disbelief.

For a moment, with eyes glued to the white card, he had a fleeting vision of driving past an aristocratic looking building up at Lincoln the night after a basket-ball game at the University Coliseum. It had great cathedral-like pillars in front, and was brightly lighted on three floors. Cars were drawn up at the curb and fellows in dress suits were getting in and out of them. There were girls in velvet evening wraps--.

He raised his head and spoke eloquently: "Oh, my *good gosh!*"

CHAPTER 5

Miraculously, to Allen's way of thinking, he was pledged Pi Tau and the aristocratic house with the cathedral-like pillars became his home. But Fate, that old woman of the loom, snapped the bright colored thread of her weaving in the spring after his initiation. For Allen's father died suddenly, and Allen went back to the square white house at the end of the lane of walnut trees to take complete charge of the work.

But something had happened to Allen. He was not satisfied,--not with himself, not with the old-fashioned methods of his father, with the machinery on the farm, nor with his limited knowledge of the management of the business side of it. To his surprise and deep mystification he was not even satisfied with Verna Conden. He lived only for the day when he could go back to school,--could tie together the broken strands of the weaving and see the whole of the design.

Herman Rinemiller's death had done something to Old Christine, too. She spent most of her time over at the square white house talking of Herman, handling things that had been Herman's, recalling childish anecdotes about him. "A calf . . . he vas sick once . . . my leetle Herman t'ought he vas *todt* . . . dead. Und he took off his coat and put it over him . . . and ven ve looked out, leetle Herman's coat vas all around de yard runnin'." She told it gently in pride and sorrow. It had come to her out of a harsh past, from the life of her little son whose boyish playtime had been given to work,--a sacrifice on the altar of greed. Poor Christine! She had long ago spent the days of her young motherhood in the marketplace, and now that they were all squandered, she had so few pleasant things left to remember. So she crouched low over the dull embers of a few half-memories in order to warm her old heart.

Lucy, Allen's mother, was always kind to her old mother-in-law, as hard as it was to do anything for her. "You can come here and live with Allen and me now, Grandma. You know you're as welcome here as though Herman was alive."

Old Christine's pale blue eyes filled with unaccustomed tears. Two or three dropped down on her leathery red-brown cheeks with immodest abandon. "A good girl you are," she said suddenly, and wiped the miscreant water away with the back of a red hand as hard as wood.

Allen, always tenderhearted when it came to old people and children, seeing her unusual distress, added his own brisk: "Sure, Grandma, I'll set you up a little stove in the east room and make you a wood-box so you can have your own heat and not depend on ours."

After which, old Christine tied a veil over her head, took her basket of eggs, and in her blue calico dress trudged over to town, went into John Deal's office and gave Allen two eighties of land via a will to which so many codicils had been added that, with more amendments than body, it looked much like the Constitution of the United States. She signed her name with a cross, saw it witnessed, and trudged stolidly back to the farm in her blue calico dress gathered full at the waistline.

High School to Laura Deal proved to be what High School is to any young person in the Cedartowns of the country,--a period of youthful ups and downs, illusions and disillusions, of long-lived friendships and short-lived enmities, of study so interspersed with play that youth does not always understand where the one leaves off and the other begins.

Laura's achievements in those four years were of extremely varied results. She was the shining star member of all English classes and the dumbest integral portion of all mathematical ones. Composition? Although verbally as noncommunicative as her father, she wrote reams on any and all topics with girlish abandon. Algebra? Eloise, varying her home instruction with scolding, sarcasm, and plaintive encouragement, managed to assist in pulling her daughter through it. American Literature? Laura had read and absorbed most of the assignments before they were assigned. Physics? Her father, beginning with extreme patience to try to augment the teacher's instructions, admitted toward the middle of the term an inglorious defeat, and quite frankly worked out the rest of the problems for her. Shakespeare? She read all the plays demanded in the curriculum, and all the others not so nominated in the bond. Plane Geometry? John and Eloise together in combined effort, dragged, tugged, and pushed their offspring through part of that science which treats also of the magnitude of space and its relations, to a passing grade. Advanced composition? Laura dashed off essays, poems, parodies, stories and biographies, both for herself and for such of her girl friends as stood in dire need of material assistance. Solid Geometry? Instructor and parents, for once in peaceful united decision, gave up with calm resignation and allowed her to substitute something which, like that portion of her mathematical head, was not so solid.

Laura was prettier now in her Senior year than she had ever been. Her clear olive complexion with its warm underlying pink, her brown eyes, the softness of her well kept dark hair, the suppleness of her body, all helped to make an attractive whole. But Laura herself was odd. Every one said so.

For one thing, in an age when High School dating was the most important of the extra curricular events, Laura did not enter into the pastime with any degree of pleasure. She did not care for boys. Dating, perforce, meant boys. And because things that are equal to the same thing are equal to each other, it followed that Laura did not care for dating. Q.E.D. As skating companions, tennis partners, and members at large of any other form of out-door sport, she not only tolerated them, she liked them. But when it came to rear-seat riding, semi-gloomy-corner sitting, and all similar modes of entertainment, Laura was just not among those present. More likely, she was curled up in some cushioned corner reading or dreaming dreams of her own. She was used to hearing people say she was odd. But for the most part she did not even care.

"When Laura gets her nose in a book, she's just dead to the world," was Eloise's complaint. "She's not wide awake about housework, either. She does her work mechanically as though she didn't have the slightest interest in practical things. At times I think she's lazy."

"Oh, I don't know," John returned, "she's young. She isn't lazy about things she likes to do. Maybe we don't understand her. Mother always seemed to understand her so well."

Immediately he saw that he had said the wrong thing. Eloise's firm lips gave an example of one of the few theorems which had been comprehensible to Laura,--that a straight line is the shortest distance between two points. "I'm sure, John, that no one can understand a child so well as the mother who gave it birth."

To which conclusive biological statement John made no reply. He had long ago learned that it was less trying not to argue. And for that matter, he did not understand Laura himself. He loved her devotedly in his busy way, but he did not understand her. But Eloise would not let the subject lie. She had to dig it up again and worry it around as a dog digs up the bone he has buried and stands barking foolishly at it.

"I'm as fond of books as Laura. She takes that from me as much as the Deals. But I don't moon over them. I go in for knowledge and data and not the emotion to be obtained from them."

Eloise took a keen delight in her club assignments. For days before the club meetings, she would work on her paper surrounded by an array of text books and encyclopedias. She would write and rewrite, hitching a sentence from one text book onto a sentence from another in an intricate form of rearrangement, and read over the result with deepest pride.

"When I go into a subject, I go thoroughly," she would say, "I marshal all the facts to be obtained."

"Facts--facts . . . what good are just facts?" Laura would say to herself, for to her a new phrase of lovely words was infinitely more alluring than all the facts of her Mother's cherished club work. "Mother never wrote an original thing in her life," she would admit to herself. And then in a sudden feeling of revulsion at the disloyalty of the thought, would throw her arms around Eloise, who stiff as a ramrod, would submit to the hasty caress with: "There, there, Laura, let mother get at something practical now."

Eloise's life seemed not rounded out. One may work at trivial uninteresting tasks and be neither small nor tiresome. But Eloise chose to dwell on the fact that she was doomed to a life of trivialities. She gave the impression that Providence, through some oversight, had neglected to place her in the way of a larger life, whatever that was. One inferred that having been formed of more artistic, less dusty dust, as it were, than the Deal family into which she had married, by some great voluntary loss of potential possibilities, she had made herself more practical than they.

She dilated long and enviously upon the fact that her Uncle Harry and Aunt Carolyn Wentworth had a great deal of money, lived in the East, traveled long distances frequently, and that by comparison, her own life in Cedartown was a constant sacrifice, but cheerfully borne. A card from the Wentworths mailed at Havana or Miami or San Diego always set her off. "Just think of it, some folks have all the luck. At least they have plenty of money which amounts to the same thing these days. Where will Uncle Harry and Aunt Carolyn go next? They've been everywhere--just everywhere. Japan . . . Philippine Islands. Imagine just packing up and going places like that. I haven't seen them for years. I do wish we could all see them." To be sure, Eloise had other uncles and aunts but only these two possessed the golden aura so necessary to peace and comfort.

In the former years she had harbored a secret ambition to get her Uncle Harry and Aunt Carolyn interested in her oldest son, Wentworth, inasmuch as he carried the family name, but for some reason Uncle Harry never seemed to warm to the subject of Wentworth via letter, inquired more often about Laura, when he saw fit to write at all. And now that Wentworth was in the South these years, married there and settled down, Eloise had given up the thought of connecting him in any way with the affluent uncle.

Laura, however, she urged to take time and pains to write to Uncle Harry. "How can I correspond with some one when I don't know what they're like?" Laura would insist.

"You seem able to write everything else," Eloise would point out. "Why not to as important a man as your Uncle?"

"Because I have to know the kind of person any one is, and then I can be like them. I can feel just like anybody," she explained. "I can feel like an old lonely person, or a happy young one, or *any* kind, and then when I get into the feeling of it, it is easy to write it."

Eloise often grew out of patience with her, and because she could not understand her little daughter, there were many trying scenes. And because there were many trying scenes, Laura retired more constantly into the privacy of her own thoughts and dreams. "I like to talk to people that nobody understands or likes," she confided to Katherine one day, "and make discoveries about them. It interests me just as it interests some people to dig for Indian curios along the Platte and the Missouri."

"You're the oddest creature, Lolly. Well, what do you find when you dig into Old Uncle Lutz,--buffalo bones and chunks of sod houses and skeletons of those grasshoppers that 'et all the crops in 1874'?"

Laura laughed as she always did at Kathie's light and airy chatter and her imitation of old Oscar Lutz's high cracked voice.

Katherine was laughing a great deal these days, too, and almost entirely at herself. To hear Kathie's comments on the subject one would have thought that the process of reproduction was the joker in life's deck of cards.

For in the tag end of the winter, with almost as much pomp and ceremony as royalty demands, Katherine's daughter was ushered into the world. She was christened Patricia and arrived home from Omaha a month later with the highest priced carriage in Nebraska and a nurse whose services, as well as those of the smart vehicle, were presented to the little Buchanan family by that unfailing source of all luxuries,--Mackenzie Deal. Kathie having given life to her child, proceeded to call the obligation square and to take up her countless social duties exactly where she left off.

It was spring again, with Laura seventeen now, ready to graduate, and old man Lutz home.

From March until the last of October the community would see him: dreamy old man Lutz sitting on the porch in the sunshine watching Cedartown go by, rugged old man Lutz walking over the paved streets, his cane thump-thumping on the walks that lay over the prairie where the oxen had traveled, grizzled old man Lutz laboriously climbing Cottonwood Hill to stand with his hand on the gnarled old trunk of the cotton-wood tree he had planted over a half century before, wistful old man Lutz thump-

thumping along the graveled walks of the cemetery where all the old friends lived in their little narrow houses.

He lived next door to the John Deal family so that Laura saw him often.

His house was as old-fashioned as he himself. Many years before, the Cedartown newspaper had carried the item that "Our distinguished citizen, Henry Lutz, is moving into the beautiful mansion which he has just completed. This is now the finest house in Cedartown," and other descriptive matter in small town hyperbole.

One year later, the same paper carried an item so similar that it might have been the identical one with the name changed,--"Our distinguished citizen, *Oscar* Lutz, is moving into the beautiful mansion which he has just completed. This is now the finest house in Cedartown." If any sinister motive of brotherly competition lay under these items, no one of Cedartown's citizens was bold enough to mention the possibility, for Oscar and Henry Lutz had been unusually close companions. If, perchance, there flowed any competitive corpuscles of blood through the veins of Martha and Sarah Lutz, the brothers' wives, no one felt equal to the task of mentioning that, either. And, in any event, Oscar and his Martha held the advantage over Henry and Sarah, for they waited until the latter had expressed themselves in a cupola and fancy cornices and gingerbread rosettes, and then put on two cupolas, made the cornices more fantastic, and spiced up the gingerbread with what was supposed to be an Egyptian lotus effect, but which proved, when Asy Drumm, the local architect-and-carpenter, had finished the job, to look more like the heads of wild cows which needed dehorning.

Laura in her pretty white sport dress was sitting on one of these gingerbread railings of the old man's porch now. He was in his element to have an audience.

"When Marthy and me moved to Nebraska, we built a little pine and cottonwood house over there on the hill north of what's the cemetery now. Nothin' to be seen but the prairie grass a wavin' and a scraggly fringe o' trees along Stove Creek. Henry and me built together,--that is, we all lived in our wagons while we was gettin' his house ready; as soon as his was done we all moved in it and worked on one for Marthy and me. Hauled the lumber from Weeping Water by oxen,--it was only ten miles but it took all day to get down and another day to come back."

Laura let the old man ramble on with no comment from her.

"Lots of wind those years. Just had a little thin layer of ship-lap between us and the wind. Nebraska and wind used to mean the same thing. Died down now all these last decades. No more wind here than anywhere else. That's what trees does for you. You can thank J. Sterling Morton and a whole lot of others of us for that,--your grandfather Deal and Henry and me set out hundreds through this part of the county and got a lot more to take time to set 'em out. But in them days the wind just blew across the country most of the time with the tumble-weeds comin' along for company. Marthy's and my home was pretty thin, I'm tellin' you. Used to lay and listen to the wind. Told Marthy once, it seemed like we was in a great holler drum with the Lord a tappin' and rappin' on the drum."

Laura, listening, said, "Why, that's quite a clever thought, Uncle Oscar." And immediately she was thinking out a poem:

"The little house was like a drum . . ."

That was the way Grandmother Deal used to be,--sort of poetical. She wondered,--did living close to the prairie soil the way they had done, give them some inner consciousness of the beautiful?

She liked to remember how she and Grandma Deal held the same liking for lovely things in literature. It was queer that an old woman like Grandma with very little education would like the things she did. There had never been any one since who could fill her place,--to whom she could talk so readily. But she could not have held converse with Grandma Deal ten minutes without deep interest. They would have touched upon some topic attractive to both, laughed at some anecdote toward which they displayed the same sense of humor, winked back a tear over some happening about which they felt the same sympathy. Yes, there had been some deep and definite understanding of life in Grandmother Deal to which she herself held the key. She did not know what it was, could not define it, found it impossible to put into words. She only knew that in this kinship, mortal or spiritual, there had been a unity of thought and expression, a oneness of dreams and desires. And because she could not describe the unusual relationship between them, which had seemed so much more important than the mere relationship of blood, she made no attempt to tell any one about it. And because, even to herself, she could not put into the limitation of exacting words the vague yearning for something beautiful which life was to give to her, she thought of it always as a white bird flying. It seemed in some indefinable way to connect itself with the dreams and desires of her Grandmother. It was like a legacy from her, a benediction. She would say to herself:

"Pain has been and grief enough and bitterness and crying,
Sharp ways and stony ways I think it was she trod,
But all there is to see now is a white bird flying,--
Whose blood-stained wings go circling high,--circling up to God."

She knew that in some vague, undetermined way she was always to follow with wistful eyes this far-off sheen of silver wings, that by some unexplainable magic she was always to see from the window of her heart, a white bird flying.

CHAPTER 6

And then, one day in the summer after Laura's graduation, with no previous announcement of their coming, and as nonchalantly as though they were arriving at a large hotel to which they had wired for accommodation, Uncle Harry Wentworth and Aunt Carolyn, a chauffeur and a maid, came into the driveway. Cedartown is used to good-looking cars slipping unconcernedly along the graveled highways which cut through the town. Indeed, Cedartown's residents, themselves, and the owners of the surrounding farm land close their garage doors on as many fine cars as do their city neighbors. But the Wentworths' car, an audaciously long affair that sported more de luxe equipment and trimming per square foot than the most pretentious one in the community, made all the children stop their play to stare, and the old men on the post-office corner temporarily cease whittling out the affairs of the nation.

To say that Eloise was upset when Uncle Harry Wentworth and Aunt Carolyn arrived is merely to make a trite statement such as "dogs bark" or "the world is round." And to look out and witness the descent of Uncle Harry Wentworth from that leviathan of a car, was as devastating to Eloise's poise as to have been an eye witness through the centuries to the entire descent of man. But not for long was Eloise's mind a mental gyroscope. She took hold of the situation with heroic efficacy. By eleven o'clock, Aunt Carolyn was on the davenport with pillows under her shoulders and a cup of hot tea in her plump hand. Uncle Harry was in an overstuffed chair with a foot-stool under his immaculate spats and a glass of iced lemonade in his slim hand. Watson, the chauffeur, was in the garage rubbing down the car as though it were a thoroughbred horse. Annette, the maid, was unpacking. Lunch was well under way and John was being summoned home from the office. Laura was assigned the task of visiting with the heretofore unknown relatives (although she had begged to fix the salad instead) and Trib, was turning the ice-cream freezer under the grape arbor. Whatever faults may have been Eloise's, she was not inefficient.

Uncle Harry and Aunt Carolyn, having come from Denver, were now about to go up into the woods of northern Minnesota. And so it came about after lunch that Uncle Harry, in as matter-of-fact manner as though he were offering to take them around the block, suddenly decided that Eloise and Laura and Trib were going, too, as their guests. "We'll take them, won't we, Carolyn?" All at once he seemed remembering to ask his wife's opinion, although Laura had a swift intuition that Aunt Carolyn assented to everything.

Uncle Harry was slim, debonair, pink-cheeked, his snow-white hair and snapping brown eyes forming a striking contrast. His hands were long and slim, the nails as pink as his cheeks. He was nervous, unsettled, never still a moment when talking. He rocked up and down on his heels and toes when standing, fidgeted about when sitting. He darted his bright brown eyes here and there as though looking for something he never saw. His mind, too, seemed darting about in the same agile way, seeking something it never found. Aunt Carolyn was a complete antithesis. Physically fat, shapeless, and two-chinned, her mind also seemed fat, shapeless and two-chinned. She answered questions slowly if at all. Much of the time she merely smiled in answer to Uncle Harry's rather exaggerated statements. Having been left behind on most of her husband's mental flights, apparently she had now given up the breathless pursuit and settled back in obese complacency.

Eloise was delighted with the invitation but unable to see how it could be done. Uncle Harry assumed all details of the plan. The front seat was wide,--he and Watson and Annette could all three sit there very comfortably, Aunt Carolyn and Eloise in the back seat, Trib and Laura on the adjustable ones. They would start early the next morning, get to Okoboji for lunch, Minneapolis by night, and the second day easily reach the north woods hotel to which they were bound. Eloise argued that the two should make their stay longer in Cedartown, but apparently Uncle Harry, having thought of the new scheme, wanted to carry it out immediately. He see-sawed up and down on his slim immaculate shoes, waved his hands in illustrative gesticulation, winked a roguish eye at Laura, chucked her under the chin, sat down and tapped the chair arms, stood up and rubbed his hands together in nervous glee. Aunt Carolyn lay shapelessly among the pillows of the davenport and smiled steadily without effort.

To Uncle Harry's sudden inspiration that John go up on the train and meet them, Laura's father only shook his head and named two or three important reasons for not doing so,--the Blackman estate, a guardianship case, preparation for the schoolboard suit. Uncle Harry looked at John Deal with something akin to curiosity. Here was a man who seemed irrevocably tied by a hundred chains to a desk. For a brief moment he might have been wondering how it would seem not to be able to go where he wished, whenever he wished. Then his restless mind was off again on another tangent.

When it was decided that they were really to go, Eloise rose to the management of the preparations like a bass to the lure. Her efficient brain pigeon-holed every activity of the household. Trib was to ride on his bicycle and give certain instructions to the woman who did cleaning for her. Laura was to look over her own clothes and her mother's for any missing buttons or stitch. Eloise, herself, turned off a dozen necessary tasks. Uncle Harry walked nervously about the house. Annette fanned Aunt Carolyn who lay supinely among the pillows, the bustling activity going on around her like so much wind around a granite monument. Watson groomed the flawless car.

In the midst of preparations old Oscar Lutz tap-tapped around to the back door, a mess of spinach in the gray pail with a rope for the handle. Eloise was provoked. "That old codger--whatever is the matter with him? *Spinach*--the night before we're going away. He *knew* we were going. Dad told him. I heard him out by the morning-glories. Now he'll have to meet Uncle Harry. And how well they two will mix."

Laura took the spinach. She understood old Oscar Lutz better than her mother. He wanted to do something for them, so he was saying it with spinach. She introduced old Oscar to Uncle Harry and Aunt Carolyn. Uncle Oscar was pleased to meet them, both verbally and whole-heartedly. Here was a fresh new audience,--one to whom no anecdote of his was old material. He had a full life time of experiences upon which to draw, not one of which these people had ever heard.

His hand, as hard and calloused as untanned buffalo hide, shook Uncle Harry's slim bony one and Aunt Carolyn's cushion-like soft one.

It was not five minutes later until Eloise and Laura, going on with their preparations for the journey, could hear his high cackling laugh and his enthusiastic "I mind as how--" It seemed to be something about traveling in the early days, the subject introduced no doubt by the present anticipated trip. "I mind as how I started out doin' all my travelin' on 'Shanks mares' over the hills, wadin' in mud or deep snow." They could hear snatches of the one-sided conversation. "Well, well, travelin' wa'n't what you'd call ideal in them days, but we had lots o' fun . . . more 'n' they have now, seems like. I mind as how I made a cutter out o' good stout lumber, lined the inside with buffalo so's to be warm and comfortable for Marthy. Had a soapstone we'd take along and two or three bricks--heat 'em all in the fire, wrap 'em up good, tuck Marthy in with her feet on the soapstone and put mebbe two buffalo robes all around us and away we'd go, bells ringin', and happy as larks."

There was more monologue on the subject and by the time Eloise had returned to the living room, she found Uncle Oscar going strong on the Easter blizzard of '73, Uncle Harry moving about with the peevish headshakes of an irritated animal, and Aunt Carolyn frankly asleep.

All that evening Laura was thrilled with the thought of the unexpected trip. Just one thing was lacking--her father. She felt a deep disappointment that he could not go--a sympathetic understanding of the cares that harassed him. He was like the old man of the sea,--the burdens of the community the bundle on his back.

It was a gay lark to glide along the country in Uncle Harry Wentworth's great car. Uncle Harry sat with Annette and the chauffeur, a young married couple. He had his arm on the back of the seat and sometimes he would touch the back of Annette's white neck with his nervous slim fingers. Once Aunt Carolyn said, "Annette, if you're crowded, you can come back here." Much of the time he was turned around talking excitedly to Laura and Trib who sat on the smaller extra seats. Aunt Carolyn did not talk a great deal. She sat quietly with the little fixed smile on her fat face. Laura stole surreptitious glances at her sometimes and wondered just what she was thinking. Did she enjoy her husband's nervous chatter? Did she approve of his extravagant statements? Did the little fixed smile mean she was happy? Or was it a mask? Sometimes she went to sleep for a few moments, her head against the gay cushions, and the smile vanished, so that her plump face looked flabby and sad. Laura, stealing a covert glance at her then, tried to picture her in another environment, and invariably she saw her in a washable house dress and big white apron, her plump hands, white with flour, making cookies for hungry little grandchildren. It was a foolish notion, Laura told herself, but it seemed the setting in which she really belonged, rather than the present one of traveling about the country in the palatial car with her silver-mounted luggage and her maid.

It made Laura think how different many people would look in other environments. It was queer what clothes and setting did to one. She pictured Katherine Buchanan in sleazy cheap clothes, and her own father as a section boss in overalls, thought of Allen Rinemiller in his collegiate-looking suits and hats since he had been to the University.

The group of travelers stopped for a little time by the shores of Storm Lake and again at Okojobi and Spirit Lakes. Laura and Trib were charmed beyond words. Children of eastern Nebraska, they had known intimately only the Missouri and the Platte and a small lake or two.

There was a night in Minneapolis at a big hotel, with Uncle Harry in his breezy way creating a stir and commotion in getting settled when there was no need of either, and then the long trip to the north lakes. At the first odor of pines and the first sight of white birches bending above blue waters, Laura felt that old emotional uplift she always experienced when drinking in a new atmosphere. Immediately she was reveling in the "feel" of the setting: picturing sleek-haired Indian maidens and their light-footed lovers meeting here on the sloping shores. Her palm itched for the touch of a pencil and, because she had no means of putting down her emotional disturbances just then, she sat for a long time saying nothing, but mentally composing snatches of description and bits of verse.

The two weeks spent there at the rustic hotel were by way of being a bit of heaven both to seventeen-year-old Laura and thirteen-year-old Trib. The white birches drinking forever from glass-clear waters, the tall pines massed against sapphire skies, the clear spongy carpet of sweet-smelling needles, all filled Laura with the poetry of living that she always experienced when everything was "just right." Trib's sensations were not of a poetical type. The motorboat at the dock, the box of lures, the rods and reels for which Uncle Harry arranged, constituted a large part of his own particular joy of living.

The mornings were spent in fishing, up the long lake in the motorboats, casting for the sporty bass or trolling for the common pike, with the hope always present of getting a wily muscallonge. At eleven there was bathing, and again at four, when the water was full of young people and old with water-wings and joy balls. After dinner, cards for the older people, dancing for the young, inside the hotel or on the screened-in porches into which the mosquitoes could only gaze hungrily.

Aunt Carolyn and Eloise settled themselves each night for bridge. But Uncle Harry danced, always with the prettiest and youngest girls. Sometimes Aunt Carolyn, calm and placid, watching the dancers, would send for him. She wanted a silk shawl or would he please go and see whether Watson had looked over the car in preparation for the trip tomorrow. It seemed queer to Laura. She could not quite sense what was wrong. Aunt Carolyn was pleasant. Uncle Harry punctilious in attendance. But something was not just right.

"Is Aunt Carolyn lots older than Uncle Harry?" she asked her mother once.

"Goodness, no" . . . Eloise laughed, "he's anyway two years older,-- maybe three. And you'll have to give him credit for having the same wife all these years, Laura."

Well, why shouldn't he, Laura wondered. Why was that any credit to him? She thought about it a great deal. It worried her,--the something which was not right,--but she could not quite put her finger on the defect. It was a queer marriage,--Uncle Harry, gay and slim and debonair, sipping the tips of the blossoms of pleasure,--Aunt Carolyn, fat and old-lady-like and settled, drinking her tea and cuddling her hot-water bottle.

Laura thought often of her father down home, working at the desk. She felt a great pity for him that he could not be up here, too. She wished he could do something that would make him happy and care-free and boyish. Working and working for other people without a great deal of compensation, always on the town council and the school board, always assigned to church and civic committees, his tasks never finished, a rest never earned. She wished she could do something about it, but not being able to, she did the next best thing--she sympathized with him, writing a note every day telling him of all their activities, never failing to add "I wish you were here, too." She did not know that her father put them all away in a private drawer in his desk where they stayed for years. John Deal in his silent way loved his young daughter deeply.

It seemed queer to John Deal to live alone in the empty house. He missed the lively chatter of the children and Eloise's good housekeeping. He scarcely knew what to do with himself on the few free evenings which were his. Sometimes he read, and for one whole evening he sat in a big chair in the living room and dozed or looked at the group on the mantel.

Many a descendant of some old sea captain has above his fireplace a miniature brig with sails bravely flying, to which he points with pride as the traditional embodiment of the spirit of his forefathers. John Deal had a bronze covered-wagon on his mantel, the oxen molded in the act of drawing it, well-formed and life-like, their huge horns tipped realistically with brass knobs.

Eloise had protested the advent of the piece. There was no covered-wagon episode in the life of Eloise's parents, she said. Her people had originally come over in the *Mayflower* (at which John had surreptitiously grinned and mumbled something that sounded like "poor old over-loaded boat"),--they had always remained city people and easterners, for that matter, until her own father came to Iowa. She didn't think the huge clumsy bronze thing looked in place in what she had tried to make an exceptionally dainty room. If the statue were something graceful, now, a deer, or even the long sinuous lines of grayhounds; but oxen,--huge and dull-looking and stolid,--and a wagon with every flapping piece of canvas molded in the bronze. She had said a great deal about the price, too.

"Bronze--why bronze is terribly expensive. John Deal, how much did you pay for that? I'll wager anything, we couldn't afford it."

As a matter of fact, he shouldn't have afforded it. Eloise was right about that. It had cost an even hundred dollars, the entire fee of a client. But he had been attracted by it as he was waiting for Laura to make a small purchase; had stood for a long time before the little group, coveted it with a good healthy covetousness; had thought about it many times and finally gone back to get it, half in hopes that it was gone, half worried for fear it was. He liked to look up at it as he smoked, forgetting the petty quarrels of his country clients in remembering some of the tales his people had told him. Their lives seemed hard in retrospect, but after all, there had been something free and untrammeled about them, like the winds that blew over their prairie home. To get food to eat, fuel to burn and money to pay the taxes,--those seemed the greatest problems his father had.

He remembered just how the old soddie looked,--he must have been eight or nine when they moved from it into the frame house. He could close his eyes and visualize the one main living room with the general bedroom off of it, the cookstove where they sometimes burned corn, and the deep seats in the two windows formed by the width of the sod strips. He could see his cheery mother at her endless task of mending the clothes, his big strong father coming in with the milk pails, smell the odor of cornmeal cooking, hear the never-ceasing wind blowing against the little soddie. Here he sat now in comparative comfort, complete luxury even, if likened to the soddie; and yet his problems seemed more difficult than his father's.

He wondered why, with all the added comforts, there had been no lessening of worries. Sometimes, the difficult questions confronting him seemed more than humanity could solve. There had been the question of defending the guaranty law. He had gone to the legislature with the burdens of the depositors in the failed banks heavy upon him. He had the story of old Mr. and Mrs. Kleinman losing their life savings ringing in his ears; the pitiful tale of Amy Hall, the little seamstress, saving a dollar or two a week for twenty years only to see it swept away; almost on his own cheeks the tears of young Mrs. Wise who had deposited her husband's insurance money just before the crash. How could he have gone up to the legislature and not fought to the finish for a fund with which to reimburse these? It had made Mack angry. Mack and the other bankers were lying down on further taxation. Already they had paid out several million dollars. "Poured it in a rat hole" Mack had said. For the fund was insolvent. Weak banks had been allowed to run on when it was known they were weak. Cracking down on the first few would have saved the many, he had thought.

"The trouble was long before that," Mack had said. "Anybody could go out and start a bank where two roads crossed, if they had ten dollars and a blank book and a pencil." The whole thing had been bungled. People had been led to think the state was solidly behind their deposits. Then came the land slump, depression, banks crumbling,--good bankers were required to pay for the sins of the poor ones. It made a vicious circle. Mack and the others had rebelled. Confiscatory they called it. Unconstitutional. "No state has a right to take one man's property to pay another man's debts." Mack had said it a hundred times. They had argued hotly--brother against brother. "But you didn't call it confiscating when you were playing it up big in your ads. Now that it's a heavy burden you've changed your mind." They had grown hot in their arguments,--had lost their former comradeship. Civil war in the Deal family.

Well, it wasn't a question of what might have been. It was a question of what to do now. How to compromise. How to fight to get back old Mr. and Mrs. Kleinman's money with which to bury them, and sickly Amy Hall's savings and young Mrs. Wise's only fund for herself and two babies,--and at the same time keep the other banks solvent,--keep the whole system from crashing with a far greater catastrophe than the present one.

He would go over and over it, silent, brooding, with a deep feeling of compassion for them all. Life was like the old plains before the trails were made. It took initiative and foresight to find one's way through it. The old plainsmen moved through an uncharted region with only the sun and the stars for guidance. Their children and their children's children moved now through just as uncharted a wilderness. If only the stars and the sun could guide them, too.

Sometimes he would look up to the exquisitely done bronze on the mantel and feel a touch of mental uplift. It so typified the struggles of another day, made him realize that every age has its long tiresome journey. Sometimes it is an endless lurching over miles of dry grass and sunflowers, and the breaking of raw prairie sod. And sometimes it is an endless fighting for the peace and comfort of fellow men. He was glad he had bought the bronze.

CHAPTER 7

Laura and her mother seemed in some inexplicable way to draw closer together in spirit there in the north so many miles from home. Sometimes they walked together through the needle-carpeted woods. Once they came upon the remains of a tepee set high upon the bluffs, so that Laura was transported in fancy to the days when Indians lived by the lake. She was deep in an emotional retrospection of the time, when Eloise called practically: "No, Laura; look here. It's of recent date. The poles at the top are bound together with a patented wire. Scouts or Hi-Y boys! No Indian ever put those poles together." Laura had to admit defeat. But why couldn't Mother have left her the fancy?

It was on one of these walks that Laura approached a subject long on her mind. She didn't want to go to the University--not at all. The University seemed so huge with its six or seven thousand students on the one campus. It frightened her, the very thought of it. Couldn't she stay home and read and write? She'd make good use of her time. Really, she would.

But Eloise was firm. "It's just what you *need,* Laura. Mother knows best. You need to mix with people. This is a practical world we live in. You'll just have to shake yourself out of that dreamy way of yours."

It hung over like a menacing thing; she wished she could stay forever in her blue and white room or out in the grape arbor. The middle of September grew to seem as threatening as some date of impending disaster.

"Sometimes, Laura, I think you're a nineteenth-century girl in a twentieth-century setting," her mother said in exasperation.

But whenever it fastened its hold upon her, Laura threw off the thought of the dread change, preferring to live in the happy present and make the most of her pleasures.

And then, in the midst of the other excitements, as though her experiences were not sufficient for happiness, she met Miss Westcote,-- Miss Evelyn Westcote, the writer. Miss Westcote and a friend had a cottage where the pines tapped on the roof and inquisitive squirrels ran nimbly around the chimney. To one in Laura's state of mind concerning writing, the place seemed hallowed ground and Miss Westcote a goddess who had lost her way between Olympus and some Utopia. She spent every moment near Miss Westcote that propriety allowed. Sometimes she walked past her cottage with scarcely a glance in that direction, so that she might not seem to be thrusting her presence upon the writer. If Miss Westcote was the first to notice and invite her in, Laura lived in a heaven of bliss. She could not understand, though, why Miss Westcote seldom mentioned her writing. How could she turn out a book like *The Chime of Bells* and not talk about it? She ventured to ask her one day. Miss Westcote laughed in her merry way, the lids of her eyes crinkling. "For the same reason that the candy manufacturer doesn't stand and eat his own candy. We all like to get away from our business and forget it."

"But, Miss Westcote,--it isn't like a *business,* surely." Laura was surprised, a little disillusioned. "I thought it was . . . oh, always inspirational, you know."

Miss Westcote suddenly sobered. "I rather think it always is,--when one is very young. But oh, my dear," she added, "for such a short time does one stay young."

Eloise, too, was delighted to meet Miss Westcote. Was she not to review one of Miss Westcote's novels in club that very fall? She was jubilant about the fact that they were to be thrown together for a time. "Imagine my meeting her here," she said to Laura. "I can question her all about it and get my information first hand. The ladies will certainly sit up and take notice of that."

"But, Mother," Laura was diffident about the matter. "She's here on a vacation. She's resting and playing around. Maybe she wouldn't relish an interview."

But Eloise knew better. "You can't tell me," she affirmed, "I'll wager there never was an author yet who didn't like to talk about himself and his books. I shall ask her beforehand of course. This is really an opportunity that I couldn't have dreamed would happen."

Miss Westcote was quite gracious about the interview. She would be glad to tell Mrs. Deal any time about the writing of the novel.

Eloise and Laura drove over to Silver Lake Corners before the interview to buy a notebook for the occasion. A fat man in a straw hat waited upon Eloise in the little general store that supplied the tourists' needs. People were buying fishlines, sinkers, rods, lures, ice-cream cones, movie magazines and pop, getting their mail, and sending postcards of pigmy-looking people nonchalantly holding up twenty-five pound muscallonge.

From the Corners they drove straight to Miss Westcote's cottage where they found her sitting in a long deck-chair busily engaged in doing nothing but gazing out on the lake whose waves danced under a golden shimmer in the afternoon sun. She rose to meet the two, pulled other lounging chairs forward, and slipped back comfortably into her own. Laura, too, made herself comfortable. But not so Eloise. She sat upright on the edge of her chair, pencil poised over the notebook, and the interview was on.

"My first question comes under the head of 'Author's Motive,'" Eloise said pleasantly, briskly, "Miss Westcote, why did you write *The Chime of Bells?*"

"Well," Miss Westcote said pleasantly, but not briskly, "you know, Mrs. Deal, there is one motive behind writing which all authors possess in common,--at least, after the first fine thrill of writing to reform the world is over and they have settled down to make a business of it. They would like to side-step the issue, and most of them do."

"And what is that?" Eloise was ready to write the answer verbatim.

Miss Westcote's eyes twinkled and then closed in narrow slits, a way they did when she was silently laughing. "Because we can no longer use buttons, trinkets and beads for trade and barter, and because writers are charged practically the same for food, clothing, tooth paste and gasoline that other people are charged; you will figure out for yourself what was at least one motive for writing it."

Laura laughed, but Eloise looked a little pained, so that Miss Westcote said hastily: "But that's too sordid a motive for you to tell your club, isn't it? And now I'll give you a more literary sounding reason." And Eloise copied her words verbatim in the little black book.

And then, "Who are your primary characters?"

That was easy, and Miss Westcote named them.

"Your secondary characters?"

Scratch--scratch in the little black book.

"Your tertiary characters?"

Miss Westcote's eyes narrowed again into quivering slits. "My dear Mrs. Deal, you're getting me worried. Is there such a word as 'quartuary' for the fourth in importance?"

Eloise said she thought there was one with that meaning, although she had her doubts about it being that particular word. "And I rather think the three . . . the three . . . what shall I call them . . . ?"

"Layers," Miss Westcote suggested, her eyes crinkling.

"Sets," Eloise corrected. "I rather think the three sets of characters are enough to report."

"So do I," agreed the creator of those characters.

"Now for the questions," Eloise was businesslike, thorough. A bombardment followed: "What do you consider your chapter of climax?"

"What are the main crises before the climax?" "What were your controlling factors in plot formation?"

Miss Westcote later related the incident to the friend sharing the cottage: "She had me completely floored. I could scarcely remember the names of the characters. If there was a climax I had mislaid the thing. I couldn't have sworn absolutely that I wrote it. In a maze of academic questions, she had destroyed my poor little story. It was dead,--killed on the dissecting table under an anæsthetic. If a story, Blanche, is worth milling over in a meeting at all, it's worth reviewing as a thing of flesh and blood and spirit rather than of bones and dead tissue and numerical dimensions. The girl was darling, sweet and understanding,--but the mother,--one of those highly efficient women who would have arranged the stars in symmetrical rows and dispensed with the milky way as being too messy."

Toward the end of the second week, Uncle Harry grew restless and irritable. Aunt Carolyn seemed striving to be carefully tactful. She began inquiring about a hotel in northern Wisconsin, casually speaking of the delights to be encountered there as related to her by some young woman who had been a guest the year before. Uncle Harry became interested, cheerful. With much commotion and questioning he collected data about it: distance, roads to take, prices, conveniences, kind of people there. He spent a long time sitting on the steps leading down to the dock with the young woman who had given Aunt Carolyn the information.

The two weeks were over, the beautiful two weeks. Laura thought she could not stand it, never again to see the lovely birches and the winding roads, smell the pungent green pines and hear the lapping of the cool blue water. She felt sad and depressed with that emotional thrill which always accompanied the sensations.

She went over to see Miss Westcote and to bid her good-by.

"I can't tell what it has meant to meet you, Miss Westcote." Laura's serious brown eyes met the kindly twinkling ones of the older woman.

"And I've loved knowing you, too," Miss Westcote was saying. She held Laura's hand. "Keep up your writing. Write the things you know and understand . . ." She smiled down on her, ". . . your own prairies and your own people. Write it in your own way . . . the way *you* see it. Don't imitate or copy . . . you wouldn't do that with words . . . but don't even do so with the spirit of the thing. Don't try to look at your own prairies and your own people as an outsider does. Interpret them as *you* feel about them . . . knowing that there will be others who see and feel as you do."

Laura wanted to talk more, to ask a dozen questions, to tell this wise woman many things that were close to her heart. She wanted to throw open the rooms of her mind and take the thoughts out one by one and show them to Miss Westcote. She wanted to repeat to her the verses she had run across after her grandmother's death, to tell her that no one had ever held her complete confidence since that time, to confide in her about the wonderful magic dreams and desires she and Grandmother used to discuss, to make her understand that all there was to see now was a white bird flying. But she felt that old tight-throated sense of restraint, and only thanked her, told her she would do the best she could, and said good-by. When she turned away and walked down the little path where the pine needles lay like a thick brown rug, she felt that nothing in the world could keep her from making another Miss Westcote of herself, that she would never let anything in life handicap her or swerve her from the goal.

When they parted--the Deals were to go home by train at the Wentworths' expense--Uncle Harry held Laura's hand and kissed her twice. "You're coming with me again. You're coming East to stay with me awhile," he said suddenly, as though he had just thought of it, "isn't she, Carolyn?"

Aunt Carolyn smiled and said yes, that would be lovely.

Uncle Harry grew more enthusiastic. He went up and down, see-saw fashion, on his slim immaculate heels and toes. "I'll send for you. Soon. She can come, can't she, Eloise?"

Eloise was pleased and made no effort to hide it. "It would be the making of her." She was earnest and grateful.

"I'll drop you a line when the time comes. And send you a check. I wouldn't want my little girl to be at any expense when she's visiting me." He shook hands again. He sprang on to the running board and into the car, tilting his youthful hat jauntily, winking a bright brown eye at Laura, wagging a slim, highly polished finger at her and saying: "You'll hear from me, you rascal. Probably next summer, you'll hear from your Uncle Harry. It'll be fun to have you there--and a lot of your friends around."

Aunt Carolyn settled herself heavily in the big car, with Annette fixing cushions and the footrest. She had on a loose shapeless dress for comfort in riding and wide flat oxfords.

The big car drove off with Uncle Harry waving his jaunty, boyish hat. Laura felt depressed. There was something wrong--something terribly wrong there--but she did not know just what it was. Marriage ought not to be like that.

CHAPTER 8

When they were back in Cedartown, slipping comfortably into the old routine, Laura realized that she was being swept along in the stream of preparation that emptied as it were into the great gulf of the University. It seemed a terrible thing that she could not stop it. Why couldn't people do what they wished? Sometimes she walked past the big brick High School where she had spent so many years, and looked longingly at the old building as one looks at the familiar face of a friend. She fancied it looked kind, motherly, almost compassionate that she was to go away. Strangely enough she failed to remember that she once felt the same temerity upon entering its portals that she was now feeling.

The clan all discussed her, long and openly, at Katherine's on a Sunday afternoon in August. The lovely little English home was full of Deals: Aunt Margaret and Uncle "Doc" Baker and Grace Deal, who was teaching in the University now, were there from Lincoln. Aunt Isabelle and Uncle Harrison Rhodes were there on their annual trip out from Chicago. Uncle Mackenzie and Aunt Emma Deal, their son Stanley and his wife and two children were there from Omaha. John, Eloise, Laura and Trib were all there, as well as Jimmie, Katherine and little Patty, six months old now and the center of attraction.

"Going into a sorority, I suppose, Laura?" It was Aunt Emma who inadvertently began it.

Eloise immediately answered for her. "Oh, yes, Laura's going into a sorority."

"Mother," Laura was disturbed, embarrassed. "I don't know that I would be *taken.*"

Eloise's mouth set in a firm line. "I think you'll be taken all right."

Why did mother say that out before every one? She might *not* be pledged.

Others had something to say. Immediately it became the topic of conversation. The Deals were always like that--noisy and argumentative, each one sharpening his wits against the other's judgment. There was diversity of opinion here. Jimmie Buchanan, Uncle Doc Baker and John Deal were decidedly anti-fraternity. Eloise, Aunt Margaret, Aunt Emma, Katherine, Stanley Deal and his wife were all Greek letter advocates. Because it had no direct bearing on music, the Rhodeses were not especially active in the discussion. Uncle Mack was neutral,--dipping in here and there on either side. Grace Deal, who said she ought to know, inasmuch as she taught there, declared they were necessary evils. "I don't like everything about them . . . but just suggest something constructive to take their place. You can't criticize without substituting some constructive idea."

"Dormitories . . . treat everybody alike. I've been working for that move for a long time." It was John Deal.

"Of all utterly snobbish outfits the frats get the hand-crocheted waffle-iron," was Jimmie Buchanan's verdict.

"Yes, they ought to be abolished entirely. Think of a democratic tax-supported institution . . . and a decent taxpayer's son can't go up there without . . ."

"But, John," it was Margaret Baker, "it's human nature to form in cliques. Seven thousand people can't all go together in one nice democratic crowd."

"That's it . . . there you are . . . that's the answer," several said triumphantly.

Katherine had something to add: "People *will* run in bunches. Say the charters were all taken away to-morrow, Uncle John, and the chapter houses turned over to the University . . . if that were possible . . . by next Sunday the crowds living in them would have reorganized and have new names: 'The Apache Indians,' or 'The Ancient Arabs' and 'The Dirty Devils.'"

Every one laughed at that, and it temporarily cleared the atmosphere which was becoming warmer with slight indications of a storm.

"Kathie's right," Eloise put in, "I'll say it's better to be organized nationally with creeds and supervisors."

"Maybe it's all right for the East with their older traditions, but here in this democratic Midwest . . ."

"Where men are men and women are W.C.T.U. members," Katherine inserted with her usual flippancy.

"Look what the fraternity did for Allen Rinemiller in the time he was there," some one said.

Eloise snorted. "You can't get away from your grandmother."

"Yes," Jimmie Buchanan took it up. "That's a frat for you--pounced on a green country kid like Allen because of his fine athletic record. He makes a few important plays and the frat sits back on its haunches and takes all the glory."

"But, Jimmie, look what it did for him socially--took the shine off his hair and put it on his shoes--got his hair cut right--put him in a tuxedo."

"And the Pi Tau house--you can't put a fellow in a house furnished like that and not have his standards of living raised. The Pi Tau house is a beauty--it looks like a church, and--"

"Ha! Ha! That's pretty good." It was Jimmie Buchanan, again. *"Looks like a church maybe . . ."* And he went off into a personal and private gale of laughter.

"Allen's going back again now," Laura volunteered. "I met him yesterday on the street and he told me."

They discussed the subject long and noisily--the Deals. They were like that, full of interest toward all that was going on around them.

In the midst of the brisk debate, there was a tap-tapping sound on the cement sidewalk.

"Uncle Oscar," Emma said with supreme resignation.

"Now the shouting and the tumult will die," Katherine predicted, "and we'll hear a little about the original brotherhood of fraternities, . . . the Ancient Order of Ox Drivers."

The old man came in smiling, his black hat in his hand, in his shabby coat the G.A.R. button and "68." He felt a great happiness to see so many of his old friends' children and their children in one group, a deep gratification that he had taken the notion to walk down here just at this time. He had brought lettuce to Kathie in the pail with a rope for the handle.

Although Jimmie held a chair ready for him, the old man stood in the middle of the room leaning on his cane and looking into all their faces. "There's about as many of you here as there was the time your father and my brother Henry and I fixed up a wagon to haul the whole neighborhood down to Weeping Water. I mind as how at the County fair they was goin' to give a prize to the precinct that could get up the largest representation. Well, sir, Will Deal and Henry and me put our heads together and said old Stove Creek precinct would just naturally come home with that money. Took boards and spliced out the longest wagon box you ever see . . . had four team of oxen on it . . ." Every one was avoiding Kathie's laughing eyes. "Piled all the Deals and the Lutzes and the Reinmuellers and some others in 'n' drove to the fair. You should o' heard 'em shout when we come. Equipage was so long we couldn't turn around . . . had to go on through the little street and turn around on the prairie beyond the town. Had Henry and Sarah's melodeon in the front . . . Abbie Deal was playin' the accompaniment to 'Red, White and Blue' and 'Columby the Gem of the Ocean.' Wagon was so long they couldn't keep together in their singin'. Will Deal and I was drivin' the ox teams. And Henry would run along side 'n' yell: 'Ready--set--sing.' Once Henry come up to the back end and says: 'Darn it. Quit singin' that *Who Will Lead Me Home To Heaven*--the front end's singin' *Three Blind Mice*.'" And he slapped his knee and chuckled over the pleasant memories.

If John Deal did not care about his daughter going Greek, Eloise had no greater desire than that she would. Laura knew which one would win, providing she were invited. She added the last always, feeling very young and unsophisticated and not having any too much confidence in her own appearance.

By the next week party bids began arriving. Laura was surprised beyond measure. It seemed unbelievable. Eloise was not surprised and there was nothing unbelievable about the daughter of a Wentworth having plenty of invitations. She was planning to go to Lincoln with Laura to see that the affair was engineered correctly.

"I couldn't trust Laura to see the thing through herself," she said to John. "She's such a day dreamer, and she seems to care about almost nothing about getting on socially. She'd be apt to forget to keep her most important house bids. There are the Chi Taus now . . . wealthy girls . . . and the Alpha Betas . . . *family* counts the most there . . . the Gamma Zetas are a lively bunch, prominent socially . . . the Rho Phis are awfully good nationally--she has party bids from them all . . . and it's of the utmost importance that she make one of these."

"Why is it?" John wanted to know. "Laura's a nice kid--she'll make friends anywhere."

"Of course, you would say that. I suppose you think she could go up there--and just study--and make a few frowsy friends . . ."

"I had a faint notion we were sending her up there *to study*. When I was in the University . . ."

"Yes, we know. You curried Dr. Overman's horses and stoked the Chancellor's furnace . . ."

"And made plenty of good substantial friends . . ." he returned warmly.

"Well, Laura can't stoke furnaces . . ."

"Nobody wants her to work her way when she doesn't have to . . . but it seems to me you put a lot of stress on the social side."

"I do, and there's plenty of reason for it. Listen to me, John Deal. You're a man and couldn't be expected to have the intuition a mother has. Practically every girl who leaves school, leaves it engaged. Now I'm far-sighted enough to prepare for that. If she goes Alpha Beta or Gamma Zeta or one of those--whom will she meet?"

She hastened to answer her own question: "The brothers and the friends of Alpha Beta or Gamma Zetas. See? It's as simple as daylight."

"And where's the assurance that the brothers and the friends are going to be so all-fired nice?"

But that was too much for Eloise. If one could not comprehend the superiority of the brothers and the friends of Alpha Beta or Gamma Zeta-- there was simply no use discussing it.

So Eloise fitted Laura out in pretty new clothes, and armed with the party invitations and her own efficient management, accompanied her to school.

John hated to see his little girl go. She was only seventeen. The school seemed so huge. Would she come back to him still sweet and unspoiled? Or snobbish and sophisticated? He wanted to tell her how much he loved her, how proud he was of her little talent, how happy he wanted her always to be. But he could not bring himself to say any of those things. He only pinched her cheek and waved his hand to her cheerfully, when she left. The more deeply he felt anything, the less articulate he was. He had always been that way, and Laura was like him.

Eloise and her ewe lamb stayed at a leading hotel during the rush week. Aunt Margaret Baker had offered them the hospitality of her lovely home, but Eloise said no, they would be right down town ready for anything that came up. And plenty of things came up.

Laura was herded to breakfasts and luncheons and dinners, to afternoon teas and evening parties. Some of the chapter houses were gorgeous in their furnishings. One or two were not quite finished so that they stepped over lath and plaster in part of the rooms. There seem always to be lath and plaster on the campuses of midwest colleges.

Laura could not quite understand the queer quality of the atmosphere. There was something about it she had never experienced before-- something tense and important, as though every one's welfare hung in the balance. Nerves seemed taut, manners strained. An exterior of convention seemed to cover something primitive that might at any moment break its leash and bound out. Girls she had never seen before put their arms around her. Many told her she was a darling. Some confided that, honestly, she was the keenest girl that had been in the house.

Laura said to herself: "That isn't so. I can see right through them."

But some of the girls had other qualities,--graciousness that seemed a part of them and not assumed, sincerity that showed in their conversation. Some were jolly with infectious laughter. At first, Laura met them curiously with some attention to their various characteristics; but after a time she grew tired, confused, unable to tell the ones she fancied from those she did not. And once in the mad rush, her mother happened to remember that Laura must go to the huge Coliseum to register for classes. It seemed a waste of time to Eloise, but after all, it was quite true that the studies must be given some thought also. Registration was effected with no casualties, although it was well for Laura that her own chosen course carried no science of number and quantity and all their respective relations. It was very trying, and in the midst of the confusion, she sometimes longed for an hour in which she could go out in the grape arbor of their back yard, and sit and read and think.

The rushing parties were all over at last, and, in the temporary shelter of the hotel room the potential author shed nervous tears. She was so bewildered, she told her mother, she hadn't the faintest idea with which group she wanted to align herself. But Eloise chose for her. "Alpha Beta," she said unhesitatingly, firmly. "That's your first choice, Laura. I do hope they will take you. It seemed the last word to me in an aristocratic group. Gamma Zeta is your second choice, and Rho Phi third. When you turn in your list, that's the way they are to be listed."

"And where'll I live if not any of those three bid me?"

Eloise's nostrils quivered, and her mouth became a firm straight line. One might have wondered if the whole system did not totter perilously in that moment. But the old order of things was happily preserved, for Laura went Alpha Beta. A little frightened and decidedly homesick, she was towed to the house at the specified time by Eloise, triumphant and self-complacent.

The Alpha Beta house was old, and like Westminster Abbey, fruit cake, and wine, all the better for that. In fact, its very antiquity gave it an air of superiority which is the *ultima thule* of attainment at colleges west of the Missouri, in some of which Time has not played so long in the cast that he has called in his partner, Tradition. The house had an atmosphere of mellowed aristocracy which exactly suited Eloise's aspirations for Laura. The white woodwork and mahogany doors, the delft blue hangings, soft-toned rugs and fat old furniture in the living rooms, the quaint chintzes in the sunrooms, the rather old-fashioned furnishings of the bedrooms all seemed combining to make capital of the fact that they represented one of the first chapters on the campus.

Eloise was satisfied. And as she did after most attainments of the John Deal family, cut another notch in the gun of her own efficient management;

although as a matter of fact, if the interior of Eloise's mind had been disclosed to the chapter, nothing would so certainly have lost Laura her bid as the knowledge that her mother had definitely picked Alpha Beta for Laura, before Alpha Beta had done its own picking.

When Eloise said good-by to her Alpha Beta pledge in the wide open spaces of the lower hall where the stairway with the dull mahogany handrail curved up to the higher regions, Laura thought she could not stand it to see her mother go. Not especially companionable in the deeper sense, Eloise was a good mother, and Laura felt closer to her at the farewells than she had ever felt before.

"I wish I'd planned to stay home a year before I came," Laura was winking fast, now that the parting time had come. Her mouth was trembling. But Eloise kept a stiff upper lip. "You will be very happy here. Just think what mother has accomplished for you"--(the Alpha Betas should have heard that)--"I've got you in what has seemed to me *the* very best one of all. You'll meet the best people. And maybe" . . . Eloise was archly playful: "maybe you'll have a nice young man some day . . . the brother or cousin of one of these aristocratic girls."

"Oh, no." Eloise could not have said it at a more inopportune time. "Oh, no, I don't care for men, Mother--not *at all.* I really don't. You don't understand. . . ."

Seeing that Laura was genuinely distressed, Eloise changed her tactics. "After all, I can't say that you are especially attractive that way, Laura." She was the personification of tact. "So just keep your mind on your studies. Good-by now . . . keep your head up . . . don't let any one run over you. The Deals are all good capable people--you don't need to be ashamed of the name Deal. Your father has been in legislature. Your Uncle Mack is a banker in Omaha, your Aunt Grace on the University faculty, your Aunt Margaret a leading physician's wife here in Lincoln, your Aunt Isabelle a music teacher in Chicago." Eloise tabulated them as though it were all news to Laura. "The Deals are all decent, capable people--and above all that, remember *your mother was a Wentworth.*"

With this parting dose of nerve stimulant, Eloise placed her small-town child in the lap of the gods. And University life had begun.

"She probably wouldn't have made it," Eloise said complacently to John on her return, "if I hadn't gone. She was almost ready to give up making a decision."

"And what if she had?"

"If she had . . ." Eloise lowered her voice in the hushed tones one associates with grief and bereavement, "if she had, *she might never have been bid again."*

Yes, Laura went Alpha Beta. But some did not. One girl was not taken on account of her freckles, one had been tabulated a crock the moment she stepped inside the door, and another had made the fatal error of eating a bite or two of the garnishing on her salad. In the four years of their schooling, Laura saw the tan spots miraculously fade into the background of a pink and white complexion, the crock become the May queen, and the lotus-eater--no, lettuce-eater--earn the Phi Beta Kappa key. But it's a wise sorority that knows its own child, and no fraternity can read all there is in the stars and the crystal ball in one mad week of rushing.

CHAPTER 9

In the game of roommates--in which game the freshmen are the pawns--Laura was given into the care of a sophomore--one Bernice Fowler--a brisk capable girl with so many of the characteristics of Laura's own efficient mother that one might have wondered if the two girls had not been interchanged at birth. Laura had not lived with her a full day until she had altered the position of all the furniture in the room, rearranged Laura's hair, ripped a lace collar off one of Laura's dresses and instructed her to wear brown beads with it instead, discussed a change of music teachers for her, and run over a list of male acquaintances to pick out a boy friend for her. By evening Laura also had received her first lesson in fraternal rivalry. Standing at the window of their room on third, she asked guilelessly: "Why are there so many cars all around the Gamma Zeta house?" To which Bernice Fowler said significantly: "It's probably because there's a stop button there. There are *never* more cars around the Gamma house than around ours. Remember that."

At the end of one month, Laura's newly acquired knowledge consisted of a few French words, the fact that she did not stand correctly in Phys. Ed., that there is much more to the science of botany than pressing flowers collected along old Stove Creek, that all men are not born free and equal, that all Alpha Betas are God's own children, that Pi Tau men rate much higher than Tau Phis, that Omega Gammas are the lowest species in the genus Greek, and that a barb is a microscopic organism of the animal kingdom. To be sure, some of this instruction did not assimilate easily. And when food or instruction do not digest readily, they cause distress if they can not be thrown off. Laura was sensitive, deeply responsive to the feelings of all humans with whom she came in contact; and this being so, she could neither wholly believe nor totally disregard. So she suffered a little in characteristic silence.

All the first semester she was quite depressed concerning life. But gradually when it was borne in upon her that most barbs wanted no sympathy, that large numbers of them were actually without the pale by choice; that the lowly Omega Gamma men, who did not rate well, laughed and sang and danced and slapped each other jovially on their respective lowly backs and gave every evidence of wholeheartedly enjoying life; that some of her own exclusive Alpha Beta sisters had periods of depression, homesickness, no dating, deflated pocketbooks, and disappointments; the world began to swing back into its natural orbit. Life was queer. But it was somewhat gaining its equilibrium.

Several times she met Allen Rinemiller on the campus. Allen looked very collegiate in his up-to-date clothes. And evidently he was popular, for he was always with football boys whose names were familiar to every one,--fellows who were known for their campus activities--or prominent sorority girls. Always they spoke, and once or twice Allen dropped out of the group he was with and talked to her a minute. The first time he did so Laura experienced a queer sensation, for although she despised herself for the snobbish thought, it came to her mind that their places were changed here,--that at home a Deal was a bigger person than a Rinemiller, but that here a Deal was quite grateful for a little attention from a Rinemiller. And when she attended the football games with a bunch of Alpha Betas and saw Allen, big and grimy and dependable, get through the solid phalanx of the enemies' lines, with the entire stadium gone wild, she felt quite important to think he was from home.

Some girls are apparently born with dates; some through much personal activity, achieve them; but others seem by necessity to have dates thrust upon them. By going home for week-ends all fall, Laura evaded the dating question for which she had no great hankering, but by the time their own formal party was to be staged, it became apparent that she must have a date thrust upon her.

Bernice Fowler secured this necessary equipment. And Laura was not overwhelmed with the gratitude Bernice seemed to consider her due. She dreaded the ordeal much more than she anticipated it with pleasure. She had no gift of small talk. More than ever she was realizing how much like her father she was.

Eloise saw that Laura had a pretty new gown. It was soft ivory silk, simply made on graceful lines, but all the more fetching for its simplicity. The "date" was a mere freshman, but in the abstract and unknown he presented to Laura all the horrible prospect of a masculine Gorgon. But when he was announced and she went down to the lower hall to meet him, seeing him in the flesh,--and more bone than flesh at that,--boyish and nervous in his tuxedo, in her characteristic way, she suddenly felt tactful and at ease with him. She wondered why she always felt that way toward boys, almost motherly. He seemed nothing to her so much as Trib grown tall and dressed up, painfully trying to please her. When he smoked pompously, and spoke darkly of wild parties his frat had thrown, she sensed that he was not quite used to it all yet, so that she wanted to laugh and tell him not to take the trouble to impress her with his worldliness.

The formal at a big hotel was an elaborate affair. Your Cornhuskers and Jayhawkers and Hawkeyes are not entirely what their names imply. Elaborate gowns and decorations and imported musicians made up the ensemble. Because they have been doing this kind of social thing a less number of years than their eastern prototypes, perhaps they stress the settings even more.

Allen Rinemiller was there with one Delores Thaxter, a Gamma Zeta. It was the first time Laura had seen Allen in evening clothes, and Allen in evening clothes was Apollo in a tuxedo. His superb well-built physique, his jolly clean-cut countenance, his blonde hair with its three distinct waves, his flippant ease with every one,--Laura thought she had never seen a man look nicer.

They made as ideal looking a couple as Jimmie and Katherine, Laura decided,--Allen and that Delores Thaxter. The girl was in dark red velvet. She was a sophisticated looking young woman from Central High in Omaha, and had been used to social affairs all her life. Her older sister had been a friend of Kathie's,--they had been duchesses or princesses or something important together at the same Ak-Sar-Ben ball. While she was lovely to look upon, Laura decided she did not like her. She made her think of a cat rubbing her sleek head against Allen. "I can almost hear her purr," Laura said to herself as she danced with her bony freshman.

When they accidentally bumped into Allen and Delores on the crowded dance floor, Miss Thaxter threw out a little annoyed frown at them, but Allen laughed, "Hello there, Laura . . . traffic's congested," and went on his pleasant terpsichorean way. Laura could not help but think of Allen in a tux there on the dance floor with the haughty Omaha girl in comparison with what her grandmother had told her about old Gus and Christine Reinmueller coming into Nebraska in a wagon which had been constructed from a rowboat, the bow facing the stolid oxen, the stem forming the base of the canvas doorway. It made her smile to herself to think of the change in the three generations. Nebraska had certainly been a melting-pot.

"What brings out the dimples, ducky?" It was her worldly-wise escort.

Oh, how silly! "Pardon! My mistake," Laura said coolly, and began analyzing herself even as she danced. Why was she different? Most girls would have *liked* that simple kid's remark. Yes, she guessed people were right,--she was odd.

And then by some shifting which Allen seemed to manipulate, the freshman, who knew Delores Thaxter slightly, was to dance with her, and Allen with Laura. But dancing with Allen proved to be more painful than dancing with the freshman. She could talk generalities to the freshman, but coming from the same community as she and Allen did, there seemed nothing for her to say except things that pertained to home. And she could scarcely talk about Christine Reinmueller or his old girl, Verna Conden. Allen was a good dancer and she would have enjoyed it but for that terrible restriction on conversation which took hold of her. Everything that came to her mind to say seemed uninteresting, and her tightly constricted throat seemed in league with her dull mind. So aside from a few brief answers to Allen's pleasant remarks, she had nothing to offer and quite in relief saw him go back to the dashing Delores, who from her animated appearance was in no way at a loss for small talk.

The freshman took her to supper in that nervous am-I- pleasing-you manner which he had shown from the first of their meeting. He did everything correctly with the chairs, the silver, the tipping, the wraps, but in a sort of tense manner as one who is doing something he has learned by rote. "His fraternity is doing a good job," Laura told Bernice Fowler. "But he made me think of some one driving a car who sits stiffly at the wheel and never takes his eyes from the road." Bernice was impatient with Laura's report. She had spent quite a little time and no small amount of diplomacy in arranging the affair, and she did not choose to have it looked upon lightly. In countries where matrimonial affairs are arranged by a third party, Bernice would have made an excellent go-between.

"He's a nice man,--from one of the oldest pioneer Nebraska City families, and if he pays you any further attention, you grab it," was her sisterly advice.

"Most of our pioneer families in Nebraska are all of three generations old," Laura returned, "and if you call him a man, then Allen Rinemiller is ready for the old folks' home."

It brought on a discussion about Allen. Two other girls, a Dresden-china blonde and a tall Carmen-looking one, were curled up in the two biggest chairs in the room. They were agreed in saying that Allen was one of the keenest men on the campus. Laura swung an active leg from a daybed and informed them: "Allen's grandfather and grandmother, old Mr. and Mrs. Reinmueller and my grandparents, the Deals, came into the state the very same day about sixty years ago. A Mr. and Mrs. Henry Lutz,-- those were my Aunt Emma's parents--and a Mr. and Mrs. Oscar Lutz--they all met--in their covered wagons, you know,--at Plattsmouth or Weeping Water or some place along there, and came on to their land together where they settled."

"And they all lived together in a little crooked house?" chirped the blonde.

"They did not," said Laura. "They built two little frame houses and a soddie and a dugout in the side of a ravine, and Allen Rinemiller's granddad was the one that lived in the dugout."

"Can you *feature* it? *Can* you feature it? Imagine,--that ritzy looking Pi Tau man! Who could believe it,--his grandfather living in a *dugout?* I never heard anything so perfectly unbelievable," said the Carmen girl, whose grandfather had hauled hogs dead from cholera to an oil factory in Lincoln all one summer for five dollars a load.

CHAPTER 10

Laura's first year at the University was over--a year of readjustments, perhaps, more than of accomplishments. She passed the minimum of required grades by a good margin, but with no apparent prospects of a P.B.K. ever coming to rest on the lapel of her jacket. She had made some friends, assimilated a certain amount of fairly important information, and learned to concentrate in the midst of buzzing, laughing, crying, whistling, singing, typing and arguing. She wore an Alpha Beta pearl-encrusted insignia on her breast and carried home the pleasant memories of freshman friendships, and the unpleasant ones of freshman disillusions. She had teachers who were apparently as kind to her as though she were not one of dozens who felt that they could write.

John Deal was pleased with his young daughter. He saw no apparent change in her, and felt a little conscious-smitten that he had predicted such a thing. This was not surprising, for the greatest change that had taken place in Laura was not visible. For a year she had lived with girls who had traveled more or less. For a year she had listened to instructors speak casually of the East and Europe. The greatest change then in Laura Deal was that no longer did Cedartown seem satisfying. No longer would a blue and white room and an old grape arbor constitute a world.

The day after she returned, Laura went immediately to see every one, as though she had just come from far countries instead of the distance a car could drive in a single hour. She met old Christine Reinmueller on the street and stopped to talk to her. Old Christine with her flat braided hair and blue calico dress, seemed more gentle, she thought,--mellowed the last year, as though in preparing to part with life she had grown tender toward it. Once, as she was talking, she wiped her hard old hand across her eyes. She spoke deprecatingly of Allen,--the big *faul*--lazy,--he was all for graduating from the University, such a *fehler*--mistake. But even as she spoke, Laura saw the gleam in her watery blue eye, detected that she was as proud of him as a peacock.

At Kathie's, she found Patty, sixteen months old now, as sweet as babies of that age usually are. Kathie, herself, was leaving for a bridge afternoon. "Oh, Kathie, how can you leave her just when she's so cunning?" Laura wanted to know, as Patty toddled back and forth in the nursery and did funny slobbery things with her pink mouth.

Katherine laughed shortly, "Old-fashioned as ever, Lolly. I thought the Alpha Betas would take some of that out of you. I suppose you'd have me stay at home and watch over her like a mother hen and her chicken. No, I have this new Verna trained like a seal. She's awfully good with her."

"Who's Verna?"

"The girl--a Verna Conden."

"Verna Conden? She *works* for you?"

"Yes. Why?"

"Oh, I don't know--I just was surprised. She used to be so pretty and popular in High School."

"Well, she's pretty yet. But I don't know anything about her popularity. If she gets her work done and takes good care of Patty, it's all I want to know. And don't you get it in your little brown head that I'm neglecting my baby. I have Dr. Rayburn look her over at stated periods. Dr. Moss is watching her teeth,--and she's on as regular diet as the champion heavy-weight. The modern mother puts it all over the antebellum one, Lolly, and so kindly remove that critical beam I see in your eye."

It struck Laura that Katherine was really irritated, that she was genuinely offended at her innocent remark. When she was leaving, Verna Conden, in a cap and apron, came quietly around the side of the house and called to her softly, "Laura, may I speak to you a minute?"

"Hello, Verna,--how are you?"

"I'm all right. I wanted to ask you something." She was embarrassed. Her hard brown eyes looked at Laura with level familiarity a moment and then dropped. "Does Allen--go with any one at the University?"

"Why, Verna!" It was Laura's turn for confession. "It's different at the University--you know--every one dates. No one thinks anything about it. I scarcely ever see Allen."

"That's all I wanted. Thanks. I know now." And she turned and slipped back to the kitchen door.

Laura went home depressed. Verna still liked Allen. Poor Verna, in her cap and apron, working for Kathie. And Allen, who was so popular at school,--a "ritzy Pi Tau man," dating Delores Thaxter. It was too bad. Things were awfully turned around in life sometimes.

At home she spoke to her mother about Kathie's flare-up when leaving Patty was mentioned.

Eloise's mouth drew into a firm line. "You stepped on her toes, unintentionally, Laura. I'm glad you said it though. She just gads, gads, gads. That Verna Conden ought not have so much charge of that child. Jimmie doesn't like it. He takes more care of Patty right now than Kathie." Eloise dilated at length on what seemed to her crass neglect of a child.

Laura was sorry she had started her mother off, for she was genuinely fond of Kathie and hated to hear her criticized so forcibly.

Over at old Oscar Lutz's Laura found him on the side porch watching the Cedartown small stream of life go by. He was delighted to see her, and talked steadily in his high voice. It was about odds and ends of things, with no special correlation.

"Had plenty of gum to chew and didn't have to buy it in no pink or silver paper neither. Take a can and go out on the prairies, find some rosin-weed--looked like little sunflowers,--just help yourself to gum that oozed out on the stalks. She liked it . . . get it for her lots o' times . . ." Laura, listening, knew who "she" was--wondered idly how it would seem to have thought so much of a person.

Immediately he was off on another tangent, although whatever reminded him of it Laura could not see: "I mind how the dust storm of '82 come up. She and I was on the way to old man Norton's funeral. Dust so thick, couldn't see ahead of us. She sat in the end of the wagon with Christine Reinmueller . . . Gus couldn't go and so we took Christine . . . all at once a horse come up and put its head right between her and Christine. They squealed right proper . . . guess the horse was every bit as surprised as Marthy and Christine."

In whatever he related, interwoven through all his talk, like a little silver song of accompaniment went the name of Marthy. He was always relating things that she had said, and laughing that thin high laugh about them. Laura sometimes secretly wondered why it was that he was not sad. How could he laugh so heartily? If you loved some one and that person died . . . how could you ever afterward be anything but grieving? And now he was saying: "I was telling her just yesterday . . ."

Suddenly Laura ventured it: "Who, Uncle Oscar? Telling whom?"

He stopped in surprise, "Why, Marthy."

"But Uncle Oscar, it couldn't have been just yesterday. How can you say that when she isn't here?"

He looked startled for a moment. "That's right," he said, as one who has suddenly admitted it. "She ain't here."

For a brief time he sat leaning forward on his cane, so that Laura was angry with herself that she had said so cruel a thing.

"Well, now," he began, "you see they just never leave you entirely. Now take me . . . I set here on the porch . . . and she seems to be working inside. When I'm inside, I just think of her as being out in the yard for a minute . . . sometimes I can hear her shut the door and go about her work.

Tain't so, I know,--don't think I'm off in my head . . . but it pleases an old man's fancies. And when the lilacs come out . . . always associate her with lilacs."

Laura left him sitting there saying: "Yes, it pleases an old man's fancies."

CHAPTER 11

Youth sees life as a plot, a gay, romantic adventuresome plot. But they who have lived past their youthfulness, know that life does not arrange itself forever in well-defined patterns, nor does it always arrive at solutions. Life is like a river--a groping, pulsing river, endlessly rising and falling, finding its way through mists and shadows to some far sea. Every human is a part of the interminable flow. Every human is a part of the story. One life touches another and is gone. There is contact for a brief time,--an influence for good or ill. And the river goes on, endlessly rising and falling, finding its way to the sea.

Laura's sophomore and junior years carried her a little farther toward that unknown shore, other lives touching her own, leaving their imprint. Classes in Narration and English Composition turned to Poetics and Advanced Narration. Philosophy and Child Psychology were left behind. Psychology of the Emotions and Mental Hygiene entered. Laura moved down on second floor and back on third. She roomed during different semesters with the Carmen-looking girl and the little Dresden-china blonde and a sloe-eyed freshman. She attended ball games and sang lustily with twenty-five thousand others: "There Is No Place Like Nebraska" and, carried away by mass emotion, at the moment would have cheerfully bared her breast for a sacrificial pound of flesh if Nebraska, in the guise of Shylock, had demanded it. She went in and out of the Alpha Beta house with all the intimacy of her own home, and when, between courses at the candle-lighted dinner table, the girls sang: "Alpha Beta, I Love You," and she saw the familiar faces of her sisters all about her, she would have thrown herself loyally on a burning pyre for Alpha Beta. But luckily, Alpha Beta required no such offerings to the gods. She wanted merely that one keep up to standard the honor of the house, which translated, meant scholarship, campus activities, appearance, and a high rate of dating.

The summer between Laura's junior and senior years saw her leave for the East on the long-promised but never-before-materialized invitation of Uncle Harry. It saw Eloise in a state of excited interest in the coming close proximity of her daughter to the wealthy uncle and aunt. It saw John Deal plodding faithfully back and forth his office, the cares of the community upon his shoulders. It saw Kathie flitting about, coaxing a thrill from life; and curly-headed Patty, three years old now, in a constant state of waving farewells to her mother. It saw Jimmie attending strictly to his business in the bank, mothering Patty between times. It saw old Oscar Lutz tap-tapping on the sidewalks of Cedartown, carrying gifts of vegetables to those whom he bored, accompanying every cabbage and turnip and radish with a recollection of the old days. It saw old Christine Reinmueller trudging about the farmyard, picking up in her apron a few cobs that the men had dropped from the wagon, scolding at the wastefulness, or sitting in the shade counting over and over on her hard calloused fingers the eighties she had once owned, trying to remember where each had gone.

The summer saw Allen farming his acres of rich black soil, directing his help, but with his own broad shoulder to the work, too. Allen was nearly through school now,--only another semester in which to finish a long and intensive course. He was dissatisfied with many things in his life, was searching constantly for the answer to his unrest. July saw his wheat harvest under way,--the high tide of the year for agriculturists. For those who love their Midwest it is a gladsome sight,--when the fields are half harvested, when half of the gold of the fields has turned to the bronze of the stubble.

The old glamorous days of the harvest are over. The romance of the harvest season is practically a thing of the past. The rhythm of the scythe which once stirred poets is heard no more. One-man combines do the work of six men without the spectacular aid of the brawny bodies of harvest hands. Time was when the harvesting was a struggle of many days, the workers,--men, women, and horses,--exhausted when the grain was safely threshed and stored. Once a stream of harvest workmen migrated from the southern tip of the continent to the northern border, following the lead of the ripening grain,--a subject matter for novelists. Now the migration has dwindled to a small contingent drifting across the continent with hands on their gear-shifts. The rustic daughter who once carried the jug to the field, whose favor was the prize for which the hero and the villain threshed the wheat or husked the corn, is now usually home from college for the summer, doing anything but picking her dainty way through stubble to the men who run the combine.

When half of Allen's wheat was in the shock, the rains descended for a day and a night. But Allen was also a corn and alfalfa farmer, and, as he said, what was "sauce for the goose was applesauce for the gander." It is this diversified farming as it is practiced to-day that has steadied weather conditions in the Midwest. In the days when the hot winds blew from an unbroken expanse of stubble fields and barren lands, serious damage was done. But under modern conditions the landscape is broken with such regularity by crops still unmatured, that serious damage from the winds is no longer likely.

When the wheat harvest was in, the third heavy alfalfa crop cut, and the corn tall and maturing in the fields, Allen went back to school for his last semester.

Laura, returned from the East, was plunging into her senior year. Sociology, Browning, Magazine Article, Novel Study,--she looked over her schedule with happy anticipation for the amount of constructive work for which it called.

Apparently, Allen was to date Delores Thaxter again this year. Laura saw them sometimes on the campus, standing and talking by Science Hall. Often Allen's long green roadster stood in front of the Gamma house where traffic continued to be thick, although Laura, herself, would not have admitted now that it was from causes of popularity.

Whenever Allen saw Laura he was always cordial. At sight of her he would break into his cheerful grin and give her some kind of a high sign. Sometimes they stopped a few minutes by the Administration building to talk or ran into each other at the college book store.

"What's new back in the woods?" would be Allen's cheerful greeting, or "How's every one in the sticks?"

He seemed to gloat over the fact that he came from the country. "Now us farmers . . ." he would say with an exaggerated whining drawl, and go off into a monologue caricaturing his calling.

Just how serious was Allen's affair with Delores Thaxter Laura did not know. All University affairs appeared serious to an onlooker. Laura, herself, even now at the beginning of her senior year had no deep and desperate love affair as had the majority of her sorority sisters. She accepted dates to keep away from the opprobrium of being a crock, and thereby bringing utter disgrace upon a group which prided itself upon a one hundred per cent dating. But the dates were looked forward to with no passionate longing nor back upon with any degree of heartstab. Part of the time she was frankly relieved when they were over and she could slip into her own room and read or dream and scribble. That trip east to Uncle Harry's and Aunt Carolyn's had added further zest to her dreams of a future of accomplishment, had set her apart from the world around her more definitely than ever. She felt aloof, a little like a candidate for a sisterhood, a novice who would some day take the veil. She lived and moved and had her being with her family and friends, laughed, joked, conversed with them, but was not one of them. A story accepted by *The Prairie Schooner,*

Nebraska's own literary magazine of highest type, was a thrilling reality. A poem in the same periodical, following later, added fuel to the little flame that burned so steadily within her very being.

It seemed strange that one could so thoroughly play two parts, she told herself,--that a girl could take her place in the activities of college and sorority life, genuinely enjoying most of them, and remain the cloistered nun looking out through windows upon the panorama of the world. But it was true. That was her own dual personality. And the cloistered person was the real one,--the real Laura Deal, who, looking through the windows, saw always the wings of a white bird flying.

She could now scarcely realize that this was the beginning of her senior year. Where had the time gone? It seemed such a little while ago that she had parted tearfully with her mother in the lower hall of The House. She said something of that now to Bernice Fowler. Bernice had dropped out after her sophomore year to teach, and as a consequence was to finish with Laura. She was in all campus activities,--was a Mortar Board, Big Sister, Y.W.,--everything was grist for her busy mill.

The little blonde and the Carmen-looking girl, and a red-haired young person whose talk was usually as crisp and vivid as her flaming hair, were all in Laura's and Bernice's room lounging about in the various attitudes which one finds in the illustrations of "Daily Exercises." They formed a little inner circle in the sorority, a sort of unacknowledged and unnamed sorority within the sorority. They were all seniors, and four years of habitation under the same roof had rendered them immune to gratification over compliments from each other or humiliation over insults. The talk now was desultory. By no manner of excuse could one term it conversation. It fluttered about over a dozen scattering topics as a swallow dips from one place to another. Quite suddenly it lighted, with no apparent reason, on the odd ideas which people who do not live there have of the Midwest. Every one knew an anecdote which she brought out in turn and deposited with scorn on the scrap heap.

"The Midwest,--what does it mean to people who've never been here? They've the craziest notions. My cousin . . . a kid in his teens . . . was visiting in one of the New England states, and something was said about a story he'd read in the *Saturday Evening Post.* The dumb-bell he was visiting said, 'Oh, do they have *Saturday Evening Posts* in Nebraska?' Can you *beat* it?"

"Prof. Newton told me, himself, he knew just two things about Nebraska when he came out to be on the faculty--the new Capitol and William Jennings Bryan," Laura said.

"A woman in Omaha, a musical critic and smarter than smart, told my mother she was in England and met an Englishman,--you know, girls, Englishmen inhabit England,--and when the introduction took place, the one who did the deed said, 'I want you to meet Miss So-and-So of Omaha, Nebraska.' Whereupon the Englishman toddles around and hunts up his wife and says, 'I want you to meet Miss So-and-So of Omaha, *Alaska*.'"

They all laughed, and Bernice Fowler said, "Anybody can forgive an Englishman . . . I'll bet *you* think that Manchester is on the Isle of Man,--but what bums me up is Americans, themselves. A neighbor of ours in Nebraska City was some place East . . . I forget where . . . on the coast anyway, and some woman said to her, 'I expect the trees here look odd to you?' Shades of J. Sterling Morton who gave Arbor Day to the world!--I ask you, could you beat it? If there's any place on God's green earth where trees grow bigger or thicker than around Nebraska City! Our neighbor just naturally goes upstairs and gets a little two-by-four postcard that some one sent her from home, with a picture of the huge trees meeting overhead."

"I've an aunt who has never come out here visiting because she thinks she'd have to lug along a tin bathtub."

"How do they get that way?" some one asked.

"It's writers," the Red-Head said. "They're to blame. Nobody writes anything about Nebraska as it is now. And of course, everybody thinks it's just like it used to be when the Indians jazzed around and played 'You're it' with arrows. Say 'Nebraska' to the average easterner who has never been here, and what does he think of? Pardon!--of what does he think? He sees a picture of Pa out picking up buffalo bones, while Ma's unpacking the barrel of old clothes and seed corn and dried apples somebody sent them, and Lizzie is standing at the door of the soddie shading her eyes with her hand to see if she can see a tree sprouting on the horizon."

The impromptu club of critics rocked in glee, and the Red-Head went on: "It's the grasshopper literature that's done the dirty work. It just naturally sticks in people's minds. If writers would just lay off the darned grasshoppers for awhile. There hasn't been a flock of grasshoppers big enough to make an insect baseball team for over half a century, but people who've never been here still think we're out sweeping them off the sidewalks mornings, before we open up the wigwams."

Everyone laughed again, and the little blonde said, "The thing that scalds me is, there is no way of getting it across to them. Imagine all that stuff, and then think of the way things really are,--think of the thousands of beautiful homes . . ."

". . . country ones, too . . . scads of them . . ."

". . . and the schools and churches . . ."

". . . and the people who own first editions and paintings and etchings . . ."

". . . the finest collection of ivories in this country is right in Omaha . . ."

". . . and the people that go abroad,--hundreds from Omaha and Lincoln . . ."

". . . even *seven* this last summer from little old Cedartown," Laura put in, "and some people would think that was a whistle-stop."

The languid Carmen-girl suddenly sat up: "I just remembered something . . . something awfully good. She was a newspaper woman . . . forget which one she was on here in the state . . . my Aunt knew her,-- anyway she was a hotsy-totsy Midwest booster, and she went to New York to visit her relatives. They met her with an air of 'Now we'll thrill the poor little Main Street child.' She told afterward she had been ready to see everything there was and take solid pleasure in it, but it was their manner that got her, and she vowed to herself she wouldn't have a thrill to please them. I wish I could remember everything she told, but part runs like this:

"There was something head-lining the papers about General Pershing and she grew chesty about him being a Nebraskan. They took her to the Metropolitan Art Museum, and she said, 'I see you have the works of our sculptor, Gutzon Borglum, in conspicuous places. He's a Nebraska boy, you know, and loves his state, comes back every time he can to meet old friends.' She goes past a book store and there are Willa Cather's books stacked up in a pyramid, and she gets snooty about her being a Nebraskan. They take her to see Mrs. Fiske in a Ballard play and she says: 'You knew this playwright was a Nebraskan, didn't you?' They go to see Harold Lloyd's new picture, and she says, 'Yes, Harold's a Nebraska boy that made good in the city.' I remember the story ended by them asking her what she especially wanted to see. And she says, as big as life, 'Coney Island. You know, a Nebraska boy designed it.'"

It was the parting anecdote, for after a lusty laugh at the telling, Dresden-china uncurled her silken legs, yawned, and said that she had a heavy date with Chekhov, the Russian writer, and that she was quite ga-ga about him. Carmen followed suit with plaintive murmurs about mental testing. Red-Head lingered a moment, and said it broke her heart to leave, but there was a sociology paper, that if Papa Morgan didn't like her paper it was just too bad, and anyway she was going to write at the end: "Shoot-if-you-must-this-old-red-head, but-spare-my-sanity-she-said."

They all yawned and stretched themselves across the hall.

Laura closed the door after the retreating army of invasion, and turning to her own work, stood trying to decide whether to tackle her term paper on "Criticism In America," make out a list of English idioms, or write a poem to Bernice Fowler who was taking up swimming, and entitle it "Ode to a Water Fowler." The last seemed the most attractive of the three, and she was just beginning:

Whither, midst falling spray,
While flounder the pledges with the last fatal plunge,
Far, through the murky depths, dost thou careen
In thy solitary lunge?

when a freshman inserted snappy black-button eyes between the door and the casing, and said in pert sing-song: "Mr. Allen Rinemiller in the north living room . . . calling for Miss Laura Deal . . . and if Miss Laura Deal doesn't want to talk to him . . . here's a lady who will . . . ah . . . men!"

Miss Laura Deal raised curving eyebrows.

"Did you say 'lady'?" she asked acridly, and the pert freshman withdrew in some haste.

Laura went down the long stairs that turned in three directions, a slim hand slipping along the mahogany banister. Allen, who had been standing by one of the French windows with his back to the stairway, turned and watched her unflurried descent. Laura's sleek brown head rose from her shoulders with perfect grace, her dark eyes were lovely, and the browns and tans and a bit of orange which she wore with taste, seemed melting into the clear olive of her skin.

"Cute kid," he thought, ". . . different, too." Just what he meant by "different," he himself could not have told. For the brief space of a moment, it flashed through his mind that he could not have asked any of the other University girls he had dated to do this thing he was asking of Laura Deal--least of all, Miss Delores Thaxter.

"Hello, Allen, welcome to our happy home." Laura was cool, unperturbed. She had that detached air of looking on at life. But she was no longer diffident. Her conversation no longer choked her; she had perfect poise, plenty of small talk. There was no situation which she could not handle without embarrassment. Some would have said the sorority had done it for her, some, the University, others,--just life, itself.

Laura rather admired Allen, but he was a mere character in a story. She liked his humor, his looks, his big physique, well-knit and compact, his blond head with the three distinct waves in his hair, the way his blue eyes crinkled and his mouth drew up when he grinned. Sometimes she had even pictured him in various settings of the current story in her mind, trying out different girls as the strange fictional characters,--never Delores Thaxter or any of the real girls he had dated. She liked thinking out these plots. Sometimes, when she was deeply interested in the outcome of her own fanciful creations, she would purposely wait until the girls had all gone to their eight o'clocks, so she could walk alone and finish the story in her mind.

"Busy?" Allen wanted to know now.

As there was nothing more pressing than the term paper on "American Criticism," the outline of English idioms, and the unfinished but scarcely important parody, Laura said she was not busy,--not at all.

"Then I wish you'd do something for me, Laura." Allen's clean-cut face was serious, his cheerful grin gone. "And not so hot either. Would you?"

"Why, yes, Allen--if I can."

"They took Grandma over to the State Hospital yesterday."

"Oh, Allen! The State Hospital. She's not . . . ?"

"Yes . . . gone nuts."

"Oh, I'm sorry!"

"She's not very bad. Most of the time she's O.K., but right in the midst of being perfectly normal, some one will say something,--innocently enough,--that will set her off, and then she's just . . ." he threw out his hand, "not there."

"Clear out of her mind, you mean?"

"Yes,--and the folks think I ought to go out and see her. She calls for different ones of us when she's all right. Told Uncle Emil she wished I'd come and see her. Rather be shot than go, but it's got to be done, and I thought as long as you were one of the few here in school who knew her, maybe you wouldn't mind going along."

"Why, no, Allen,--I'll be awfully glad to go with you if you want me." And she was up the stairs again on third to get a chic little brown hat and a fur. Red-Head, Dresden-China and Carmen all met her in the upper hall.

"Lolly Deal, however did you work it?"

"Headlines for the *Daily Nebraskan*: 'Alpha Beta Gets Big Burly Football Man Away From Gamma.'"

"You sly little vamp . . . good work."

"You silly things," Laura was coolness itself. "I'm going out with him to see his Grandmother."

At which perfectly true statement, the trio howled with laughter, and called after her:

"Look out for the wolf, Lolly."

"What big teeth you have, Grandmother!"

"The better to eat you, my dear!"

Laura turned at the top of the stairs, said succinctly, "Go sit on three tacks," and went down to Allen.

CHAPTER 12

From the sorority house they drove in Allen's long green roadster through the shaded streets of Lincoln, where elms and poplars bordered the close-cropped lawns, past lovely homes set in emerald frames of shrubbery untouched yet by frost, until they came to the group of buildings which make up the little city of unfortunates. Up the long curving drive they swung and parked the roadster near a graveled path. They went first into the office, but were there directed back to the yard.

They found her under the trees with one of the nurses in uniform. Under the trees sat old Christine Reinmueller, this little German peasant woman of the old school, with her shapeless body, her seamed red face, and her faded hair braided in its thin flat braids like a colorless little rug pinned to the back of her head. Idly under the trees sat old Christine Reinmueller, her gnarled red hands with their broken and blackened nails, lying in her lap.

"Do you know me, Grandma?" Allen bent low over the shrunken little figure.

She looked up at him with dim blue eyes, blurred and watering.

"You're . . . one of 'em," she said.

"Yes . . . I'm Allen . . . your grandson . . . Herman's and Lucy's son."

"Ya . . . I know." She was listless, inattentive.

"And this is Laura, Grandma." Allen drew the girl forward. "Do you know her . . . Laura Deal?"

The old eyes turned to Laura for the first time, squinted, peered.

"Deal . . . Deal." She brightened. "Ya . . . you I know, too." She put up her hard old hands and drew Laura's soft white one into them. "So? For so long . . . I not see you . . . huh? For so long a time, you not come by me. And so many tings togedder ve do. Ya . . . I know . . ." She nodded wisely. "Of me you take care ven my babies are born. Of you I take care ven your babies are born . . ."

"Oh, I say, Grandma . . ." Allen reddened a little.

Suddenly, Laura knew. "Never mind, Allen. She thinks I'm my grandmother. She thinks I'm Abbie Deal."

"Ya . . . dats it . . . Abbie . . . I remember hard now. Abbie! My frien' . . . my frien' for all my life. Ya." She stroked Laura's pink palm with her own calloused ones, and uttered little soft purring sounds. Once she put the hand up to her cheek with caressing motion. "Oh . . . so? You remember. Togedder ve come . . . by de Veeping Vater . . . togedder ve build de houses close by . . . I remember. De long grass wave . . . de sun shine . . . all vas *freundshaft* . . . friendship. Togedder all vas *freunde* . . . frien's. How you not come see me . . . my Abbie frien'?"

Laura's ready emotions were stirred unaccountably. She was winking back the tears. How dramatic! How story-like! "I'll come now . . . often. I'll drive out again."

"I'll bring her. Grandma." Allen promised solemnly. He was a little embarrassed, anxious to get away.

"Ya! Bring her . . . you!" She was evidently not fully conscious of her relationship to Allen. "Of old times togedder ve talk . . . togedder ve remember . . ."

"Yes, Grandma." Allen's fine blond head bent low, "we've heard you tell all about those old times. You had a pretty tough time, didn't you . . . getting all your land in shape . . . ?"

A change came over Christine. An evil expression slipped over her leathery wrinkled face. It grew malicious, cunning. "De land . . ." she said, "So? It's you knows about my land . . . all my eighties . . . eleven eighties I have . . . So? My land you take . . . ?" She was rising, menacingly, stepping toward them with threatening gestures. Involuntarily, Laura slipped back against Allen and his arms went tightly around her. Together they stood for a few moments, uncertain what to do. Then the nurse shook her head at them and nodded toward the parked car. Allen's arms slackened. Laura slipped out of them and together they walked over to the car.

They drove away silently, the shadow of the interview over them. Laura was distinctly disturbed. Part of that emotional disturbance seemed to come from the things the old German lady had said, but a little of it was from that queer moment when she had involuntarily slipped into Allen's arms. She did not go in for that sort of thing--had no taste for it--the girls at The House laughed at her for being old-fashioned, but she quite distinctly knew her own mind. She wished now that she had kept her head a little better. There had been no real danger from old Christine. It looked a little as though she had chosen to make the most of a simple situation. In reality, it had been done almost without her volition. And with Allen Rinemiller, of all people! It was foolish, of course, to exaggerate the small incident, so she ignored the memory of it and opened the conversation with:

"Poor old lady. Just think, Allen. Doesn't it sort of get you . . . to think about their coming here over sixty years ago? My grandmother used to tell me about it. Your grandparents and mine and old Oscar Lutz and his wife, and my cousin Katherine's grandparents, Henry and Sarah Lutz, all met at the Weeping Water and came on into our community the same day. Grandma used to say there wasn't a thing to be seen but the blue sky, the prairie grass in every direction on the low rolling hills, and a few trees along the creek bed. The sun was going down, the four wagons made a circle and they built a campfire in the center. The Indians camped near them, and frightened them silly. Can you feature it?"

"Lord--imagine it--the very same spot where our farm lies, and the graveled roads and Cedartown. I never thought much about it, but hearing you tell about it, makes it pretty clear. Feature the comparison--with cars going by now on the hard packed roads and aircraft sailing over the farm . . ."

"And voices from both coasts coming into the homes, and being able to talk to any one by long distance . . ."

"And a combine doing a hundred acres a day . . ."

They were approaching the turn now which would take them back to the University. "How about driving out farther? Too busy?"

American Criticism and English idioms seemed suddenly very unimportant phases of life.

"Oh, no," said Laura, "I'd love it."

They drove until there was just time to get back to the Pi Tau and Alpha Beta houses for dinner. In the meantime, they had discussed fraternities, sororities, friendships, athletics, professors, sunsets, careers, columnists, plays, moving pictures, life, love, and the best way to get rid of sparrows.

When they had driven up in front of the Alpha Beta house, and Allen had gone with Laura to the door, he said rather seriously: "I'll be seeing you again, Laura, if I may." They could see the girls passing into the dining room. There would be no time to change.

"Why yes, Allen," Laura laughed up at him, "we'll have to have another talkfest and settle all the questions Congress can't."

At the table, she came in for a sly bombardment.

"How did you find Grandmother, Lolly?"

They called it softly across the candles and low bowls of flowers, in the gentle well-bred tones required of Alpha Beta ladies at dinner.

"Did you lift up the latch and walk in?"

"Any nice young woodsman rescue you, Lolly?"

Laura laughed at their nonsense. She felt gay, light-hearted, buoyant. A very nice thing had happened,--she had made a new friend. In one hundred and twenty minutes ticked off by her jeweled watch, a strange thing had happened. There flashed through her mind all those past years of inhibitions,--that period in which she had been groping for some one to whom she could talk intimately. There had never been any one but Grandmother Deal to whom she could turn her mind inside out. Even as the girls thrust verbal pins into her with smooth suave voices, she was thinking of her father's taciturnity,--her mother's lack of understanding,-- of cousin Katherine,--of Aunt Grace,--of her teachers,--the girls here and those at home,--there had never been any one of them to whom she could tell her innermost thoughts without confusion. Not until now. And just to-day something had happened. This afternoon a very lovely thing had taken place. She had found she could talk about anything to Allen Rinemiller.

CHAPTER 13

Laura went home over the week-end. But this time she rode in Allen Rinemiller's long green roadster. Allen was trying, as he said, "to keep one eye on the farm, one on the football field and one on the last of his studies." The ride over the hard packed graveled highway was a pleasant one. October in the Midwest presents some days that are flawless. Blue skies, splashes of gold and scarlet along the river's banks, fields of winter wheat as faintly green as fairy carpets, huge oblong patches of newly plowed earth, and whispering cornfields ripe for the husking.

To top one of eastern Nebraska's low rolling hills in October and see the entire hollow bowl of the world fitting the entire hollow bowl of the skies is to glimpse a bit of Infinity. Often there is a haze in the atmosphere, faint, ethereal, clinging in the hollows of the far hills as though smoke from Indian campfires of long-gone Octobers lingered in the valleys.

Allen and Laura, riding home in the green roadster, spoke of it often-- the beauty of the day. They were both quite touched with gratitude at the generosity which Nature was displaying for their benefit.

Home seemed restful and quiet to Laura after the noise and confusion at The House, which usually resembled a martin-house with girls' heads protruding from all the doors in lieu of swallows. But to her disappointment she had to give her Saturday afternoon over to attending a funeral service; Kathie's Grandmother Lutz was brought from Kansas City to be buried in the old home cemetery. She had been a dressy old lady, smart and bright-eyed up to her last illness. Looking at her in death, Laura could think of nothing so much as a little waxen doll with curly snow-white hair, pink cheeks, and dainty waxen hands across a satin dress, sunk down in the elegance of a white satin box.

"My, my, how my brother Henry loved that girl, with her snappy black eyes and her pink cheeks and her merry ways," Old Oscar was saying.

It gave Laura a moment of shocked surprise,--to think that the eighty-six-year-old waxen doll had once been a young girl. And evidently Oscar Lutz still thought of her as youthful.

In the early evening Laura had strolled over to his yard when she saw him covering his roses with leaves and tying gunny-sacks about them. Old Oscar was getting ready for his yearly California trip, which meant not so much getting himself ready as his house and garden. He had sat down on the edge of the porch when he saw her coming. "And now Sarah's gone . . ." he was saying, "and Old Christine babbles about her land and I guess folks think I'm not much better. My, we was a lively, husky crowd,--Marthy and me, Henry and Sarah, Will and Abbie Deal, Gus and Christine Reinmueller . . . Well, I'll go soon, too."

How could he, thought Laura, how *could* he speak so cheerfully of it, as though it were a casual trip into the next county. "One of these days I'll catch up with 'em all . . . my old crowd . . . I've lived way beyond my allotted time now. Don't fear it a mite, not a mite. Only fear I have is that it'll be a long-drawn-out sickness, slow like a tree rottin' down . . . crumblin' to pieces by inches . . . sufferin' all the time and puttin' somebody to a lot of trouble. No, I want to go quick like a sturdy tree crashin' in the wind."

"Don't think about it, Uncle Oscar. Everybody would see that you had a good nurse."

"Wouldn't want a nurse," he snapped. "Couldn't afford one."

Laura wished that he did not have that trait of stinginess. Every one knew he had money, plenty of it. Every week or so he went into the bank and took his tin box back into her father's office and looked over his bonds and mortgages. Laura liked the old man, but she wished he did not have that unlikable characteristic.

"Queer--ain't afraid to die. But hate to leave, too. Hate to hand over the community to the new generation for 'em to run it. Always seems as though the country around here just belonged to us old ones that got here first. 'Spose Columbus and Balboa and the rest of 'em had that same feeling of ownership." He laughed at himself deprecatingly.

She had never heard him put it in so many words before, but she had always sensed it in him,--a sort of brooding over the community as though he were personally responsible for its sins and virtues, its shortcomings and its good points. It was his state, his land, his people. Laura, listening, and only half attention, thinking that it was almost time for Allen Rienmiller to drive up, wondered idly if people understood the old man,--realized that what they chose to look upon as meddling was in reality not that at all. Thumping along the graveled highways, tap-tapping on the cement sidewalks he went his way, advising, discussing, recalling, watching, planning. "Old Mind-As-How" they called him. She decided people didn't understand him. It was not that he wanted to meddle. He had merely never lost his sense of ownership. It was not that he wanted to bore. He had merely wanted them not to forget. His state, his land, his people!

His cracked old voice went on its musing way: "Sarah was buried there to-day in the very land Henry gave for the cemetery. Sarah's little orphaned nephew died . . . she'd brought him out on the long journey from Michigan.

He was down by the creek bed one day and got snake bit. Doctor worked with him all night, but it killed him. He was the first one to be buried there. I made him a pine coffin and Abbie Deal and Christine Reinmueller lined it with one of Sarah's quilts. Marthy helped Sarah wash and dress him. Henry picked out a knoll on his land, and him and I dug a little grave up there . . . the sun was hot and the wind was blowing the dry grass . . . and there wasn't a sign of shade tree nearer than Stove Creek. That was the beginning of the cemetery. My father was buried next, and then a newborn baby of your Grandmother Deal's. We put a little wooden fence around them three graves so the cattle wouldn't step on 'em nor the coyotes bother 'em. The tumble-weeds would come rollin' across the prairie and bunch up like dried brown snowdrifts."

Laura thought of "Hillside" as she had seen it that day,--the lovely well-kept city of the dead with its hundreds of markers, its graveled paths and its huge shade trees, and could scarcely believe that old Oscar had seen the beginning.

"Don't know what'll come of us,--whether we'll just lay there a long time . . ." Laura heard him going on as one hears the wind in the trees,--an old man talking only of death to a young girl who was thinking only of life. ". . . Don't see much difference, however it is. The bodies anyway go back to the good old soil. Leaves and flowers, animals and people . . . under my eyes I've seen 'em all turn to the composition of the earth itself. In time the elements run up through the trees and grasses and come to life again. If I thought I'd just help along that way, it don't seem so bad. I like to think that I'll always be a part of the prairie round about here somewhere."

"Do you know, Uncle Oscar,--you're full of poetry?"

"Me? Snappin' crocodiles! Ain't never read any poetry in my life but 'One Hoss Shay' and 'Barefoot Boy' and a few like that."

"Well, let me say one to you then and see if it isn't just about what you've been saying." And Laura, who always had poetry at her tongue's end, told him the verses about:

"Never gravedigger shall shovel me under,
I shall arise with the loam's mellow thunder
To drift in the gray of the moor-mist yonder.
"Never in grave's maw I'll be lying,
With the wild geese in heaven flying
And the sea birds over the white wake crying."

"Pretty . . . awful pretty . . ." He mumbled it over several times, as though he were alone.

Allen drove up to the curb at her home and Laura slipped away. For a long time the old man sat there on the porch, through his mind running the pleasant thought of the mist on the prairies and the sound of the wild geese honking.

CHAPTER 14

Old Oscar was distinctly interested in the fact that he had seen young Rinemiller drive up for Laura. On Sunday morning he tap-tapped over to the Deals' and took walnuts in the old pail with a rope for a handle. When Laura emptied them, he said slyly: "You wouldn't want never to marry Allen Rinemiller, Laura."

Laura was amused at the old man's meddling. "No, I know I wouldn't," she agreed amiably and added: "But why wouldn't I?" so that old Oscar smiled behind the wind-break of his beard.

"Nice boy . . ." he mused, "but now take Gus . . . his grandfather. Tightest-fisted Dutchman you ever see. Was so tight, that when he built their new house back in the old days, he picked up all the little pieces of stone no bigger than these walnuts and saved 'em for another foundation . . . so tight, he used to pick the seeds out of the ground when they didn't sprout . . . tighter than the bark on a tree . . . and Christine worse than him . . . used to put her flatiron down in the coals so she wouldn't have to use much fire for ironing . . . used to sit up close to the stove so she wouldn't have to light lamps . . . not just savin' . . . plain skinflints for stinginess."

"But those were his grandparents," Laura said, "and Allen's no more like that than anything. He's the third generation, Uncle Oscar."

"You wouldn't want to marry Laura Deal," old Oscar said confidentially that afternoon, when he cornered Allen at the curb in front of the Deal home.

"Who said I wouldn't?" Allen asked, so that the old man smiled behind the duck-blind of his beard.

"Nice girl . . ." he mused, "but sort of thin and slimsy and delicate, not robust and hearty like the kind of girl you ought to have on a farm. Pick out a good stout one when the time comes--one with big bone and muscle, and you'll have a partner instead of a plaything."

Allen laughed good-naturedly at the old man's meddling. "When the time comes, it'll be a wife I'll want, not a hired man."

Old man Lutz tap-tapped back home. "Well," he said cheerfully to himself as he packed his battered old bag for the California trip, "I don't know much poetry, but I mind as how there's a verse that says:

"He was warned agin' the woman,
She was warned agin' the man;
And if that won't make a weddin'
Why, there's nothin' else that can."

Laura thought it was very kind of Allen to take her back to school Monday morning in the green roadster,--neighborly and friendly. Allen thought it very kind of Laura to go back with him,--neighborly and friendly.

Late that night, with the sorority house locked and barred, and lights in the big brick structure snapping out one by one, Laura, in yellow pajamas, brushing her soft brown hair, heard the Carmen girl across the hall say:

"Hot news, girls,--they say over at the Gamma House that Allen Rinemiller is about to hang his frat pin on the dashing dapper devoted Delores."

Laura paused with the brush in her hand and frankly listened. It was not so surprising, but even so, it startled her a bit. She could see the three girls through the open door lounging about on the couch beds.

"I heard it, too." It was Dresden-china. "She'll be the next to pass the candy over there. And if you ask *me,* they're beating us with announcements. We'll have to pep up a bit. Carmen, can't you do something for God, home and country?"

Brush in hand, Laura walked into the room with: "All I can say is that Thaxter person will make a hot farmer's wife. I'll bet she doesn't know any more about farm life than a kid from the sidewalks of New York. She probably thinks you plant winter wheat in winter and that a silo is a new kind of vegetable."

"Well, what do *you* care, Lolly?"

"*I* don't care. But I hate to see Allen taken in. Don't forget he comes from my home town."

"That's right, we forgot, Lolly. 'Our families are friends. His grandmother knew my grandmother. His grandfather knew my grandfather. His Uncle knew my Uncle. His Aunt knew my--'"

"Oh, choke her with the curtain tie-backs." Laura would not laugh. "The Rinemillers have lots of land and Allen has big things ahead of him. He's up on the very latest things in scientific farming . . . he gave a talk on some of the new methods to our Commercial Club at home . . ."

"Listen to the little press agent."

"Not sour grapes about Delores?"

"Acid raisins, Lolly?"

The Red-Head chanted:

"Lolly's mad and I'm glad, and I know what'll vex her,
When the big green car has gone afar
And Allen no longer necks her."

They all howled. Laura said in her most courteous tones, "I hope your children all have hangnails." Then she went into her own room and shut the door.

Allen took Delores Thaxter to the Military ball for which he had already dated her. But to the amazement of Alpha Betas and Pi Taus at large, he took Laura to his own fraternity formal.

"How about it, Lolly?" The girls teased her. "Off again, on again, gone again . . ."

"Who gets the nice big football man for a prize--Gamma Zeta or Alpha Beta?"

And the Red-Head stood on one foot, bent her body forward and shading her eyes with her hand, recited dramatically:

"The girls came around the bend with chariot wheels almost touching. Black horses and white were neck and neck. Eyes glued to the front, they urged on their sweating steeds. Laura Ben Hur was a little in the lead of Delores Messala . . ."

Laura, herself, had to laugh at that bit of foolishness, but she retorted: "You girls give me a pain in the neck."

To which they returned an immediate musical answer in soprano, contralto and tenor form:

"We give her a pain in the neck
We give her a pain in the neck
We're awful sad to make her mad
But we give her a pain in the neck."

"And what's more," Laura spoke after the last musical chord had died away: "Delores can have him when it comes to marrying. I wouldn't marry him if he were the last man in the world."

"You wouldn't *have* to marry him, then, Lolly," the Carmen-girl drawled languidly.

After the Pi Tau formal, Allen very frankly went only with Laura. No Alpha Beta knew just what happened, but quite suddenly, Delores Thaxter was importing a medic from Creighton University, and Allen Rinemiller was ringing the Alpha Beta door bell one hundred per cent of the evenings in a week.

Eloise was upset beyond measure. She talked about it most of her waking hours: "Imagine sending her up there with several thousand young men running around loose on the campus,--some of them from Lincoln's and Omaha's best families. She doesn't pay much attention to *those,* of course,--and then, out of the whole University, starts going with a

Rinemiller." In Eloise's cold nasal tones it sounded as though it were "Rhinoceros."

"I can't think of a nicer chap," John retorted. "Clean, decent, smart, good mixer, well-fixed. What more do you want?"

Eloise snorted. "Every time I look at him I see old Gus driving to town on a load of hogs and Christine in her blue calico dress."

"Every time *I* look at him I see a good old product of the Midwest's melting-pot--German and American. He has the thrifty ambitious traits of the grandparents--his father's honesty and decency, his nice mother's refinement. Good kid, I say."

But Eloise's mouth was straight and fixed in grim determination. All her life she had managed the family and not yet was she ready to yield the scepter. That night she wrote a long explanatory letter to Uncle Harry Wentworth. And she mailed it herself.

CHAPTER 15

Allen finished in the mid-year and left for home to begin the real business of farming. He had a dozen changes he wanted to make, plans which would increase his business materially, he believed. And business it was to Allen. He turned the southeast room into an office, installed a desk, two filing cases and a typewriter. He was keeping a full tabulation of figures on production and cost and profits. If the wraith of old Gus could have hovered over the scene, it would have been heard to say: "For what you expect to use them furnitures and books . . . to plow it and harrow? Mein Gott!"

But though Allen had many plans, the one Plan which preceded all others was now definitely formed. It was spring and Allen was young, and Springtime and Youth are a call to the rainbow's end.

Laura was home in April,--home to discuss with her father and mother which of two positions she would take. Pretty lucky, she told herself, to have two from which to choose. Some of the girls had heard nothing yet from their applications.

April in Nebraska is a moody creature, soft and hard, gentle and ferocious, as capricious as a girl. Saturday was cloudy, with warm languorous sprinkles of rain smelling of moist loam and plum blossoms. There was an odor, too, of bonfires smoldering on through sudden gentle showers. Laura, in a snug-fitting raincoat, full of the joy of living, did errands for her mother in the morning. When she came out of Kathie's on the way home, Verna Conden stopped the sweeping of the front walk, and with that same air of embarrassment Laura had noted before, said: "I guess you must have been laughing in your sleeve at me . . . that day I asked you about . . . Allen." Her voice was tense, a little bitter.

"Why, no, I didn't, Verna." Laura's brown eyes looked frankly into the girl's.

Verna laughed shortly: "Well, it doesn't matter, now," and turned away.

Laura went on, but she was disturbed, the spring morning a little spoiled. Verna had referred to Allen's and her friendship, of course. It bothered her all the way home, like a gnat that sung about her head and irritated her.

At home again, she found two things had happened in the short space of time she had been gone. Old Oscar Lutz had arrived from California. And her mother had received a letter from Uncle Harry Wentworth. Eloise seemed nervously elated. She wanted Laura to get out of her things at once and find an easy-chair in which to sit while she read. The letter was important, so important that Laura's whole life would be changed by it, her mother told her. Laura slipped out of her wet coat, took the letter over by the east windows, and read it.

Eloise was right. Eloise would have said she was always right. So different was it to be after the arrival of the letter, that on Sunday afternoon when Allen said, "What about the decision between the two positions?" Laura was ready to say: "I'm not taking either, Allen. I'm going to my Uncle Harry Wentworth's in New York and stay,--well, until Christmas, anyway."

He was taking Laura back to the University, driving on a side dirt road rather than the graveled highway. The road dipped down little hills, trudged up steeper ones, turned a bit across small bridges set cornerwise to cut across a vagrant brook. There were wild plum blossoms along the right of way. The box-elders were pale April green, the maples dark April green, the winter wheat vivid April green. Fields were mellow for the planting; pastures lush for the feeding. Pert robins darted across the highway, flying low and saucily in front of the car. At farmhouses, purple martins were doing nose-dives and other spectacular aeronautics. A little brown pheasant then stepped daintily out of the grass and with slow unflurried movements stepped daintily back again. The air was sweet with the odor of fresh spring winds from over the prairies. Blowing into their young nostrils, it might have been like the breath of life when man became a living soul.

They were at the top of the highest of the hills between their home and Lincoln. They could see in every direction to the horizon line, which became for them a circle complete in its visible circumference. It seemed to them half the world and they the center of the hemisphere. Allen stopped the car at the side of the grassy road on the hill top. They were alone in the center of the world,--their world. And Laura was tumbling a little of that world about Allen's ears now by saying some strange words:

". . . go to my Uncle Harry Wentworth's in New York . . ."

"Until Christmas?" He said the words as though Christmas were some date in a future century.

"Well, I'll be home by Christmas; and after that, I can tell you about other plans. But, of course, the biggest one of all is to write."

"Other plans? Going to marry?" he asked teasingly.

"Oh, heavens, no. I'm never going to marry."

"So?"

"Yes. I've known that ever since I was twelve."

"That's bad news. I thought . . . Laura . . . maybe you'd marry me."

Laura raised frank brown eyes to Allen and then dropped them immediately. It is not given to femininity to look unabashed into the muzzle of The Great Question, however flippantly or awkwardly that question may have been asked.

"You? Ah, Allen . . . that's nice of you . . . and everything, if you mean it . . ." For a sudden fleeting moment, she was human enough to think of the pleasure of telling the girls at The House.

"Of course, I mean it. Gee, Laura . . . I don't know . . . ever since that first day you went with me out to see Grandma . . ."

"But I . . . wasn't counting on that . . . Allen. We've been such good friends this year."

"There's something greater than friendship."

"I know, Allen. But I couldn't . . . not at all."

Allen was trying to save his self-respect, sustain a balance between the expression of romance and his usual cheerful banter. So he said lightly, "You could do worse."

"Yes . . . but if I didn't, I could do *verse*," Laura countered. And they both laughed. Youth is youth, laughter comes easily, and the great American Youth dearly loves his own wit.

"That wasn't such a good wise-crack,--but it's true. Allen, I'm going in for a career in good earnest. There's something in my life that I want to confide in you about . . ."

"You're the duke's daughter, kidnaped by the Deal family," Allen guessed.

"You can make light of it if it pleases you, Allen; but it's really an awfully serious thing to me. Do you remember a day, ages ago, when I was a kid, and you brought wood to Kathie's and you saw for the first time that painting of my grandmother's grandmother?"

"'I mind as how,' as old man Lutz would say."

"She was my great-great-grandmother," Laura went on. "Imagine it! Her name was Isabelle Anders-Mackenzie, and she was one grand aristocrat. My own Grandmother Deal used to tell me how she always thought of this lovely lady, and when she was young, how the thought of her was kind of an inspiration to want to do something great,--sing or paint or write,--some genuinely creative thing. Well, Grandmother Deal never did,--not any of the things she planned to do when she was young. You know how she just married and came West and raised and cared for her family, and died an old woman without doing any of those things that had so inspired her when she was young."

"She was a fine old lady," Allen said stoutly, as though he were shielding her from criticism.

"Don't I know she was, and her life in its way was full and wonderful. I think at the last she wouldn't have had it any different. But just the same, when she told me all that,--her cherished hopes that never were fulfilled, I could sense that she felt she had missed something,--and she said to me: 'Laura, you'll have a fine education and you'll do some of the things I never did.' Well, I'm going to, Allen . . . I'm going to do some of the things she never did. Now, this is the mysterious thing I was going to tell you . . . that very day you brought the wood, standing there in front of the lovely lady who was an inspiration for my grandmother when she was little, I said that I'd have that career which Grandmother missed,--first of all, selfishly . . . I guess we're all more or less self-centered . . . but secondly, for my grandmother's sake. She had so much faith in me doing what she always wanted to do and never did."

"I'll go down and talk to the painted dame myself . . . tell her king's excuse, you've changed your mind."

"Don't make light of it, Allen; I'm serious."

"But that doesn't keep you from marrying." He too, was serious again--serious and earnest. "Marriage doesn't keep women from careers now, any more than screens keep out the breeze."

"It would me."

"I thought you were modern and up-to-date. As a matter of fact, you're as old-fashioned as the dickens. There's nothing to keep you from going on with your writing, if you'd marry me. Look at the people who keep on with their chosen work outside their homes. And you wouldn't even have to leave your home to do your kind of work. Look at your own Aunt Isabelle Rhodes in Chicago. Hasn't she been a professional singer and music teacher ever since she and Harrison Rhodes were married?"

"Yes, but they're different. They work together. He composes and she sings."

"Well, so could we. You'd write, and I'd sharpen your pencils." Modern youth may be as romantic as the swain of other generations, but he bestows the sweets rolled up in acrid flippancy.

"No, Allen. It just doesn't work,--marriage and a career. I'll modify that statement and say, it may work for some women but it wouldn't for me. I would want to do one or the other well and thoroughly." She named two famous unmarried authors. "They're my ideals, and I'd like to follow as nearly as I could in their footsteps."

"I'll raise your bid. Three clubs." Allen retorted, and named three equally famous ones who had married and raised families.

Laura chose to ignore the scored point with: "And you'll always live here, Allen, of course, and I couldn't."

He was genuinely amazed at that and at Laura's stating flatly: "Not here, Allen, I couldn't do anything worth while here."

"Why not?"

"Answer it yourself. What is there to write about here? No material here and no attractive atmosphere, and atmosphere is what counts. Look at all successful literature--in it the atmosphere of old New England, the atmosphere of London nights, of romantic New Orleans, of California's Spanish missions and the gold rush, of New York's Ghetto and Broadway and old Hudson river romances, of queer hill-billies, of Alaskan settings. The first writers who used the midwest pioneer material got all the pickings--just all there was. I ask you again, What is there left to do?"

Allen looked around rather helplessly. The late afternoon sunshine of the mellow April day touched the tips of the low rolling hills and lay in shallow lakes of light on the fields and meadows. It looked very beautiful to Allen. He felt young, alive, strong, virile--one with the maples in which the sap had long been running, with the newly opened cottonwood buds that had burst into green life, with the fallow fields calling for the seeding, with the mating songs of robins, with swallows on the nuptial flight.

"Oh, I can't tell," he said helplessly. "But those things are easy for you. I should think you'd know. It looks . . ." he waved his hand around at the landscape, "mighty good to me."

"Scenery," Laura said, "just setting. And there's no story in a setting."

"But the people," Allen was stanch in his groping. "Where'll you find more substantial people?"

"I'm not arguing about their characters, but just 'substantial people' don't mean a thing in the literary world. In fact, 'substantial people' are about the poorest material one could find . . . there's no dramatic interest in them, whatever."

"If you mean they don't kill their offspring or run away with other men's wives, I'm glad I don't live in a dramatic community."

"Oh, you don't get the point at all, Allen. This is my home as much as yours. Don't I love it too, every bit as much as you do? I intend always to come back to it. But my life work calls--see? If you were an explorer, for instance, you couldn't stay in Cedartown to explore."

"Too deep . . . can't follow."

"Professor Throckmortin says it's because there's no spiritual uplift here."

"Spiritual fiddlesticks. Throckmortin has indigestion."

"He says there's no great beauty here,--that without mountains and seas, the monotony of the landscape brings out in Midwesterners a pessimism of the spirit and a depression of the soul,--and that it's reflected in our writings."

"Good Lord. Does he say that? I'll stack the Midwest up any time by the side of any other part of the country he'll bring on. Think of the ten thousand lakes of Minnesota with their birch trees. . . . Tell him to go out and see the colored Bad Lands of Dakota as I did last year, and look at the Grand Canyon's rival. Take a look at the blue skies over the sandhills of northern Nebraska when a crane flies across it . . . Look at this right here . . . Gosh, I call that a sight for sore eyes."

"Well, don't get all hot and bothered, Allen. I like it, too." Laura turned to take in the circle of the landscape as it lay under the lights and shadows of the spring afternoon--the whole picture of rolling hills and dipping valleys, a lovely thing of greens and tans and blues, as dainty as a Corot, but painted on a canvas the size of a half world.

"I love my home as much as any one, but you'll just have to admit it's the common or garden-variety spot of the map for atmosphere, speaking in a literary sense."

"I'm not speaking in a literary sense; but I'll be darned if I'd go back on my part of the country in *anything*. And, anyway, we've wandered fourteen miles from the original argument. I'm telling you, I love you, and you're telling me everything about American civilization and medieval literature in answer. You've cluttered your answer all up with other issues. What I want to tell you is, that I love you and you're the one girl in the world for me. And what I want to know is, how much do you care for me, if any?"

"I think a lot of you, Allen,--as a friend. And knowing very definitely what I'm going to make of my life, I won't even analyze my feeling any further."

"Aha! You're afraid to. I'm coming on."

"Not at all. I'm just thinking of other things; my career most of all. Going East to Uncle Harry Wentworth's again in the summer, for another. They go about a great deal, and he's wealthy and they're childless . . . and

Mother thinks it's a great chance for me, and I do too." Laura was unaware that her mother had assisted Chance materially by adroitly worded letters concerning the young man in whose car she was sitting. "It reads like a story, Allen,--it's drama itself. I've told you about Grandmother Deal's aspirations that never amounted to anything. And here's more about it: When Grandmother was a young woman, she had a choice of two things . . . came to the parting of the ways, as it were. Two men loved her and wanted to marry her. She had to choose between Grandfather, whom she really loved, or a young doctor . . . I don't know his name, but he became a big New York surgeon. She chose Grandfather Deal, and came out here and went through that hard pioneering with him . . . whereas, if she had chosen the doctor and gone East, she might have had the career, for she had a lovely voice. Do you see the connection? Just like Grandmother, I'm making *my* choice . . ."

"To get yourself a nice young surgeon?"

"No, foolish. Carry out the thing Grandmother didn't do. It wasn't surprising that she didn't. Life was different then. Everyone was tied down. The old inhibitions were masters of girls' fates. She could hardly break away from any thought but doing the thing she did. But here I am . . . different . . . in a modern setting . . . a University education . . . free . . . sort of 'heir of the ages,' all that stuff, you know,--and I can choose deliberately. But I've got to be free . . . as free as the wind that blows, with no entanglements of any kind."

"You sound like a mule in a wire fence."

"Thanks, Allen . . . lovely simile."

"You're welcome."

They both laughed, and Laura went on: "I think and eat and sleep and talk in terms of writing." It was true. Even as she said it, that other person, who played so great a part in her life, was composing in her mind: "The girl spoke, earnestly, without emotion. . . ."

"No one in my life, up to date--not my parents--not even Miss Fisk or Professor Throckmortin, my two favorite instructors--none of the girls at The House, no one person has had as much influence over me as my Grandmother Deal. She had me with her much of the time and she always inspired me to do something fine--to find what was the most worthwhile thing in life and see it through. Soon after she died, I ran across a poem. It was like this:

"'Pain has been and grief enough and bitterness and crying.
Sharp ways and stony ways I think it was she trod,
But all there is to see now is a white bird flying
Whose blood-stained wings go circling high--circling up to God.'

"I haven't the faintest idea what or whom the author meant when she wrote it, or the real significance of it. That's the beauty of poetry, anyway. We can all put our own interpretation on it. To me, it was my grandmother who had known the bitterness and crying and had trod the sharp and stony ways, for her life, like all of those pioneer women, was terribly hard. And the line that just *thrills* me with meaning is, 'But all there is to see now is a white bird flying.' This is the first time I've ever told this to a soul . . . in fact, I don't *know* any one else I *would* tell it to, Allen--"

"Thanks."

"Don't mention it."

Allen grinned and Laura laughed lightly. "But that line has grown to be sort of . . . what shall I call it? . . . an influence or an ideal or inspiration or something like that . . . to me. It's kind of a vision of things to come--happiness and success in a career. '*A white bird flying.*' I say it to myself lots of times . . . I don't know that I'll ever capture it, of course. . ." She turned to him, lovely and serious, all the laughter gone. "I've only *one* life to live, Allen, and I do so want to get the most out of it."

He, too, was serious. There was no laughter, now, for either.

He slipped an arm around her and caught up her hands. "And doesn't a home of your own and all it means . . . doesn't it seem to give 'the most out of life'? Can't you see that it would?"

"No, Allen," she shook her head. "I can see nothing at all . . ." She smiled up at his face bent low over her own. ". . . Nothing at all but a white bird flying."

CHAPTER 16

The month of May brought all of those final events so important to college students. One of the early dates was Ivy Day. When the smoke of battle had cleared, Bernice Fowler, efficient and capable Mortar Board, emerged triumphant as May Queen. Many of the co-eds on the campus shrugged their shoulders and said it was an empty honor, the result of intensive political strategy. Most of them would have given their souls to have been in her shoes.

A shower in the morning, swift and sudden, threatening disastrous results for a time, suddenly stopped and left in its wake glorious sunshine and a sparkling campus. Suddenly there were the townspeople and students massing themselves for the annual parade. There were the processional by the military band and girls carrying the daisy chain entering the green triangle set aside for the ceremonies, a chorus of sorority representatives singing "Who will plant the Ivy?" and the pages announcing on silver trumpets the entrance of the queen. There was a great white throne encompassed about, not quite with angels, but by pretty coeds in appearance falling not far short of that appellation. There were the crowning of the Queen, the competitive inter-fraternity sing, the reading of the Ivy Day poem, the giving of the Ivy Day oration and the planting of the traditional ivy plant. In the outside world stocks went up and down, stores sold their commodities, hospitals cared for their sick, ships sailed to far countries. But here on the campus was a world within the other, a little world that had eyes only for the traditional exercises, and for the tapping of the Innocents and the masking of the Mortar Boards, with all their attendant enthusiasms and disappointments.

Now that the time was coming to leave, it seemed to Laura a far sadder occasion than she had dreamed. She had a recurrence of the same feeling she had known when she was to be thrust out of the grades into High School, when she was to be pushed out of Cedartown into the University. Now, it seemed she could go on longer here more easily than she could take another new step.

The month of May and the few days of June remaining on the school calendar passed into the shadows of days gone by. And Laura was in cap and gown in the huge coliseum where she had registered four short years before, standing with several hundred others, and hearing the Chancellor pronounce the end.

Then she was home, and Cedartown seemed strangely quiet and uneventful, the blue and white room a silken cocoon that she must soon burst, the old grape arbor nothing but a shelter from the sun. She set the first of August for the date to leave home for Uncle Harry's. In the meantime, she assisted her mother with the homely daily tasks, read and wrote, strolled down to Kathie's often, chatted some with old Oscar Lutz, and drove almost every evening with Allen.

Allen seemed older and more mature this summer. Away from the University, he had lost a little of that snappy way which had always come to him so readily. He seemed more serious, talking often about his work to Laura. To her surprise, she found herself growing interested in his experiments with feeding, his plans to set out a grove of walnut trees in his lower pasture, the success he was having with sudan grass, and she grieved with him over what he termed a piece of blundering on his part, losing some sheep with sweet-clover bloat.

He talked no more of his love for her, although he often spoke of Christmas and when she would return, as though some great change might have taken place in her mind by that time. Any reference to this, Laura only evaded, putting aside the thoughts that came to her as one avoids unpleasant realities. June and part of July drifted along dreamily enough. Sometimes Laura chided herself for being a two-faced person who pretended one thing even as she planned another. She ought to tell Allen all about that trip to Uncle Harry's. She ought not let him look forward to Christmas as he was doing. Just as Allen was too fine to be trifled with in any foolish, flirtatious way, so was he too fine to be hurt by the bungling of a friendship. Sometimes she wakened in the night, thought of herself with deepest scorn, and decided to tell him the truth. When she saw him again she would lose her courage, and all her nocturnal resolutions would go into nothing.

Sometimes she thought she would talk to Kathie about it. But she and Kathie lived in two different worlds. As much as Laura admired her cousin, she was admitting this summer that she was disappointed in her. Always light-hearted and gay, Kathie seemed more than that now. There was something strangely restless about her. She went to Omaha too often, and left Patty with Verna. It was as though both Cedartown and Omaha were her homes and she must attend every social event in each. She and Jimmie were seldom out together any more. The banking proposition had been a hard one the past few years and Jimmie, serious and conscientious as always, was giving the business the best that was in him. Uncle Mack came down often and together they would go over the notes. Laura had often heard her Uncle say, "The heart of the bank is the note-case. A good banker keeps his note-case clean, just as a housekeeper keeps her kitchen clean." And Jimmie, with his inclination to put his whole soul in anything, had been giving his every thought to keeping the bank in good condition in these perilous times. Kathie, in her light-hearted way, did not think it necessary that he give it so much thought and worry. She made sport of his conscientious endeavors, and not always with good taste. Several times Laura suspected that she openly embarrassed him before their friends. Lately she had been going to Omaha for longer periods, leaving Verna to take the entire charge of Patty. Laura disliked to speak of it to her mother, for Eloise was radical in her criticism, and Laura was genuinely fond of Kathie, even when she was disappointed in her.

Old Oscar had changed too, this summer, but his was the natural change of age. He seemed much more feeble than at this time last year, Laura thought, as she lay in the hammock watching him now, fussing among his roses. Poor old man. He would be gone one of these days. She ought to do something for him. "I'll walk over and let him talk to me," she told herself, "that's about the biggest treat any one can give him,--to make an audience for him."

It was true. He was delighted beyond measure to see her slip through the opening in the privet hedge. There were low-hanging clouds in the west and when she spoke about it, the suggestion opened up a whole stream of talk: "Speakin' of storms,--" He sat down on the edge of the porch, and was off on a monologue highly pleasing to himself, if not his audience. "You know that there big cottonwood left standin' north of the cemetery? Well, I'll tell you somethin' about that. Marthy's and my first old house stood right over there a few yards beyond the pasture fence north of the cemetery. That big cottonwood up there on the hill is the last one of those I planted. It's powerful old . . . I could figger it up exact, but I won't stop. I mind as how, if I was away from the house in the field or at the barn or down in the pasture and see a storm come up, I'd always hot-foot it up for the house. She was always scairt o' storms. Never got over it. Lived through Injuns coming, rattlesnakes in the yard, wind and snow and blizzards. Never complained about 'em. But let a thunder and lightnin' storm come up and she was just a little girl. Always was. I mind as how, I never could see a storm comin' without droppin' everything and hurryin' up to the house to her. After she died . . . the first time there was a storm . . . Queer! . . . I come hurryin' home here. There she was . . . gone . . . safe, you might say, from storm . . . but couldn't get over she was waitin' for me to come and stay with her."

In his tiresome old way he was repeating: "When we lived out there in that first house, no matter whether I was in the north cornfield . . . in the east quarter or down in the pasture . . . I'd always come up there through the draw. If it got dark, she'd set two lights in the windows. We had a kitchen with two windows about three . . . four . . . feet apart." He measured it off with his hand and the hoe. "There was a little cupboard atween the two windows. And if it got dark she'd set a light in each one. Always said most any one would have a light in one window, but I need never mistake anybody's lights for ours on a dark night, for she'd always have them two, about three . . . four . . . feet apart. Used to joke her quite a little about that. 'Marthy,' I'd say, 'suppose I'd come home tighter 'n' a fiddle some night . . . and be seein' double and get in the wrong house?'" And he laughed his high cracked old laugh.

"Well, as I say, when a storm was comin', I'd hot-foot it up there, and when I'd get to the top o' the knoll where the big cottonwood tree still stands, I'd hoo-hoo and call out to her I was comin'. And when I'd come in she'd run to me and say: 'My! Oscar! I'm glad you're home. Now I'm not afraid.'" He said it diffidently, almost shyly, like a young lover. Laura looked at him, so old, so gaunt, with his huge bent frame and his ashen-gray cheeks flabbily wrinkled above his beard. How queer! How could one, as old as that, remember? How could love for another last through the years like that?

"Queer, how all three little girls had to die one after the other." He was evidently speaking of his own children now. "One was diphtheria . . . never heard of anti-toxin. See her just choke up and die. One was tuberculosis . . . consumption, we called it. Didn't know what to do . . . just stuff up the cracks in the window so she wouldn't get night air. One was probably appendicitis, but never heard of it, just called it 'acute inflammation' and watched her go, too. Queer! Us old codgers ain't got any call to say times ain't better now."

Suddenly he said, with complete change of subject: "I used to play a jew's-harp: 'There Was an Old Miller Who Lived by the Mill' and 'Comin' Thru the Rye.'"

Childish, Laura thought. First you were a little child, and then you were mature, and then you were a child again. Well, that thought wasn't new. Others had thought that all out long ago. *Second childishness and mere oblivion, sans teeth, sans eyes, sans taste, sans everything.* And--*desire shall fade and man goeth to his long home.*

CHAPTER 17

Laura had one more week at home and the thought tortured her even while it satisfied. She wanted to make the most of it, to hold it to her heart as one fondles a precious thing. There was something vaguely painful in seeing her father come home from the office, care-worn and tired, and her mother go monotonously over all the household tasks each day. They would miss her. But so would they miss her no matter what she might be doing away from them. She felt a sort of patient fondness for Trib, now that so soon she was to see him no more.

Trib was seventeen now,--a queer mixture of man and boy. All his young life he had ridden hobbies up hills of enthusiasm, abandoned them one by one, and trudged down into valleys of neglect, only to find there steeds of different hue and temperament. One year it had been an enthusiasm for carpentering, in which he had made countless tool chests and benches and more or less wobbly pieces of lattice-work. One year he had been an embryo naturalist, every waking moment spent in watching birds through Laura's opera glasses or constructing nests for them, every spoken sentence a statement concerning his feathered friends. He had filled all available places with wrens' nests, made a martin house large enough for all the relatives, both blood and law, that might arrive, and built various fancy habitations for bluebirds, brown thrashers and flickers. When the winged bipeds for which the houses were intended failed to understand his kind motives, and the sparrows moved in en masse, Trib abandoned the whole interest with superb scorn. There had been a year of photography, with part of the cellar curtained off into dungeon-like quarters, where one, venturing in, fell over old magic lanterns and electric light bulbs, became entangled in coils of wire and rolls of films. Eloise had been in a state of exasperation and actual concern over these various interests, dilating long and with much detail upon her difficulties with Trib. This summer he had grown strangely quiet and read too many lightweight magazines. Laura, looking at his sleek dark head bent over one, felt a warmth of tenderness for her young brother, a vague disquietude that she was not to be near any more, not again to be an amused and exasperated onlooker at those boyish enthusiasms.

July was slipping away in a procession of hot "corn weather" days. It made Laura think in contrast of the lovely times in the northern woods. She wished her father and mother might go up there, but the former seemed tied always to the day's grind and the latter with martyr-like spirit stayed by him, though she called attention quite frequently to the grace she exhibited in so doing. Some day, Laura thought, she would be in a position to take them all on such a trip, and others still more interesting. It gave her a warm feeling of contentment for her lot.

In the late afternoon of one of these last July days, dressing in cool white after her bath, Laura decided as she slipped into the fresh things, to go down to Kathie's. She could not have known the disturbing conditions in the lovely little English house or nothing would have taken her there.

Jimmie was home from the bank, with the information that he was going to Lincoln on a business trip. Katherine had expected Jimmie to go with her on one of her all-too-frequent Omaha social journeyings,--and Jimmie was not going. Furthermore,--and aye, there was the rub,--Jimmie was quite frankly saying that he thought Kathie ought not to go either, that the weather was hot and Patty needed her. Words, which at first were only ironically polite, grew into words that were strong and bitter,-- incriminations,--denunciations. And now Jimmie was stooping and kissing four-year-old Patty, giving one of her light corkscrew curls a playful pull, saying with pronounced sarcasm: "If your business interferes with your pleasure, Patty-girl, put off your business," and cool and calm with no word to Katherine, walking on out of the house.

Katherine's temper rose in a perfect storm of anger. So this was what their marriage had come to, had it? They were not on speaking terms. So she had married a man who was no gentleman, had she? Even as she said it, some inner voice reproved her, told her flatly that she knew "gentleman" fitted Jimmie in its finest sense. She felt furious and thwarted. She, Katherine Deal, who might have married any one of several Omaha men- -men in her own set--was being treated like a child. That's what one got for marrying out of one's sphere, she told herself. Jimmie, earning his way through the University,--his mother a dowdy widow trying to make ends meet! Why had she gone out of her way to be crazy about him? She had been a perfect fool. Jimmie was commonplace,--plebeian, his people farmers. Blood would count. She had proved that. With no sense of the ludicrous, she was saying all these things to herself,--a girl whose grandparents on both sides had the same background that had been Jimmie's ancestors'. Like leaves in a whirlwind her thoughts rose fast and furiously. She would show Jimmie. She wouldn't be dictated to. Any time Jimmie could tell her what and what not to do! Criticising her, as though she were a poor excuse of a mother. Poor mother! She'd given birth to Patty, hadn't she? Little did a man know what that was.

Jimmie had wanted a child. Well, he *had* a child now, thanks to her own agony. If she never did another thing for his child, never lifted her finger to care for her, she had already done enough in going through that; no father could know it. And now to be virtually told to stay at home and look after Patty, as though she were paid by the week. Bitter things, cruel things, chased each other through her infuriated mind. She would go now for sure. She would leave him. She would divorce him. That was easy nowadays. Dad would see her through. Dad always got her anything she wanted. All right. She had a new desire now,--the biggest desire in the world,--to hurt Jimmie,--to divorce him. Dad would help her see it through. And to-night she would go right along to Omaha to attend the party at the Fontenelle. She, a former duchess of Ak-Sar-Ben, staying home from a party to look after a man's child because he had virtually told her to. He could have put off the trip,--"bankers' called meeting over the assessments of the guarantee fund." Blah! That was good, that was.

She began packing, throwing things in a bag without much thought. If she only had her car. Jimmie had his nerve to drive it. The car was hers. Oh well, *she* could ride on a dust jolting train or in a bus while Jimmie sped toward Lincoln in the new convertible coupé. The house was hers, too. Dad had given them both to her. Dad had done everything. Jimmie's very position was made by Dad buying the controlling interest in the bank. She would think a man would be ashamed to take all that from his father-in-law. Again that little inner voice which seemed keeping up with all her furious statements was reminding her that Jimmie had protested the gift of the new house, discouraged buying the banking interest if it were purely on his account, absolutely refused the gift of a car for himself. She would take the afternoon train to Omaha, and when she returned, some one of the old crowd would take pity on her and drive her back. She enjoyed the pitiful thought of herself accepting a charity ride from some one.

She would come back this time. But not for long. *Not for long.* There would be a lot of things to see to and then she would take Patty and go home for good. To take Patty away from Jimmie! That would punish him more than anything in the world. Evidently he didn't care anything about *her* any more. It wouldn't be any punishment for him to lose her. He could be free then to go and pick out some prissy thing that would cook and bake and scrub and have his babies. That was the kind of girl he wanted. Maybe he had her in mind already. In the meantime, she could make him suffer to lose Patty. She was cramming things in the bags.

She finished packing, took her bath, and gave directions to Verna about Patty. It was then that Laura came in.

Katherine's fury rose again. Now that she had Laura to talk to, she freed her mind of countless bitter things: "Imagine! Dictating to *me!* Telling me I can and can't do this or that. Insinuating I'm neglecting his child. What child *ever* had the care Patty has? Tell me that. Neither you nor I. Dr. Rayburn for one thing, Dr. Moss for another, Miss Lawrence's model pre-kindergarten school. He said I cared more about playing bridge when she was at the pre-kindergarten school than I did the psychology of it I was always pretending I was interested in. He said, 'Psychology be damned. A baby needs her mother and not a scientific textbook.' He said she'll always remember Verna more than she will me,--that Verna's with her more and understands her better." The words tumbled over each other in their harshness and anger.

Laura had never seen Kathie in such a state and the sight was unlovely. She was deeply astonished and grieved and so embarrassed that it seemed she could not endure the sensation. Kathie and Jimmie! She had loved them, idolized them. Ever since they were married they had seemed to stand for all that was attractive and ideal. Fine, clean, upstanding Jimmie, and lovely, laughing Kathie. She thought of them as the bride and groom who had settled in this beautiful little home a few short years ago. With an ache in her heart so intense that it hurt her very body, she listened to Kathie's tirade, dully watched her write and tear up and rewrite several notes to Jimmie in the vain hope of getting one which would be scornful enough to suit her. She saw her kiss Patty good-by, give Verna a final direction and leave.

All the way on the train to Omaha, Katherine Buchanan constructed and revised her tale of oppression in readiness to tell her mother.

At seven, she was in Omaha--at seven-twenty in her girlhood's lovely home.

Emma Deal was delighted to see her daughter, her youngest child. Emma in her sixties, now, was gray haired, beautifully preserved with all the modern preservation that money can accomplish. She had a complacent, easy, good-natured way about her which gave her a certain serenity.

"Dad's not here," were almost her first words. "Has to miss the party. Larry Albrett and the Millers are going with us."

"Where is Dad?" Katherine's head ached a little from emotional fatigue.

"Lincoln. A called bank meeting. He phoned just before he left." Her mother was serene, unruffled.

Katherine emitted a feeble "Well! Jimmie's gone, too." Suddenly it seemed a little ridiculous to tell her mother all she had intended. It was rather flat to blow in with a tale of being the victim of a tyranny as terrible as she had conceived herself to be, and find her mother apparently a victim of the same cruelty, and taking it as unconcernedly as though it were of no consequence. However, that did not account for the other bitter things Jimmie had said,--those about her neglect of Patty. She steeled herself against the thought of him. So Larry Albrett was going to be in the party, was he? Larry had liked her a lot at one time. And Larry was fun. Later, in her own old room, she slipped the rose-colored gown over her creamy white shoulders and looked at her slim, supple figure in the glass. "Kathie, you don't look a day older than when you left home," she told the lovely girl, looking out at her. "But you would. . ." She curled a scornful lip, "You would, if you took your family as seriously as Jimmie thinks you should."

Laura went home from Kathie's in such an unhappy state that it bordered upon physical illness. With that old sense of allegiance to Kathie which she always possessed, she would not tell her mother of the agitated scene. She was in her blue-and-white room with closed doors, trying to settle her own agitation before helping her mother with the supper. As much as she thought of Kathie, she knew Kathie was the one to blame. Jimmie was fine. Jimmie had no doubt said bitter things. But they were true. Kathie *was* in the wrong. She *didn't* pay much attention to Jimmie or Patty or her house any more. Over and over she thought of the miserably unhappy atmosphere in the lovely little house, all the more bitter for the contrasting thoughts of the happiness she had seen there. "I guess Tennyson was right," she said to herself, "that 'a sorrow's crown of sorrow is remembering happier days.'"

She wished she could confide in Allen about it for the sheer sake of self relief, but she knew the old clannish attitude of the Deals would not let her. Even then, her thoughts began running riotously through a newly discovered by-path. If it were she and Allen--they would not have handled the situation so poorly. They would have--She called back her truant thoughts sharply, soundly provoked at their strange stampede, and concentrated on Kathie and Jimmie. Kathie was selfish. She had always had everything she wanted. And now, having everything, she was restless and self-centered. Jimmie, having stood a great deal, had evidently exploded to-day. So that was marriage! Luckily she was not going into it.

She went downstairs with the sensation of an emotional depression too deep for comfort.

CHAPTER 18

Katherine went back to her home late in the evening of the second day. Larry Albrett drove her down. The night was lovely. Larry, who had "thought a lot" of Kathie, once, had not changed. Which is to say he was still single, still flitting about taking his pleasures where he found them, still thinking a lot of Kathie. At least so he told Kathie. And Kathie, not yet thirty, gay, blithe, loving the flesh pots tremendously, listened. The night was lovely and she was a little foolish. It was very late when they drove up to the house. Lights shone from Verna's room and from the upper hall. Kathie had a swift intuition then that something was not right, but put it aside, and asked Larry in. She was not going to slip in like a young girl sending her lover away, she told herself. Whether Jimmie liked it or not made no great difference now.

They went in, and Kathie, excusing herself, ran upstairs to see how everything was after the two days' absence. Jimmie was not in his room. She slipped down the soft carpeted hall to Verna's room. Verna was there in a chair and Jimmie in pajamas and robe was bending low over her, his arms . . .

Oh, not that! Not Jimmie! Katherine felt a definite illness. Not good clean stolid dependable Jimmie!

She stepped unnoticed into the room. Slim, cool, disdainful, she gazed at Jimmie's broad back. Verna looked around and caught Katherine's scornful expression. Immediately Jimmie was turning and raising miserable, angry eyes. And then, Katherine saw for the first time that Verna held Patty in her lap, a limp little Patty with scarlet cheeks and half-closed eyes.

"She's sick," Jimmie said shortly. "Dr. Benton is on the way."

Katherine was hanging over Patty now, remembering Larry only long enough to say: "Go down and thank Larry Albrett for bringing me, Jimmie." And Mr. Lawrence Albrett, standing awkwardly about for a few moments, made his escape comfortably.

"She didn't feel good before Mr. Buchanan came," Verna was explaining. "She wanted to come here in my bed."

Dr. Benton came,--and the next morning, Dr. Rayburn from Omaha. By afternoon old Dr. Baker, Katherine's uncle from Lincoln, and young Dr. Fred Baker, her cousin, were both there.

There followed days of fighting,--dark days, with the doctors coming and going, with a Cedartown day nurse and an Omaha night nurse, with townspeople slipping around to the back door to inquire how things were now; with Katherine, hollow-eyed, and without make-up, her hair skinned back tightly over her ears, and with Jimmie home from the bank, each avoiding the other's eyes.

The day came and passed that Laura was to have left. It did not take Kathie's pitiful "Don't go, Lolly," to keep her. She put the leave-taking completely out of her mind until--Laura's heart ached with the uncertainty of what that awful word "until" might mean.

Eloise was worried with the others, but she did not hesitate to say: "Well, I'm sorry, but Katherine needed just such a lesson."

"Oh, Mother." It was Laura. "I think that's hard-hearted. How *can* you?"

Katherine's mother, well-gowned and well-groomed and sick with worry, came down from Omaha in a Packard. Jimmie's mother, in a homemade dress with a biscuit of hair on top of her head, and sick with worry, came over from Meadowville in a rattling Ford. And Mrs. Mackenzie Deal, the Omaha banker's wife, and Mrs. Hattie Buchanan, who managed her own chicken farm, held on to each other in the depths of their despair. And upstairs in the dim light, there was a little Patty who moaned and cried out and threw herself about or lay quietly and inert in her coma. There were temperatures that hovered between 105 and 106, and one frightful night when they dropped suddenly to 96 and she began chilling.

Sometimes she called out sharply, and always when she did so, it was "Daddie" or "Verna" she wanted. Laura sensed Katherine's agony.

"She's delirious, Kathie," Laura tried to tell her. "She doesn't *know* it's Verna and Jimmie she's calling."

"That makes it all the worse," Katherine said in a dry dead voice. And there was nothing for Laura to say.

Mackenzie Deal, bald, heavy, prosperous-looking, his big round florid face looking grotesquely scared and flabby, came down with another child specialist. He had been able to accomplish a great many things in his life on account of his executive ability and his money. Only once or twice before had he been face to face with a great Force before which he was helpless,--the time Stanley had gone to war, for one. It brought back that old helpless sensation now,--that some tremendous Force, before which he was puny and impotent, was stepping in between him and his deepest desire. He had always been able to give Kathie everything she wanted. Every whim had been granted, and now he was not able to give her the thing she wanted most in the world,--her baby.

He sat out on a garden bench in the back yard, and watched the windows of the room where the white-gowned nurse passed and repassed.

His brother John, home from the office, had come over. He came around into the back yard and sat down with no word. He and John had not been on the best of terms the last few years. That banking controversy had always loomed between them. Sharp words had been spoken. Now, they sat together on a garden bench and said nothing. Once Mack cleared his throat: "Queer how Mother always pulled us through all the sicknesses, wasn't it? No child specialists,--no modern drugs."

"I was thinking of her, too," John said briefly. "Onion poultices and castor oil and catnip tea."

For an hour or more they sat there and said nothing, while the white-robed figure passed and repassed the upstairs windows.

In the house, Kathie, watching the nurse, was hanging on the very lift of her eyebrow. The young woman had been a classmate of hers in Central High. She had never paid any attention to her then. Now she was saying to herself: "If Patty pulls through I'll have her down here often. I'll ask her if she wants to have a room here with us when she's in this community nursing."

She hung on to Jimmie's mother, too. How good Jimmie's mother was, so capable and motherly and confident that Patty would make it.

Old Oscar Lutz came tap-tapping around on the cement walk to the back door, bringing a bunch of carrots tied with a red string. Kathie would have laughed at any other time. Now she took the carrots, scrubbed to a salmon polish, and asked the old man to stay awhile. She had never voluntarily asked him in before.

He came in and sat miserably in a kitchen chair, his cane between his legs.

"Why couldn't it be me got to go?" he said to Kathie. "I wouldn't a-cared."

Kathie laid a slim hand on his head for a moment, and then slipped back upstairs.

"Sometimes they pull through," the old man said to Laura. "You can't tell. I mind as how when I was a little fellow back in Michigan, Henry had the scarlet fever. For two days they thought he was just about gone. Watchers set up with him . . . nothin' more to do . . . just wait. Sudden like, he seemed to take a bit of a turn. They thought he was brightenin' up a little before goin'. People do sometimes."

The nurse came in and got a hot-water bottle. Laura went out of the room. Katherine came back in. People moved about, paying no heed to the old man's tale. He told the first of it to one person, the middle portion of it to another, the end to a third. It was Katherine who was near him now. "When he got over the crisis . . ."

"Oh, did he pull through, Uncle Oscar?" She did not even know of whom he was telling the long-winded story. All she wanted to know was that sometime, somewhere, some one pulled through a severe illness.

"Did he? I just tell you, he did. Wasn't he your grandfather? But he couldn't talk. Had lost his little speech entirely. We was all sad about Henry never being able to talk again. I mind as how when he was convalescing, Ma and Pa had to go to town on business . . . sign some papers or something . . ." Katherine had gone and Laura and Jimmie's mother were his audience. "Ma cautioned us to watch Henry good and keep him amused, and under no consideration to let him climb down out of the old crib she had him bolstered up in, with pillows at his back. We kept showin' him things and tryin' to amuse him, and we sort o' run out o' things to entertain him with. I mind as how I climbed up in a chair and was rummagin' around on a shelf, and come across an old yellow-handled jackknife that Henry had thought a lot of and cut himself on a half-dozen times, and I turned around from where I was up high on the chair and said: 'Looky, Humpy, . . . that was our nick-name for him . . . 'looky, Humpy,' I says, 'what's that?' And Henry reached up both hands excited and says: 'Dat's my knishe.'"

Laura was listening in spite of her lack of interest. "And mebbe you think us kids didn't holler that he talked." His cracked old voice went on. "We was all crazy to be the first to tell Ma and Pa. We took turns of stayin' by Henry fifteen minutes at a time, and lettin' the other kids go down the road a piece to meet the folks. I mind as how I was in the bunch that was down the road when we see 'em come over the hill. I can hear us kids yet in my mind yellin' and screechin' at the top of our voices, 'Humpy can talk.' 'Humpy can talk.'"

Those in the kitchen sat ready to obey the order for ice or hot water; one never knew what the next moment would bring.

"I mind as how Henry got his nick-name,--Humpy," the old man told them. No one in particular was listening. He did not seem to care especially. He appeared to be telling it more for his own pleasure than anything else. "Was too little to go to school, but was bright,--always pesterin' Ma to learn to him to read. Ma gave him his letters and he was doin' right smart with 'em. Give him a few little words to spell, but he was always gettin' *m* and *n* mixed up, so Ma says, 'You can always tell *m* because it's got three humps and *n* has just got two.' Next day, Ma give him the word 'man' to spell, and Henry says as chipper as a squirrel, 'Three humps, a, two humps.' Everybody roared, and we called him Humpy clear up to the time he got to sparkin' Sarah, and he said he'd lick anybody that called him that again." And the old man, in complete forgetfulness of the sorrow in the house, chuckled to himself for a long time.

The great crisis impending plunged Laura into the depths of an emotion more painful than she had ever know. Flesh and blood seemed to cry out against the terrible delay. Each night one wondered what news the morning would bring, each morning what secret the coming day held. Sometimes Allen drove up and went over home with her. Once she turned to him at her own doorstep: "Allen, life is too terrible. How can one stand it? It holds such heartbreaking things."

"And that," said Allen simply, "is one reason why two people who care for each other should meet it together."

And then, when there seemed nothing more to do, when one almost asked for relief for Patty, one way or the other, there came the faint indication of a change for the better, so extremely slight that it seemed the waft of a butterfly's wing would change the brighter symptom. Another bit of hope,--and another,--while doctors and nurses hung over her and waited,--and then the verdict,--she would pull through,--with Katherine crying and crying, with Jimmie's arms around her. And Jimmie crying, too. And Laura crying because they cried.

Laura went home, worn to a shred, mentally and physically. So this was marriage! Down to the depths of the valley of the shadow of death and up to the stars of the heavens with gratitude and joy. All this then she would avoid. Life for her would not hold such depths and heights of emotion. In more pleasant places her life would be lived,--by the side of still waters her work would be accomplished.

CHAPTER 19

With that amazing power for recuperating that children possess, Patty made noticeable strides toward a complete recovery. There was only one nurse on duty now; only one trip each day by Dr. Benton. All of Kathie's latent motherhood was in the supremacy. She half quarreled with the nurse over serving her child. "Anything you want Mother to do, Patty?"

"Yes." Patty knew her mind immediately. "Daddie read me some stories. I wish you'd read 'em all over to me, too."

"What were they, darling?"

"Bible stories. One was about David and Goliath and the Lord let David cut down a big bean stalk; and the other was about Jack the giant killer, and the Lord come to him and told him to take a little stone and put it in a sling and when the giant come out, to shoot him in the stomach."

Katherine, seeing Laura come in, slipped down to tell her the funny thing Patty had just said. The two girls laughed together. "Isn't it lovely and comfortable just to stay home and have Patty back . . . back from wherever she was . . . ?" Katherine broke off.

"Lolly . . . do you know something . . . all the time the doctors were fighting and I was just ice and stone, all that time . . . day and night . . . I kept thinking I had tight hold of Granny Deal's hand, and I kept saying over and over: 'Granny Deal, ask God not to let her die . . . please, Granny Deal, ask God not to let her die.' And I said it so much, sometimes I had it turned around the opposite way and would be saying: 'God, ask Granny Deal not to let her die.' Anyway," she added, with a little deprecating laugh, "they've always seemed kind of alike to me . . . God and Granny Deal."

Gay, laughing Kathie had known her first real anxiety and temporarily, at least, it had left her serious.

"Isn't life lovely anyway?" she said to Laura in an exuberance of thankfulness. "I mean just common, ordinary, everyday life, when there's no black cloud hanging over you,--just hollyhocks in the back yard, dinner cooking, Jimmie coming home. . ." She broke off and averted her eyes momentarily. "Lolly, I want to get something out of my system. I know you'll be shocked, but I think you'll be forgiving too. You and I have always looked at things differently. And I can't imagine you getting into the muddle I was in. But that day when my temper blew up like a new oil-gusher . . . and the day after . . . I played around a lot with Larry Albrett. Well, Laura, when I came home I was thinking of divorce."

"Kathie . . . not divorcing Jimmie! Why . . . how *could* you . . . I can't think . . . he's so altogether fine . . . and there's no grounds anyway."

"Incompatibility," Katherine announced blithely. "It covers a multitude of things . . . selfish and otherwise. It's true. And then, Patty . . . why, Laura . . . listen,--isn't this the funniest thing you ever heard?" She laughed gayly as though at a huge joke. "Listen to this, Lolly: *In-com-pat-i-bility,* and then *In-Come-Patty*-bility. Isn't that *funny?"* And she went off into another gale of high laughter. Laura looked at her in amazement. Wasn't that just like Kathie? You could not change people. No matter what happened, people never really changed. Out from under the black cloud of impending death, Kathie was her old self. Having slipped away from the shadows, Kathie would face life again as always,--light and careless, and airy as thistles in moonlight.

Laura set the third Thursday in August then for leaving. On Tuesday afternoon she and Allen drove down to Nebraska City, in order that Laura might see Bernice Fowler before going East. The hush of a warm August afternoon hung over the old town on the river that had seen so much of Nebraska's early history. From there, William Hill had gone out to blaze a path through the wilderness. From there, had started the long trains of oxen-drawn freighters to cross the then barren plains to Cherry Creek, later Denver. From there the first attempt was made to freight across the plains by means of steam. There slaves were once sold on Nebraska soil. There lived J. Sterling Morton, the man who originated Arbor Day, and the first Secretary of Agriculture. There the first newspaper in the state was printed, and prophetically enough, the first article set in type was entitled "Agriculture." The promise of the prophecy is magnificently fulfilled, for the rich soil of the rolling hills in this portion of eastern Nebraska is covered with corn and great orchards and vineyards. One of the greatest apple, cherry and grape countries in the world lies in this hollow of the Missouri Valley.

There was no one at the Fowler home, and a passing neighbor volunteered the information that the family had gone over into Iowa for the day. There was extra time then on their hands, and the two young people decided to spend it out at Arbor Lodge.

A mile west of the city it lies--this estate called Arbor Lodge--on a highway known as the old Steam Wagon Road because of its connection with those early attempts at steam transportation. There are sixty-five acres of ground surrounding a beautiful colonial mansion of a half hundred rooms. There are acres of maples, elms, oaks, pines,--all the planting of J.

Sterling Morton, the original owner, or of those in charge of the estate. But when Mr. Morton brought his bride, Carolyn Joy Morton, to the spot in 1855 it was native prairie with no sign of a white inhabitant. Indeed, Indians had ceded the land to the Government but a short time previously, and were still ambling freely over the homestead site. The Mortons selected a spot on a hill near the Missouri, looking toward the high Iowa bluffs, and built what was then considered a notable structure,--even though but three-roomed,--the only shingled house between Nebraska City and the Rocky Mountains. Here they lived and raised their sons, and with open-house hospitality welcomed all comers in that early day.

Soon the homestead blossomed under the hands of these two nature lovers,--fruit trees, shade trees, evergreens, flowers, shrubs, vines surrounded the home,--and that portion of the prairie was transformed into a spot of beauty. Twice the original home has been remodeled, until now it stands, a stately white mansion of fifty-two rooms, with white semicircular porches on three sides, supported by massive two-story columns. Mr. Joy Morton, the oldest son of the sturdy pioneer, and who became the owner upon the death of his father, formally presented the entire property to the State of Nebraska in 1923. J. Sterling Morton gave Arbor Day to the nation. And now, Nebraska, with the same hospitality shown by the original owner, welcomes the nation to Arbor Lodge.

Allen and Laura entered the park through its wide brick gates and stopped on the driveway a moment to gaze upon the monument of the great tree planter,--the huge bronze statue standing in front of a background of dense evergreens. Across from the monument on the other side of the drive, they looked over at the log cabin erected there as a memorial to the old pioneers,--a replica of the typical house of the day for those settlers who made their homes along the wooded river banks.

"Not anything so gay and giddy for our ancestors, though, Allen," Laura said. "The soddies and the dugouts farther out in the state for them."

"I'll say. I'll bet there weren't enough trees in the whole Stove Creek district to put up this house," Allen added.

"If humble beginnings have to start all over after every third generation, Allen,--it's your sons that will have to roll up their shirt sleeves again," she laughed.

Up through the brick-paved driveway between the stately trees they rode, turned to the right and passed through the arboretum, skirted the tall pines and parked the car near the stables. On foot then they went over to the stately white mansion, walked past the huge white columns of the north wing, through similar white columns at the main entrance and into the reception hall with its blue hangings. There they registered in the guest book: *Laura Lee Deal, Cedartown,* and *Allen S. Rinemiller, Cedartown.* Granddaughter of Will and Abbie Deal and grandson of Gus and Christine Reinmueller, who only a few years later than the Mortons, had come into the state in their covered wagons on the same day.

A bunch of tourists was just ahead of them, and the two joined the sightseers who were being conducted through the mansion by the caretaker. There was the usual conglomerate group of people to be found in any sight-seeing trip,--an old lady being helped along by another scarcely less old, a middle-aged man and a fat daughter in her teens, a woman with two children in a chronic state of pushing noisily forward and being as noisily yanked back, two bored gum-chewing youths, and a deaf old man who wanted to argue dates and data with the lecturer,--and they two. The only sightseers of their own age and apparently education, it gave them a sense of oneness, a closer companionship because of the contrast and strangeness of the rest of the group.

Looking on and amused, they followed the little group into the room at the north of the hall, a huge room with high beamed walnut ceiling and deep red hangings. "The family library it was," the lecturer was explaining, "but called the Title Room now." On the walls the various owners of the property were represented,--the buffalo and the Indians as claimants of the first rights, the Spanish ownership, Napoleon representing the period of French ownership, and then Uncle Sam who came into possession by the purchase of 1803. Straight from the Federal Government J. Sterling Morton had secured the rights to the land, and now, a gift from his son, the State of Nebraska owned it.

It gave the two a sudden sense of pride, that so recently as their own grandfathers' time, a friend of their grandparents had wrested this garden spot from the raw homestead lands of that day.

Retracing their steps to the south of the main hall, they came to the drawing-room with its silk tapestried walls, and its fine old mahogany furniture. They were enjoying themselves. They nudged each other at times, in a moment of suppressed and ingrowing mirth, and caught at each other's hands once or twice as the conductor related a bit of historical pathos of those early days. For a time they stood in front of the pictures of J. Sterling Morton and Carolyn Joy Morton as they looked when, bride and groom, they had crossed the Missouri and come into the new land not yet ceded to the Government by the Indians.

"Just think what it meant to her . . . and to our own grandmothers, for that matter," Laura said in a low voice. Every one was speaking in that hushed tone of voice one uses before a shrine,--every one, that is, but the two noisy children and the deaf old man; the former constantly pushing forward to look up the cavernous fireplace, and being as constantly yanked back by their mother's hand in some sort of hasty posterior clutching, and the latter raising his voice in occasional querulous contradiction of the guide.

"Pretty fine work, I'll say," Allen was looking at the firm, strong features of the man who did so much for the raw new state. But Laura, questioningly, looked only at the sweet young face of the bride.

Through the sun-parlor they went, with its cathedral-glass skylight and its French doors opening upon the wide expanse of lawn; and came then to the Denver room which the guide explained was part of the original building, and that it was named the Denver room because General Denver occupied it while he was negotiating the treaty with the Pawnees. This and the Document room, where the glass cases were lined with letters and documents all relating to the events of an early day, gave the young people a sense of closer connection with those days than they had ever felt. But it was when they had crossed the hall to the dining room with its beamed ceiling, its walnut woodwork, its china closets with portions of the first set of dishes used by the bride and groom, that Laura began to sense a feeling of reality of those young people who had made a home on the prairie. A little colored china hen placidly spreading her little colored china wings to form the cover of a dish, quite suddenly brought a swift mist to Laura's eyes. It was foolish, she told herself; she knew nothing about the history of the quaint little dish,--but something moved her unaccountably for a moment. Legal documents and letters, Indian relics and mementoes, pictures of steam wagons and of Presidential Cabinets; not one had possessed the quality of bringing home to her the life of the young bride so far away from family and friends as a little china hen spreading her little china wings over a dish. Had Carolyn Joy Morton brought it from her old home across the Illinois and Iowa prairies? The other tourists were asking of this and that, having pointed out to them the silver-marked chairs in which President and Mrs. Cleveland had sat, surveying the old silver service presented to Mr. and Mrs. Morton on their twenty-fifth anniversary; but Laura Deal stood looking only at the little humble dish, unaccountably touched by the living presence of a young woman who had left all, to brave the unknown.

Allen was waiting for her at the portieres of another room, and she came out of the mood into which she had fallen, to follow him into the music room where there stood an upright piano, one of the first to come into the state. She let her fingers slide over an octave or two and the keys gave forth a faint tinkling sound, that to her vivid imagination seemed a musical note from out of the past. "You can't quite think of playing 'When My Sugar Walks Down the Street' or 'Yes, Sir, That's My Baby,' can you?" she said to Allen.

Up the wide mahogany stairway they passed to the landing, where hung the huge J. Haskell Coffin painting of the Pawnee Indians signing away their claims to Nebraska Territory.

"It was signed right out here near Arbor Lodge in 1857," Allen was saying. "Doesn't that sort of get you?"

For some time they stood looking at the shining brown skins of the Indians in ceremonial dance, and at the figures of Mr. and Mrs. Morton and General Denver as they watched. Then they were going up the stairway to the room that was still furnished as it had been the day President and Mrs. Cleveland occupied it. From the balcony under the porch, they looked down the long brick paved driveway separating the pine grove from the arboretum.

Laura was unaccountably touched again by a visit to Mrs. Morton's bedroom, which stood just as she, herself, had furnished it a half century before,--bird's-eye-maple furniture, oil paintings, tidies, splashers, washbowls and pitchers,--all the old-fashioned furnishings of another age. There was a little glass inkstand--Had the young bride used it in writing home? Had she sent words of loneliness and homesickness? Or pride and pleasure in the new undertaking? She wondered why she, herself, was always touched by such infinitesimal things. Their very homeliness and lack of worth seemed connecting the past with the present all the more. It was true, she thought, that the big things awe us but the little things touch us.

The other second-floor rooms contained countless relics of that early time,--an old sewing-machine and melodeon, slippers and hand-made baby clothes,--mementoes of a bygone era.

When Laura and Allen came out of the mansion, something hung over them,--something which made them strangely quiet,--a bit of glamour from the early days, a sense of the heritage that had been bequeathed to them, a common knowledge of that close companionship they had just experienced, and above all, a sudden realization that the afternoon was waning and that a train was going east.

From the mansion they passed through a graveled path in the lovely lawn to the stables, used now as a storage for the various old equipages that had been used in different periods of the past. In the first room stood a coach once used on the old Overland line running between Lexington and Fort Kearney, and driven by Buffalo Bill; so high that the driver's seat was far above Laura's head, and the musty-smelling antique seemed a top-heavy affair. The leather had hardened into a substance resembling cracked and brown wood. The wheels were enormous wooden affairs, the back ones rounding up over the windows of the coach.

The two peered into the dusky interior; Laura, with some misgivings that the spirit of a departed Indian might not suddenly utter a ghostly war-whoop and send a phantom arrow through the old vehicle.

"I can't see that times have changed so much, though," Allen said. "Now, a highwayman merely rides up in a high-powered car and instead of the arrow, shoots off his mouth with 'Hand 'em over.'"

Next to the coach stood a vehicle still higher, but of a later vintage,-- the four-in-hand brake used by one of the Morton sons in the days when he drove four sleek high-steppers.

"'The king's horses *and* the king's men,'" Allen sang in his unmusical voice. He was gazing into the glass case that held the harnesses which had once graced the proud four. It, too, looked hardened and dull, all the life of the leather gone, like the sap from old trees.

They sauntered into the next room, where a dozen outmoded vehicles stood in two lines facing each other across the sunny room. An old fire-engine of a half century before came first, then the worn-looking phaeton used by J. Sterling Morton in his trips to town. A Stanhope phaeton, a surrey with frayed fringe still jauntily rippling around the canopy top, and a heavy cumbersome carriage completed the one row. Across from these more common vehicles stood those evidently for formal occasions; a three-seated affair all in gay tan-colored leather, a taxi, a Chippendale, and two broughams. Laura was fascinated, as she always was with anything which roused her sentiments. She peered into the dark interior of one of the broughams, with its elegant tufted leather upholstery, so glossy that it looked like ancient black satin; into the dusky inside of the once gorgeous taxi; imagined gay parties of young people going out in the Chippendale; wondered which one of the equipages was driven up through the long paved driveway with President and Mrs. Cleveland.

They appeared human, the dozen or more vehicles of other generations, standing there in mute memory of a day that was dead. They seemed the epitome of a grandeur that had come to the prairie country, of a long gone hospitality that had been fostered by a prairie lover. The whole period seemed to come alive to her sensitive imagination,--the people of the times, substantial and courageous, walked and talked with her. For the first time she was sensing to-day a romance in her own Midwest, a glamour over the lives of her own people. She wished she could hold to her heart the fleeting sensation until she could get pencil and paper. She wished she could catch it and hold it between the covers of a book.

CHAPTER 20

Leaving the stables, Laura and Allen strolled around for a time among the trees of the arboretum and perfunctorily read the names on the brass plates of the shaggy old trunks, criticizing each other pertly about their pronunciations.

"Juniperus virginiana, Red Cedar, 1868."

"Acer saccharium, soft maple planted in 1871."

"Pinus nigra austriaca, Austrian Pine, 1871."

In front of the mansion in an oval plot of lawn, they came to a dwarfed spruce with a stone collar about its base. "It's the tree Mrs. Morton brought from Colorado in a tomato can over fifty years ago," Laura told Allen. They both stooped down to read the words cut into the stone, for the low hanging branches of the Englemann spruce hid the carving.

Laura read the inscription aloud and very slowly, for the words were not especially clear in the rounding cement: "Arbor Lodge Homestead," she read in her low throaty voice, "was settled June, 1855, by J. Sterling Morton and his wife Carolyn Morton. Together . . . they lived . . . hereon . . . up to June 29 . . . 1881 . . . when . . . the . . . light . . . went . . . out."

They stood up, neither speaking, both touched by the simple words, as though into the brief poignant statement had gone all the love of a man for a mate. Instinctively, Laura's fingers sought Allen's, and together without words, they turned and walked down the graveled path and on down the steps to the sunken gardens.

Sturdy J. Sterling Morton and Carolyn, his bride, Grandmother Deal, old Oscar Lutz and his Marthy, Allen's German grandparents, Gus and Christine Reinmueller,--what did they have in their lives that gave them such fortitude decades ago here on the wild prairie?

Past the old brick walls and lovely close-clipped hedges separating the different parts of the Italian gardens, the two young people strolled to the rose arbors, scenes of a thousand thousand blossoms in the earlier part of the year. Retracing their steps back past the geranium beds, they walked on over the lush green grass to a sundial. Simultaneously and haltingly, as they made out the hewn words, they began to read aloud the quaint inscription cut from the gray stone: "Hours Fly," they read, and "Flowers Die." They paused for the next wording and then went on in their fresh young voices together: "New Days, New Ways, Love Stays."

The spoken words, deep with meaning, seemed to ring reverberatingly for a moment over the old timepiece which had seen so many hours fly, and so many flowers die.

Still facing the old sundial together, Allen slipped an arm about Laura and drew her close. "Stay, Laura," he said suddenly. "Don't go. Stay and make a home with me . . . as they did. After all,--it's best."

For a brief moment Laura rested her cheek against Allen's arm, felt the touch of something big and beyond her. In that fraction of a minute she had the sensation of being swept on to some new existence, in which she was greater than herself, larger than humanity. The feeling of a great contentment came upon her. In that brief space of time she seemed to have slipped into her place in the scheme of things. It was as though she were the center of all existence, the reason for a Great Plan. But she straightened and said quickly: "Don't, Allen,--please. Don't spoil our last nice hour here. I've told you how I feel; I'm just not letting myself in for that sort of thing. It isn't what I've planned . . . oh, Allen, try to understand me . . . you've been so understanding this last year. I've dreamed wonderful things for myself,--you know that it's just the spirit of the place that sort of got us both for a minute . . . the spirit of the times . . . J. Sterling Morton bringing his bride out here and the wonderful thing they and all the other young couples did. It *was* wonderful, and it sounds romantic, but that's all in the past. And after all, on top of the experiences of the other two generations before me, there must be something more for me in the world than just a supine giving up and keeping house. Why, *that's* what my grandmother did with her meager education and slight advantages. Surely there's more for me, now, than just that. If *that's* all, we wouldn't have progressed a bit. I've only one life to live, and it must be lived to the fullest. Surely there's something more for me than life gave my grandmother."

She turned earnest brown eyes to him, eyes without banter or evasion.

"I don't know anything about all those generalities," Allen said stubbornly. "I don't flounder around in a lot of philosophies and vague possibilities. All I know is, you're the girl I want . . . the most natural . . . and the most wonderful thing in the world."

"I think a lot of you, Allen. Why, you're . . . Allen, you're the very best friend I have, but . . . .well, this will hurt, but it's better to be honest . . . we've always been honest, and I think that's been the secret of our good friendship . . . but I can't think of anything more prosaic than settling down here . . . and sort of letting the world go by."

"I don't call it letting the world go by," he returned quickly. "I call it tackling a small piece of the world, and making something of it. You admit Morton and his bride and all the rest of the old pioneers did a great thing when they crossed the river and started their settlements. You've said it was romantic and intensely interesting and quite worth while. You think their own love lay at the bottom of their acts of courage and bravery. All right,--did you ever stop to think that maybe we're pioneers, too? Haven't you the vision to see that? Why isn't it something of pioneering that I'm trying to do? Agriculture in most quarters has been a hard, wearisome proposition. People, at large, still think a farmer is the same old whiskered type of straw-chewing gent, saying, 'Wall, I swan,'--that he's always pictured in the cartoons. *I'm* pioneering, too,--and a whole lot of other young fellows from the colleges and universities--*we* have visions, too,--a new outlook on the whole thing,--that it's a business that can be looked after as thoroughly as any other; not the old haphazard type of one-horse farming, but the making of every farm into an organized center of activities. We've the vision of country homes, as fine and ample as any Englishman's estate, and a darned sight more convenient,--miniature Arbor Lodges, in a way."

He threw out his hand toward the lovely mansion on the terrace above them, its pillars cloud-white against the dark green of the ancient trees. It looked peaceful, serene, in the warm glow of the late afternoon,--the embodiment of strength in a restless time,--the symbol of all that is steadfast and durable in a changing world.

"We're pioneering, too," he went on earnestly, . . . "starting a new class . . . the Master Farmers who are attempting to develop agriculture to the *n*th degree. Why couldn't you enter into that in the same spirit your grandmother did? There are a thousand things to be worked out . . . worked out by genuine farmers, and not politicians sent down to Washington. Because you're rooted in the soil, need you be a nonentity? There's room for criticism, I tell you, in an agricultural economy which has squeezed out its best youth. Farmers have always been a sort of incoherent mass,--their best leadership drained off into city life. A scad of sacrifice had been made for this state in its early years, and it ought not go for nothing. A lot of young fellows with vision and qualities of leadership have got to tackle the problem, or we're going to have a state of increasing tenantry,--and that *would* ring the bell for agriculture."

When he paused, Laura was laughing her throaty contralto laugh. "Allen . . . believe *me* . . . at this rate of silver oratory, you'll be in Washington yourself."

"All right . . ." he grinned, too, a bit sheepishly after his tirade, "maybe I will . . . and at that, it wouldn't hurt the state to send a dirt farmer either. Well," he sobered again, "how about it? I wouldn't ask you to stay now, of course--that would be selfish . . . but how about a promise that when you come back at Christmas . . . ?"

"No, Allen." Laura, too, was sobered and earnest. "There's no middle ground for me. If life held marriage for me, I would want it to be whole-heartedly so . . . home, housekeeping, children. In that, I'm as old-fashioned as they make them. Otherwise, it's freedom and more schooling and development, and I hope, a career. I'm not going to cross life's ideas, make a sort of hybrid of myself, doing neither one very well. It just has to be a choice and I've decided for the freedom and the career. I feel too energetic, and . . . though it's not very good taste to say it of myself . . . too talented to embroider fat initials on towels and go to housekeeping. To marry and to be brought up against all the little irritations of housekeeping . . . actually to live with another person . . . would injure my dreams. And a writer's life, Allen, is just dreams."

When he said nothing to that, Laura went on: "And then, Allen . . . there's something else." She paused and looked up at him a bit queerly, he thought.

"I'll be home Christmas as you say. But not to stay. There's more to this visit than I've told you. I'm even more tied back there than you know. I just said we'd been honest with each other. Well, we have, for that matter. I'm not going back on that statement in general. But there is one thing I *have* kept from you, Allen,--not because you're not entitled to know, but I've had a sort of delicacy about telling you."

With the quick jealous instinct of the male, Allen divined at once. "Somebody else," he said shortly. "Some one East." He gave it as a statement rather than a question.

"No. That's where you're wrong. I met some men, to be sure, but no one to get excited over and write home about. No, Allen, something as opposite as it could be."

"Spill it. I'm ready."

"Money."

"What do you mean,--money?"

"Uncle Harry Wentworth's and Aunt Carolyn's money. I'm to get it, in time, Allen. Isn't it wonderful? I feel terribly humble about it, and you can see for yourself how diffident I've felt about people knowing it. Cedartown people! What would they think? You know, yourself, how they'd begin to look at me differently, as though I were some unusual species. Every time I'd turn around it would be misinterpreted as some high-hat move. Small towns are funny that way. They're far better to any one that's down and out than they are to any one riding up on a wave. If I needed sympathy, they'd shower me with kind acts. If I had a windfall, they'd watch my every action to get a chance to take me down a notch or two. It takes a small town to keep you humble. So, not anybody knows it but our clan. The Deals!" She laughed up at Allen standing silent and grim by her. "Rest assured, the Deals have all sat in council upon it--have gabbled it all over from A to Z. It isn't any of their business, as a matter of fact. The money is going to come from my mother's side of the house, as another matter of fact. But does that faze the Deals? It does not. At every clan gathering they discuss and argue it before my face. 'Once a Deal always a Deal' is on our coat of arms, I guess."

Allen was surprised and a little confused. He could scarcely get his bearings. It threw the game into one of entirely different tactics. To make love to the little Laura Deal he had known,--and then to hear suddenly that she was to come into a large amount of money! He stammered a little. "Well . . . congratulations. Why . . . that sounds . . . great. But what's the big discussion and argument?"

It was Laura's turn to be a bit confused. She looked away for a moment across the lovely hedges and the green sloping lawns. Then she raised honest brown eyes to Allen. "Because . . . if I accept their offer . . . I can never marry as long as they live. I am to stay with them . . . like a daughter . . . unmarried . . . as long as both live . . . then the major part of the estate is mine."

"Not to marry?" Allen said it over, as though speaking it aloud might make it more comprehensive.

"Not to marry." Laura answered, as though the repetition gave it emphasis. "And it's only fair, of course, Allen," she hastened to say. "You see that, don't you? You take two people getting on in years that way, and of course they would want me to make them that kind of promise, if I stayed with them. It's perfectly fair of them. And you can see now, what I've been meaning about being free--to follow out all the plans I've made for myself. You see it all now, don't you, Allen?"

Allen was staring down at her. "And you call that 'free'?"

"Of course."

"Well, I don't," he said hotly. "I call it selling your freedom. I call it selling your birthright for a mess of pottage."

Flushed, earnest, tense, the two stood facing each other, between them the old sundial where the shadow cut its dark path across the sunlit stone. A bird dipped down into the green thickness of the hedge. A faint odor of the pines came from the far side of the grounds and mingled with the scent of newly cut clover. From the high terrace above them, the pillars of the great house glistened white under the blue sky in which a few long feathery clouds sailed, as though some of the white columns of the mansion were floating off to make dream houses in another world.

Allen was the first to speak. He looked at the old sundial where the shadow finger was pointing to the fleeting moments so stealthily, so noiselessly, that no one could detect its measured counting.

"It's time to go," he said briefly. And Laura, taken back at his lack of response, for a moment felt childishly hurt.

"I expect it is," she said as briefly, and together they went down the walk through the garden of dead roses toward the graveled road where the parked car stood. The rays of the low hanging sun lay with warm mellow light across the lovely clipped lawn and hedges. At the west end of the Italian garden, Laura, through a swift mist of the eyes, looked back at the sundial that had seen so many hours fly and so many flowers die. The first part of this August afternoon would always stand out in her memory as unbelievably happy and peaceful. She had a vague feeling that she would always remember it, that she would be able to recall it when she was an old, old lady. The hours would fly and the flowers would die. She felt unaccountably saddened, foolishly homesick. But she had chosen wisely. She had kept her head. The emotion which seemed to possess her temporarily would leave as soon as she was on the train bound for the East. And Allen would recover quickly. Yes, for them both there would be new days . . . and new ways.

CHAPTER 21

Laura found Aunt Grace at the house when she and Allen drove up. She had a momentary feeling of irritation that Aunt Grace had come. The Deals were clannish, and Laura would have defended her aunt to the last ditch before an outsider, but to her own self she acknowledged that there were times when Aunt Grace's precise English, lack of humor, and didactic methods were extremely trying.

Something unusual must have brought Grace down to Cedartown on a school night. She was punctilious in her habits, and nothing short of a special occasion ever saw her in town at any time but a week-end. Added to this, she had already bade Laura good-by on Sunday.

"I wanted to see you again," she said when Laura had gone into the house. "I couldn't bear to let you go without another glimpse of you. I'm staying all night and will drive back in the morning, in time for my eight o'clock."

It struck Laura as unusual, to say the least. She and Aunt Grace had never been very companionable. In fact, she had never quite overcome a certain awe of her aunt which had persisted from babyhood, an attitude that was not materially benefited by having a class under her in the University.

Dinner over and the dishes washed, Laura, still under the spell of the afternoon spent with Allen, slipped upstairs and into her room, that old haven from countless storms of her girlhood.

Quite to her surprise and slight annoyance, Aunt Grace sought her out. "I wanted to talk to you about something," she said in her precise way when she had settled herself by the window. "I thought of it often yesterday and today. And so, when my last class was dismissed, I determined to speak to you."

Laura found her heart thumping a little, and acknowledged a vague return of her old childish fear of this aunt and her correct ways.

"I wanted to speak to you, as I said, about a certain matter."

Laura wanted to scream "For heaven's sake--what?" But she only said, "Yes--Aunt Grace?"

"You're really accepting your Uncle Harry's offer, are you?"

"Why, yes, Aunt Grace. It's lovely, isn't it?" She spoke in a sprightly tone of voice. "I feel like a little Cinderella who doesn't quite know how to clean the pumpkin off her dress."

"Yes, it's quite unusual and wonderful. I'm wondering though. . . . You're . . . I suppose you think it quite without my province . . . and it isn't any of my business, Laura, excepting as anything is my business that affects a niece of whom I am fond." Of course Aunt Grace would not drag in any love stuff. "You're sure you're quite happy and sincere about the promise not to marry while the Wentworths live?"

"Absolutely. But, Aunt Grace, that's kind of funny . . . from you, isn't it?"

"No--it isn't. It isn't at all odd or funny. I'm the *one* to say this to you. I'm the *only* one among the relatives to say this to you." She was speaking fast, agitatedly, in sharp contrast to her ordinary measured voice. "You're so young to tie yourself to that promise . . . I wonder if you know your own mind. I wanted to ask you about this young Allen. You've been around with him a great deal."

Laura laughed a little dryly:

"Surely, Aunt Grace, after all those years of experience with college people, you're not joining the Village Sewing Circle and thinking every girl who is seen with a man is going to marry him."

"No--I've grown used to that. I'm just wondering if you should tie yourself, though, that way to a promise."

Laura was provoked. She felt nervous and irritable at the turn of the talk, coming so soon after Allen's own arraignment.

"It's no more than any one does when he takes up his life work," she spoke quickly. "If I were a little girl, and my people were giving me away to Uncle Harry and Aunt Carolyn for their own, there would be some room to talk. I'm not 'selling myself.' I'm grown, and my own boss, and quite capable of deciding. It's no different than your own work, Aunt Grace. You teach in the University--you've sold your services to the state for the school year. Your summers are your own, to teach or go to school or travel. Uncle Harry has said I can come home at Christmas time and again in the summer if I wish. I'm just as free as you."

"Except for that promise you're making them."

"Neither is that anything unusual. I am to stay with them as long as they live and look after them. Whichever one is taken first is assured then that I'm staying with the other as long as he or she lives."

"They may live for a great many years, Laura, and become helpless and very trying."

"That's my risk, of course. But there is plenty of money for hiring attendants. I'd only be overseeing things and being what I hope would be a comfort to them. If Father and Mother were older or sick, my conscience might hurt me, but not under these circumstances. Mother is awfully happy about it. Father says very little, but neither does he talk much about anything, so that's nothing unusual."

Grace was dubious. "I know my brother, Laura. I don't think *he* is entirely happy about it."

"That's just at my going away for such long periods. But I could be doing that for any other reason. Bernice Fowler's sister has gone to Alaska to teach."

"Yes, I know. And, of course, you're resenting what I've said. I can't quite blame you. But I've seen you with this young Allen. . . ." There was a distinct air of embarrassment about her. ". . . And you've seemed so happy. I just wondered . . . if you really knew . . . how happy you were."

Laura was further surprised and not without an embarrassment of her own. Whatever had come over this icicle of an Aunt?

"I wanted to tell you . . . I want your life to be happy, at all costs. . . ." Evidently she was driving herself to speak of that which was painful. "I've had two chances to marry . . . one of them doesn't count . . . at least, as far as I'm concerned. But the other. . . . Oh, Laura, don't make a mistake. Know your own mind, for sure." Laura was amazed. She had never before seen her Aunt Grace drop her mask of unruffled calm. "He was one of the teachers . . . I enjoyed him more than any man I knew . . . but I didn't think I cared . . . that way. Later, I knew I cared. I was too slow in knowing my own mind . . . too cautious . . . too afraid of the sentimental side of life, I guess." She was making pitiful little attempts to get control of herself. Laura was moved to the depths. If it had been anyone else! But Aunt Grace, with her precise way,--"prissy" was Katherine's word for it,--it seemed unbelievable that she had known this romantic experience.

"Mother never knew that I regretted my decision. I couldn't add it to her troubles, so I kept it to myself. She would have suffered with me. She always wanted to see me in a home of my own. She had the old-fashioned notion that it was the most satisfactory life. Well, at that, I guess she was right,--providing, of course, that home can be all that it should. And it would have been,--oh, it *would* have been." Her face was red and contorted in its distress. Laura wished nothing so much as that the painful interview might end. "He was fine in everyway. I should have known my own mind, sooner. Mother was right. She tried to tell me. I never told her how I came to feel, and I never told any one." She was speaking fast, catching her breath quickly to cover her emotion. "I don't know what was the matter with me." She rose and walked over to the windows, fingering the draped curtain nervously. "Oh, I can have a home of my own . . ." she explained apologetically, "every capable woman can. But it will never be just what that one might have been. So you see, Laura," she was gaining her composure, "it's because I . . . am fond of you that I'm telling you . . . because I don't want to see you make the mistake I did . . . if mistake it *is* you will be making . . . that is something no one but you can know."

She was calm again, quite unruffled. The waters from the depths of her being had moved in and up, with some vagrant tide of emotion. And now they had receded. And there was nothing to disturb the serenity of the surface.

CHAPTER 22

At dawn the birds outside Laura's window woke her. A woodpecker was beating a monotonous tom-tom on some hollow drum of a tree, and a rain-crow called. With returning consciousness, the thought that this was the last full day at home sprang nimbly to the foreground. For a time she lay and thought of many things: that Allen's personality had developed into something finer than mere attractiveness,--that life was like a forest in which one walked blindly,--that good judgment, like a forest ranger, watched for the earliest sign of smoke and flame--And then, suddenly, the simile weakened and had no meaning, for it occurred to her that the lookout can only give the alarm. By no means is he expected to reduce the conflagration, alone and single handed. There was something so disquieting about the thought that she rose, threw a robe across her shoulders, and sat by the window.

Some one was stirring. It was Aunt Grace, up early in order to get back to school on time. She felt a sudden tenderness for her, a definite pity that she had experienced a disappointment in life, all the more keen, perhaps, because it had been of her own making.

Aunt Grace had said that no one was to get up when she did, that she would slip out very early. But hearing her moving about that way, gave Laura a sense of compassion, a desire to do something for this aunt whom she had never really known. What a good woman she was,--so conscientious and faithful to her duties. So she, too, dressed and slipped down to make toast and coffee for her. Through the kitchen windows, as she worked, she could see old Oscar in his garden, walking through the rows of cabbages and selecting one or two with the dew still fresh upon them. "I can foresee that our family or Kathie's or some of the other neighbors will have cabbage presented to them to-day." She smiled to herself at the old man's habit. "He's vegetable-conscious," she thought, and told herself she must repeat that to Allen to make him smile. She loved making the corners of his mouth draw up in that cheerful grin. This made her think of that particular young man again, which brought her around in a circle to the point where the morning's thoughts had started.

Aunt Grace came down then, a little neat overnight bag in her hand. She was surprised, and evidently a bit touched at the early attention from Laura. The two ate together, but with no great degree of ease. They were both conscious of the intimate talk of the evening.

Eloise came down, energetic and capable, with much criticism of the slight breakfast: "Laura, you should have made cocoa. Your Aunt Grace likes cocoa. Did you measure the coffee? The toast, Laura,--oh, surely you didn't use the bread in the white square box. The bread in the round green box is always for toast."

John came down. "You're going to have a hot day for your last one, I'm afraid, Laura."

Trib came lumbering down, looking sleepy and a little watery as to the sides of his dark hair. "Wish I could pound my ear once 'til noon," he was growling.

How common and natural everything was,--the day starting like a hundred other days, with duties and ordinary events. And yet, it was not an ordinary day at all. It was the last one to be spent at home.

Aunt Grace was leaving. They all stood in the driveway with her. She brushed a little dust off the windshield of her coupé. She hoped she hadn't put them all out, getting them up early. She would be very pleased to have a letter from Laura, any time she felt like writing. She looked at her wrist watch. She must start in order to have plenty of time. She thought the day was going to be rather trying. She shook Laura's hand stiffly and wished her a pleasant and safe journey. She slipped driving-gloves on her immaculate hands, the brown cuffs coming well over the white of her sleeves. And she was off to her daily war upon split infinitives and double negatives.

Looking after her a moment, Laura had another feeling of tenderness toward her. How we live our lives side by side with those whom we never know or understand. Some day she would like to write about Aunt Grace.

She turned and was about to slip her arm through her mother's in a moment of deep feeling, but already Eloise was stepping briskly up on the back porch. "Now, Laura, we must systematize everything to-day. The packing, the work, the last calls to make. I always say, the way to accomplish anything is to organize and then concentrate on the--" Her voice died away in the interior of the kitchen.

For several moments Laura stood on the back steps looking out over the low rolling hills to the east. There was an opening between the neighbors' houses and the trees where one could see, as in a dark frame, a section of the rich rolling farm land under the yellow morning sun. Then she, too, turned and went into the house.

All day there were necessary tasks to do. The phone rang often and friends dropped in to say good-by. Old Oscar Lutz brought a cabbage and some onions in the battered pail with rope for a handle. Eloise was provoked. "Imagine it! *Onions* for you, Laura."

Kathie called and asked Laura to come there for dinner at six. She was having Allen too, and to pay for their meal, she informed Laura laughingly, Laura and Allen were to drive Jimmie over to Meadowdale to catch the evening train. Yes, Patty was fine and wanted to see Lolly. All day Laura moved in a half daze. It did not seem possible that she was leaving for good.

And all day John Deal worked at his desk in the office back of the bank. Not until he closed the desk did he realize how tired he was. The day had been particularly trying. He had been attempting to work on the Statler case, a suit for damages. Old Oscar Lutz had taken up an hour or more with a minute change in his will, and an incredible number of reminiscences. And as a climax, the warring factions of the Neidlemann family had descended upon him, with long drawn out recitals of their respective grievances which consisted for the most part of such important injuries as the unwarranted removal of a chicken brooder and the unauthorized disposal of an old bucksaw. A country town lawyer's greatest trial is the inability to get rid of clients with any degree of speed. To hire a lawyer in a small town is to hire him body and soul, to compel him to listen to all the minutiae of all the experiences, physical and mental, that have attached themselves to said client or all the relatives, both blood and law, of said client.

And so, as John Deal closed the office door, the words of the old poem came to him:

"And the cares that infest the day
Shall fold their tents like the Arabs,
And as silently steal away."

He wished it were possible that they would do so. But he could not shake them off. They rode home on his shoulder, like so many little red devils. He had always been that way. He guessed he took life too seriously. Other men seemed to be able to leave their business cares behind them like lizards' skins. Mack, for one. Mack had made lots of money and apparently more easily than he himself had made a mere living; was not tied down to it especially, either,--did a great many social things in Omaha, played golf, was a good mixer.

His jaw set as he thought of the arguments he had staged with Mack. Bull-headed, Mack was. Mack had started out on that guarantee law fight with only his own interests at heart. Had hidden behind that word "confiscatory" every time the matter was discussed, like a kid behind his mother's skirts. Confiscatory! He had heard that word so much he wished he might never hear it again. Let the bankers pay. Let them pay and pay until it hurt. They would yelp at every assessment, but it was no harder on them than the calamities of those poor people who had lost everything. To be sure, the fight for the old law was over, the fund was insolvent and the law repealed. But there was that other obligation, that gradual liquidation of the fund, the back assessments and the future assessments. The supreme court had decided for the state against the bankers. And still the bankers refused to pay and had started another suit. It would work a great hardship on the banks, they said. To be sure it would. So was it working a great hardship on old Mr. and Mrs. Kleinman to lose their life savings; so was it a great hardship on Amy Hall, the little seamstress, to lose all she had; on young Mrs. Wise and her babies, to see their insurance money swept away. And yet,--

In his trained way of looking at both sides of a question without prejudice, he made himself again look the other side of the issue squarely in the face. The assessments had called for an immense sum from the state banks,--millions. Thirty-six thousand dollars from the Cedartown bank alone had been paid out since the weak banks started going,--probably over a half million from Mack's bank in Omaha. Should they pay longer? The depression had taken its toll in withdrawn deposits, in slumping of land values, in losses on bond investments and in individuals' failure to pay obligations. Was it true, as Mack insisted, that the whole state system would be badly weakened, as a bridge would weaken if a portion of the bolts were removed? Perhaps he, himself, had been wrong. Good bankers ought not pay the debts of the poor ones. Perhaps the lesser evil was the individuals' losses. His mind went back again to old Mr. and Mrs. Kleinman, to Amy Hall, to young Mrs. Wise. It was for them,--and their kind,--he had fought so hard. And to what end? It made him feel very old and very tired.

As he turned the corner on his home street, the thoughts of his business cares were suddenly forgotten in remembering that it was tomorrow morning that Laura was leaving. It gave him a sudden stab of regret like a physical pain. He wished she wouldn't go so far away, and especially under those circumstances. He wondered if she knew her own mind, that she was virtually selling her youth to the old couple. It was tempting, he realized,--but ten years from now Laura would be in her thirties, the first fine flush of youth over. Eloise thought it quite wonderful. That was to be expected.

Eloise had always counted success in dollars and cents. He had not pleased her in that way, he knew. She had not particularly nagged him about it in so many words, but he had learned to translate the straight set line to her mouth, when fees were discussed. And this move of Laura's meant success in both her own and her mother's minds, he knew.

He was not sure he liked the plan. He wished he had talked more to Laura about it. Had always found it difficult to express himself to the children. Something about the whole thing seemed like turning your back on your own people and your own Midwest. That last was all sentiment, of course. Because one was born in Nebraska was no reason he had to take root and grow there. But even as he refuted it, he vaguely knew that he had a brooding love for it. There was something of the old raw prairie in his blood, a little of the stubborn old buffalo in his sinews. It was as though having been born near the sod and under the northwest winds, companioned by the prairie grasses, and wakened from sleep by the prairie-lark, this was the only home he could know.

Young Rinemiller had told him once he felt the same way, as though the very loam and skies and winds were different. He liked the young fellow. Going to make good, too. Had a fine start from the old Reinmueller holdings, and with his technical knowledge, he would make a big estate out of the old farms. Had a notion that Laura liked him pretty well. She had certainly been around with him enough, but that didn't mean anything these days. Joke and laugh and make love and ride away seemed to be the general trend of the times. Well, Laura ought to know her own mind.

When he went up the steps at home, the sight of Laura's steamer trunk in the hall and an open bag on it, gave him a heaviness of heart that he could not throw off. He felt depressed--and very worn.

"Where are Mamma and Laura?" he asked Trib who, legs over the arm of a big chair, was devouring an apple and the contents of a movie magazine.

Eloise came in at the moment. She was flushed and warm. "I'm all ready," she said, "Katherine sent for Laura to come to dinner. She thought she ought not to go on account of it being her last night. But Katherine insisted."

The three ate supper. It was hot and sultry, so that immediately afterward, John went out on the front porch with the evening paper. The sun was dropping in the west and low sullen clouds like gray smoke hung along the southwest horizon.

Old Oscar Lutz came thump-thumping around his house, stopped to speak to John about the warm day and the promise of rain, recalled other Augusts with his everlasting "I mind as how" and thump-thumped on up the street for his evening walk.

"He goes to the cemetery so often," Eloise said, with a sudden unexpected touch of tenderness in her voice. "Funny old codger. No one could ever say he forgot his old 'Marthy.'"

Trib went out on his bicycle. Eloise repacked part of Laura's bag. John read here and there. But the paper did not seem to interest him. He was thinking of Laura when she was little, remembering how happy she always was out at Mother's. He let the paper fall in his lap and his mind linger on his mother. What a combination she had been of strength and tenderness, of courage and love. He believed he'd walk out past the old place. Hadn't been out that way for a long time. Had a distinct longing to see it to-night. He called to Eloise that he would be back in an hour or less and started out.

Arrived out there, he was almost sorry he had come. The empty old house looked more decayed and tumble-down than he had remembered. It gave him a feeling of depression and pain to see the place that had once meant so much to his mother, looking forlorn in the glow of the late afternoon sun. Young Rinemiller owned it now,--had said it was the best building site in the county, and that if he ever built, he was going to tear down the old house and built right there on the same spot.

Foolish notion,--but he couldn't help but wish something had come of that affair of Allen and Laura. Fine young chap, and Laura would be right here--

He broke away from the thought of the vague desire almost with embarrassment, as though he had spoken it aloud. For Allen Rinemiller's roadster was coming up the street, and the people in it were waving to him. It was Allen and Laura and Jimmie Buchanan. He wondered where they were going.

CHAPTER 23

It was not quite five-thirty when Laura went down to Kathie's. She was fresh and dainty in creamy white, an ensemble in which she was at her best, for the pale olive of her skin, her shining brown eyes and soft brown hair were thrown into lovely relief by the very lack of coloring in the costume. As she walked, her thoughts skipped about, quite like children at play, with no special objective. She thought of the physical ease that life would bring her at Uncle Harry's and of the long free hours in which she could scribble to her heart's content. She thought of her youth, and how true it was that a young person's eyes were always on the future. That made her think of old Oscar Lutz in contrast, whose thoughts were always with the days that were gone. Age and youth! Her father, then, must be at the stage where one thought only of the day's work,--the present. She would not like that age very well, she decided,--the time when one looked neither hopefully forward nor longingly back.

She thought how pretty Kathie's house looked down the street, in its trim lawn with the white hydrangeas massed against the reddish-brown of the brick. Allen had said it was the kind of house he wanted to build--At that, she concentrated on the vision of Uncle Harry, and was annoyed that she could think of him only in his most exasperating moments of see-sawing nervously up and down.

A girl was coming up the street. It was Verna Conden. She, too, was in white,--a pretty girl, if she only had some grooming. Her hair was dry and rough, on her cheeks two vivid spots as round as dollars, her generous mouth outlined heavily in scarlet. She passed Laura with a brief "Hello," her eyes straight ahead. It annoyed Laura, but there was nothing she could do about it. Verna had always acted that way. She probably still cared for Allen. Life was a strange mixup. The thought troubled her a little, so that when she went into Kathie's she had not thrown it off.

With that high-handed manner for which she was known among friends and relatives, Kathie immediately poked her finger into the sore spot even before they had moved out of the hall:

"Lolly . . . you're unhappy about something. I can see through you like tissue paper. Look me in the eye. Tell me . . . is it about Allen Rinemiller?"

Laura flushed and evaded Katherine's bright all-seeing eyes for the space of a moment, and then she spoke with composure. "Since you've asked, Kathie, I can tell you that it's not the pleasantest thing in the world to hurt as fine a fellow as Allen. We've been friends for a long time . . . and

I'm terribly sorry he's grown to . . ." she faced her cousin ". . . care." They had moved into the living room. Laura sat a little stiffly in a big chair. Kathie curled up on the davenport.

"And what about you, yourself? Katherine was not one to stand on the ceremony of polite evasion.

"I . . . you mean me?"

"Quite naturally, when I said, 'What about you, yourself,' I meant you. Looks suspiciously to me, Lolly, that you were stalling for time to get a neat little well-bred answer ready for me."

"Oh, no, I wasn't. I'll answer you, but it's awfully hard to define the way I feel. I really don't think you'd understand."

"Oh, I'd understand, all right." Katherine grinned cheerfully. "I'm not such a nit-wit at times. I've even been known to see through a sorority roommate of mine who was marrying a man for his money . . . a match her dear mother made for her . . . and how that girl did talk against time to make us think she was crazy about Louie. She called attention to his honesty and his ability and his nose and the shape of his feet and his blue blood and his energy and what-have-you, and all the time, I was dying to quote that smart old Billy Shakespeare who was just as wordy as she was: 'Methinks the lady doth protest too much.'"

Laura laughed. "Oh Kathie, you're the limit. Whatever has that got to do with me? If . . . just *if* . . . assuming that I *would* marry Allen . . . instead of *for* money, it would be I who would be giving up money."

"The whole point being, my dear Miss Deal . . . and *misdeal* it might be, Laura . . . don't forget your unfortunate, unlucky name. Anybody's who's handed that Miss Deal for a name ought to change it . . . that's why I did. The point is, that if I had the wit to see through my roommate, who was marrying for no reason *but* money, wouldn't it follow, inversely, that I had the wit to see through a girl who was *not* marrying . . . all on account of money?"

"That's unfair, Kathie,--perfectly unjust. Money or no money, I'd think of my own best good. I've settled it quite definitely in my mind that I'm going to bend all my energies toward making something of myself in the writing line. I think I inherited this little talent . . . if talent it is . . . from Grandmother Deal. She used to talk to me about it. She wished so much she could have written . . . she'd say 'Some day you'll write for me, Laura.' And I'm going to. I feel it in me." She wanted to tell Kathie about "a white bird flying," but it would sound silly and sentimental to Kathie, she knew. Kathie would only make some wisecrack about putting salt on its tail. "I say, you can't serve two masters. If you want to be any good at something, you'd better just cut out everything else. That's why I said I thought you couldn't understand. I do like Allen. I like him immensely."

"So you do love him?" Katherine looked with level blue eyes into the brown ones of the younger girl.

"I didn't say so," Laura insisted. "I said I *liked* him. I like him better than any man I know. I'll go farther . . . since you're putting me through an examination . . . I'll say maybe I'd love him if I'd let myself go. I don't know. But I just won't do that. Ever since I was a youngster, I've been deliberately holding myself to this one thought,--that of accomplishing something worth while. And I'd be absolutely crazy to throw away Uncle Harry's offer. I told Allen once I wasn't going to be a hybrid,--a sort of cross between two desires in life, amounting to nothing much in either. Apparently I'm keeping my head as I choose. What do you say?"

"If you ask me, I'll say that if you love him, you're a little coward."

"That's a strong word, Katherine."

"Good! She called me Katherine. She's getting dignified and mad."

But Laura, unheeding, went on immediately: "A coward being, as I supposed, some one who is cravenly afraid, I ask you what I've given you reason to think I'm afraid of?"

"Nothing much," Katherine said coolly. "Nothing but life."

"That's good. That's awfully good." Laura's olive cheeks were flushed to the forehead, and she was sitting on the edge of her chair. "Why, it's life I'm starting out to see. It's life I'm starting out to study . . . to feel . . . to know. . . ."

"To smell. You've left out one sense, Lolly," Katherine laughed gayly.

But Laura would not laugh. She went on earnestly: "I'm going East. I'm going to do the thing Grandmother had a chance to do and didn't take her chance. I'm going to see life, and I'm going to write about it. And nothing you can say will change me."

"All right, Lolly. Let's not fly at each other's throats. Go on . . . go on East . . . it'll be lovely. In time, you'll have gobs of money . . . and if your slippery Uncle Harry Wentworth and his fat frau don't hang on until your arteries harden, you'll enjoy it mightily. It's none of my business, honey. And anyway, I must see about the dinner. Verna struck . . . just walked out on me. Said she had a headache, but I noticed she was as gay as a chorus girl until I mentioned my guests."

She rose and moved toward the dining room. At the door she stuck her head back in the room. "When you go East," she was smiling mischievously, "be sure you take all your baggage . . . dresses, shoes, hats, undies, pocket-book, toothbrush, heart,--everything . . . don't forget your heart, Lolly."

And she went off toward the kitchen with one of her high merry laughs.

Jimmie came home, the fatigue of the hot day and the wrestle with various business problems showing a bit in the lines around his eyes.

Allen came only a few moments later. He was tanned, but he looked immaculate and well-groomed in his summer flannels. He had not seen Patty since her illness and at Katherine's suggestion, he and Laura went with her upstairs to see the little girl.

Patty was sitting up in bed with several pillows behind her back, and a village of cardboard houses roaming up and down over pink coverlet hills in front of her. The nurse went down for the supper tray as soon as the group came in.

"How are you, Miss Buchanan?" Allen sat down on the edge of the bed, and immediately the two were engaged in a guessing game in which Allen, shrunken to two inches in height, was supposed to be hiding behind one of the houses from which he was to be dragged by a pygmy Patty of one inch. How nice Allen was with children, Laura thought.

When the nurse and tray appeared and the three were leaving, Patty's squeals of laughter over the miniature hide-and-seek game changed to pouting and a suggestion of tears. Katherine plead with her small daughter to be a little lady, the nurse painted the description of the supper tray in glowing colors, and Laura promised a story when the tray was cleared. Even then, it was Allen who brought back the sunshine with his watch on Patty's own dainty wrist, the band making two trips around before it was fastened. Yes, Allen was nice with children, Laura admitted it again. People always said that if a man was nice to old people and children--Laura hurriedly returned a group of little thoughts back to the portion of her mind from which they had come, as one would shoo a flock of chickens back to their coop. Thoughts must not get out that way and run unheeded all over the nice clipped lawn of her mind. But it was true that every one liked Allen,--young and old, she was thinking as they went downstairs to the dinner table.

The dinner was not an unqualified success.

Jimmie was pleasant but tired, and was having to leave as soon as they would finish. Allen, unaccountably for him, was quiet. He seemed to have lost his gay banter, and with it, the ease he usually possessed. He was preoccupied, roused himself with an effort to take his part in the conversation. Laura, too, was quiet and apparently incapable of any small chatter. So many big things were happening to her that all the little gay things of life seemed inadequate, not worth noticing. Katherine did the best she could with her usual nonsense, succeeding in getting them to laugh a time or two. But for the most part, the little foursome was merely a matter of gastronomics.

The meal was scarcely finished until Jimmie was getting his bag to leave, in order to catch the through train at Meadowdale.

So it came about that Allen and Laura, sitting in the car, waiting a moment for Jimmie to come out, were quite without conversation.

When through the front door Laura caught a glimpse of Katherine's and Jimmie's farewell, it recalled to her the narrow escape in the little household. She wished she could tell Allen all about it. Allen was always so understanding. But the near tragedy had happened to a Deal, and the Deals were too clannish to betray each other's confidence. There was something queer about Allen to-night, anyway. He seemed quiet, constrained, a little stiff. He had no gay inconsequential chatter, and no laughter.

Sitting between the two men as the roadster headed north, Laura thought that they were, without doubt, two of the finest men she knew. And something alike too, when one stopped to think about it,--clean, straight-shooting, dependable. Yes, that was the word she decided that fitted them both,--utterly and unequivocably dependable. She felt terribly sorry for Allen. It was no small thing to hurt a man like that. She would make it up to him as much as she could with letters. She would write him gay interesting letters,--letters that would bring that cheerful grin to his lips, and the crinkling laughter to his eyes. And Christmas . . . when she came home . . .

There was her father, sauntering along in the northeast end of town. She wondered what he was doing out here. A warm feeling of tenderness toward him came over her, and a touch of anxiety. To see him walking along in that leisurely fashion so contrary to his usual brisk pace, gave her a momentary thought that some day he would be like old Oscar Lutz, thumping along the sidewalks with a cane.

They turned to the west and again to the north on the main highway. They were passing the west end of the cemetery now. Thinking of Old Oscar, there he was now, leaning on his cane and looking over toward the west.

They waved him a friendly salute, but he did not seem to notice.

"He probably can't see well any more," Laura explained.

"What do you suppose it seems like, Allen"--it was Jimmie Buchanan--"to be approaching the end of a lifetime of that length?"

"Lord,--I don't know. It seems rather terrible to me to think about it at all . . . feeble and dull and all that."

"With all your emotions dead . . . hope and love and your dreams all done for. . . ."

"That's so . . . hope and love and your dreams all done for . . . nothing left." Allen's voice sounded dull and flat.

"Think of being lonely like that . . . no matter how many people are around you . . . lonely in spirit, not being able to recall what happened yesterday."

"Not being able to recall what happened yesterday."

Laura glanced up at him quickly, but Allen was merely repeating it, parrot-like, as though he had no real idea of what he was saying.

The car shot on toward the north.

"You're forgetting one thing," Laura said.

"What's that?" It was Jimmie.

"You're forgetting memories," she said. "Old Oscar Lutz has his memories left."

CHAPTER 24

Old Oscar Lutz, bent, and as wrinkled as one of the walnuts under his ancient trees, had trudged sturdily along in the early evening, his cane tap-tapping on the cement. At the end of the walk by the cemetery he had stopped and leaned for a while on the heavy gnarled stick. From under his shaggy white eyebrows he gazed long and lovingly at the prairie landscape, with the sun slipping down behind the green rolling hills. The graveled highway like a tawny path through a sea of green, stretched as far away as his blurred old eyes could see. As he stood there wrinkling his eyelids, squinting to see the farther, a long green roadster shot by to the north. People in it waved their hands to him, but his slow moving thoughts had not been able to send their message speedily enough to his own calloused old hands, and the car was far in the distance before he could collect himself to respond.

He stood looking after it helplessly. It made him feel stupid in the face of such speed. He had recognized the car, though, as Allen Rinemiller's. He was proud of that. Eyesight was pretty good, yet, he bragged to himself. That would probably be Laura Deal with Allen. Nice little girl. And nice boy.

His thoughts turned to Allen who was farming his own old place now. Queer, to think of some one else farming the old land whose virgin sod he himself had turned so many decades ago. He looked over into the pasture and longed suddenly to feel again the sponginess of the ground under his feet, the velvet of the lush green grass. Cement,--how it tired your feet!

In the slow hesitating ways of the very old, he stood for some time trying to decide whether he should make the attempt to get through the fence and over into the pasture. Then he caught a strand of the barbed-wire in the hook of his cane, and with slow painful movements, his hat dropping in the grass and his long white scarf catching on a barb, he pushed through the wire into the pasture,--formerly his own farm land.

Retrieving his ancient headgear, he walked slowly, laboriously on through the green growth, his cane flicking the jimson and milkweed. Here was the very spot where his house had stood. How many years had it been torn down? Twenty . . . thirty? Oh, well, what was the use of trying to figure it all out? Whatever the number of years, it seemed like yesterday that it stood there.

He walked over the lumpy ground flipping his cane about, trying to find some old landmark of the house yard. There was nothing left but a few flat stones in a pile over which the wild morning-glories were sprawling. Those stones had been hauled from Weeping Water,--ten miles,--a full day's trip. He had hauled them with oxen; old Roxy and Roll, the brass buttons on their horns glistening in the sunshine as they swayed their huge heads from side to side. All day it had taken; and now the youngsters piled in cars evenings and, bareheaded, drove down to the picture shows in Weeping Water in a few minutes. Somebody ought to tell the youngsters about the way it used to be, make them appreciate the times in which they lived. But nobody ever seemed to remember or care. Everybody taken up with his own affairs. Who would there be left in the community to tell them about the old days when he was gone?

Sarah Lutz was dead now and Christine had no mind, and he alone was left, the last of the group that came into the country when there was nothing but virgin prairie. He tried to tell folks about it. Sometimes they listened, but more times they seemed unheeding. Did any one care about those old days? Apparently not. But how could a group of people do what he and the Deals and Reinmuellers had done,--come in their prairie schooners to the wild prairie, dig their very homes out of the ground, brave the storms and the droughts and the blizzards and all the wild ways of the raw new country, establish the community,--and be ignored? How could they do it,--and be forgotten forever?

There was a rusty piece of iron. He pushed it over with his cane,--a part of the pump. A piece of a rusty pump and a pile of stones,--all that was left of the place he and Marthy had called home. *Home.* What a big word that was. Lots of attempts made lately to belittle it. Plenty of fun poked at it. Young folks laughed about it,--called it a place to park. Everybody wanted to get some place else, seemed like. They'd find out. They'd understand some day. When they got old, they'd know. They'd want to go home. Sometime in their lives, everybody wanted to go home.

He looked over to the low green hill where the mighty cottonwood still stood. Marthy used to say she didn't like cottonwoods,--they looked lonely and homesick-like. But he liked them. They were the settlers' first friends, and he would never go back on a friend. Their little shining leaves twinkled merrily all day long,--shimmered when everything else was still. Happy sort of trees they were. Only trees he knew that liked to laugh and joke. The leaves were not stirring now. That was because the breeze had died down and there were low threatening clouds hanging in the far southwest. Going to rain. It would be midnight before they got the shower though. Good thing,--keep the pastures green for the stock as they were now,--not like some of those old summers when the corn baked on the roots and the fruit died in the blossom.

Up the incline he toiled, digging his cane in the ground to help him ascend. He was out of breath. At the top of the little hill, he leaned against the tree, his bent, gaunt body dwarfed by the size of the massive trunk. He laid a trembling hand against the bark,--one was as gnarled as the other. He had a warm friendly feeling for the old tree, as though having been planted by him, it was born of his flesh and blood; as though having come up through the years with him, it was one of the old crowd. He and the old cottonwood,--the only two old settlers left. All of the old cottonwoods had been replaced by newer trees,--all of the old settlers replaced by younger men.

From the rise of ground, he could look off in every direction. To the north and east and west were prosperous farms, with their huge barns and silos and granaries. To the south lay the town, looking quiet and peaceful under the pink light of the waning day, its great trees apparently massed in one huge bouquet of green, spires of churches piercing through it. Not far from where he stood, motor cars purred swiftly along the graveled road. Following the highway, a huge powerline sent its electricity to the farms and into town. Telephone poles stood on duty, conveying messages from the town to farm and farm to town. What a change since the days of the oxen and the soddie.

For a time he stood, trying to call up the picture of the same view as it had been from this identical hill in those days. He could vision only an ocean of grass, here and there a hut of a settler and a few cattle herded on the prairie. With the dim picture came a sudden "feel" of youth. For a minute the sluggish blood within him stirred, so that in fancy he felt a touch of reality in the memory, as though for a short period the dim picture brightened and hung there colorfully before him. The brief moment of vividness made him feel that the old days were best. But immediately, his good sense told him the feeling seemed true only because he had been young. And youth is best. These were the best days, now, for all who were young. The old days here in the state had been the foundation days,--days of digging and delving and laying the stones for the structure. Lots of hard work. Lots of sacrifice. Primitive ways. Crude methods. Lots of sorrow. Three little girls dying. No anti-toxin. No knowledge of tuberculosis treatment. No hospitals. Everything changed now for the better. Folks would be surprised--some day--when his will would be read--two grandsons in California would get their father's share, all right, but what would have been for the three little girls was going to be a hospital for Cedartown. Nobody but John Deal knew. *Martha Lutz Memorial Hospital.* Place where they'd know about anti-toxin and operations and tubercular treatment for other little girls.

Slowly he walked around the summit of the knoll and looked at the creek bed beyond. It looked inviting,--seemed more like the old place than any other part of the farm. Allen, with his smart up-to-date farming, had changed everything around now. Only the old pasture and the creek bed gave back their memories. Only the lush green grass and the winding timber were familiar.

Half aware of the foolishness of the venture, he walked on down the slope of the hill to the creek bed. It seemed homelike down there--friendly. He had not dreamed that the creek bed would show so little change. Always before, in recalling the old scenes, he had been obliged to imagine half of the picture, but here he seemed absolutely back in the past. It gave him the happiest sensation he had known for years. Wild plum and thorn-apples, little scrub oaks and soft maples, misshapen elms and willows attempted to shoulder each other out of the way, as though all were trying to get down to the low running water. Wild grape-vines tangled and festooned themselves from tree to tree. There were declivities here, faint indentations marking the spots of old buffalo wallows. Familiar looking muskrat slides confronted him. He followed slowly and doggedly the turns of the vagrant creek, a warm feeling of pleasure growing upon him, half aware that he should go back, but losing himself in the "feel" of the atmosphere. Why, gosh all hemlock,--this time, he was not just remembering the old days. He was *living* them.

Suddenly, he knew that by comparison all his memories of the past had been dim, befogged by the years in between. But this was different. This was as clear as crystal. He could think of the house back there now just as plain as could be. He leaned on his cane, and looked back toward the hill which would have hidden it from view.

Up to now, this memory had been blurred a little, as though the old house were seen dimly through a curtain. Now it stood out in all its clearness. Every window, every shingle, every clapboard took upon itself form and clarity. Just over the hill out of sight it would be standing. He visualized the sloping roof,--he had built it steep so the great prairie snows would not pack on it. Queer how the country had changed,--very little snow last winter, they told him. And in the old days, the great blizzards half buried the house and stables all winter.

His mind turned the scene to summer, and he recalled the kitchen door with the vines over it. Marthy was great on flowers and vines. One year when nothing else would grow, she planted a squash. It grew all over the back of the kitchen, and he had to get boards to brace up the heavy Hubbards pulling down on the vine. He could see, in fancy, the two little kitchen windows a few feet apart. Marthy used to set her pies in them to cool--pumpkin or wild gooseberry or wild crabapple. Nobody could make pies like Marthy. He almost chuckled aloud at the memory of the time he had come up the draw, tiptoed to the window, hooked one of the pies, eaten part of it and hidden the rest, and let Marthy scold and wonder about it. When she accused Shep he confessed, and Marthy boxed his ears. Couldn't let old Shep be scolded. He hadn't thought of old shaggy Shep for years. Used to go after the cows with him--chase little yellow butterflies--bring him foolish little things in his mouth and lay them at his feet. Wanted a younger dog when the old fellow got so he wasn't much good--gave him to a young couple over beyond the Weeping Water. One cold night heard a scratching on the door and there was Shep,--legged it home all the fourteen miles--standing there looking up, wagging his tail, and had a piece of dried tumble-weed in his mouth for him.

Beat all, how well he could remember things tonight. It was being down here on the old stamping ground, that accounted for it. He had a pleasant sensation of knowing what to do after this when time hung heavily on his hands. Come down into the draw, where the wild grape-vines tangled in the underbrush and the old buffalo wallows and the muskrat slides looked familiar. It made things all clear, again. It took away the dimness of the pictures.

Yes, old Oscar Lutz had his memories left.

He turned and looked back to the creek bed again. Suddenly he wondered if he could still pick out the spot where the four families had camped those first nights on the prairie. He plodded along, following the bend of the creek, remembering how the four wagons had trailed along behind each other, . . . forded the creek bed about . . . There! . . . about there . . . where that clump of elderberries stood. He felt excited, the long forgotten sensation of warm blood stirring again through his veins. They had gone over this way a little . . . there . . . about there was the campfire. Well . . . snappin' crocodiles! . . . there was the old black burned-out remnants of the campfire right now. Suddenly he felt foolish. The kids came down here often . . . Boy Scouts and the like. It would be their burned-out campfire. But, for a minute, it had him fooled.

He poked at the black remnants of wood with his cane, and thought of the wagons trailing over the prairie,--his own with Marthy and the little girls, Will and Abbie Deal's with little Mack . . . Mack was a big banker now in Omaha . . . Henry and Sarah, the bride . . . lively Sarah with her pink cheeks and her snappy black eyes . . . and Sarah dead a few months ago at eighty-six . . . or was it a few years ago . . . sunk down in white satin, like a little old dainty wax doll in a fancy box . . . Gus and Christine Reinmueller . . . and Christine over at the asylum now, where she sulked or shed pitiful old tears for her lost quarter-sections of land. Yes, it must have been right about here that they forded the creek. How glad they were to get here, after the tiresome three weeks' trip. They had formed a circle with the wagons, built their fire in the middle, and searched the ground for rattlesnakes before they let the babies out. The Indians had come and camped near them . . . friendly, it turned out . . . but how scared Marthy had been . . . and the boys weren't so easy until morning either.

If he went on a little farther, he believed he could find the center spot where the land of the boys joined. Hadn't felt so strong in years . . . the walk was doing him good . . . all foolish to stick to sidewalks . . . he'd come down here often. Yes, it would be great sport to walk out into the middle of the section to the place where the farms used to meet. He felt closer to the old crowd than he had for years, as though they were all living, as though at any turn of the creek bed, he might come upon Henry or Will Deal or Gus Reinmueller. He could fancy the joking that would follow:

"What you doing here, old sneak?"

"Trying to slip up on me, was you, and steal one o' my shoats?"

Good friends . . . all of the old crowd . . . help each other out every time.

He worked his way through the tangle of sumac and wild grapevine, thorn-apple and wild plum. Nothing like that smell anywhere in the world . . . not in California, that was sure,--irrigated fields and odorless roses. Thought he'd kind of lost his sense of smell, but it wasn't so. All he'd needed was to get down to a place like this where there was something *worth smelling* . . . great heads of wild phlox and the damp sweet odor of the undergrowth by the creek bed. Laboriously working his way through the tangle, he came out to the open cornfield. Gosh all hemlock! Look at the sky.

CHAPTER 25

At Meadowdale Allen and Laura parked near the station. The train came in surprisingly on time, and Jimmie, waving to the two on the platform, left on it.

Allen assisted Laura into the roadster, walked around to the other side and slipped in under the steering-wheel, but he did not start the car. Instead, he said suddenly, a little breathlessly: "Laura, you're going to-morrow, and as this is the last time I'll be seeing you, I've a lot of things to say to you."

"But I'll be back at Christmas, Allen. I'll see you then. That's not so far away,--four months only. That's one thing I've told Uncle Harry and Aunt Carolyn . . . that's one thing I'll never give up . . . and they're perfectly all right about it. I'm to come back every summer for a visit and *every* Christmas. You see, never having had children, that way, I think Christmas doesn't mean as much to them as it does to all of us out here. It does take children to make a Christmas, doesn't it? Look at the big Deal clan gathering every year. I can't *imagine* Christmas any place else." Laura was aware that she was chattering against time. She knew what was coming, and it was going to be hard. Allen was going to talk again about their marrying. And even if she were sure of herself, she couldn't marry him, now. If only she didn't like him so well, the thing wouldn't be difficult to handle at all. But the whole situation, now, was hard. It would take all her tact and patience to deal with Allen to-night.

But Allen was saying, "Personally, it isn't going to make any difference to me whether you come at Christmas time or not. For I'll not be seeing you."

Laura had the sensation that she imagined one might have in an earthquake disturbance. She could have sworn that the car under her rocked a little.

She managed a casual, "So? Is that a threat?"

"No--self-preservation. This is the last time . . . to-night . . . that we'll see each other . . . alone, I mean . . . ever. I'm through, of course, now. I've thought it all out last night, and to-day as I've gone about my work, and I'm through. You don't care for me, of course. If you did . . . nothing,--money, career, travel--nothing could keep you from me. I know that. I've got it through my head at last. I've been thick skinned, I'll admit,--thick skinned, thick headed and a fool. Lord knows, you've told me enough times you didn't care, but I've been fool enough to think . . . ." he broke off, "until yesterday." He threw up his head. "Oh, well . . . I'm awake now, and I want you to know it."

Laura was startled, but she managed a casual, "So a friendship doesn't mean much to you?"

"Not such a darned lot--not when there's something bigger."

"Well, we can't agree on that." She was talking without much thought. Her wits seemed wool gathering. "I think a genuine friendship a very beautiful thing,--I've even thought *our* friendship was a lovely thing, Allen. You've been one of the few people I could talk to . . ."

"If you'd wanted to talk to me, you could have come and lived with me and talked to me all you wanted to."

"It isn't convenient to marry all your friends, Allen." Laura was speaking stiffly, and with no apparent sense.

"No, I see not." Allen was equally stiff.

The station agent came out, saw the parked car by the platform, and was about to tell the two young folks in it that the next train was not due for three hours, scratched his head, decided they didn't care whether it was or not, looked over at the low hanging clouds in the southwest, and went on home.

"I was crazy enough, for a time, to think I could compete a little with all the career stuff. I thought I was equal to it. I had an idea lots of girls talked that way and didn't mean it. Apparently it's my rotten luck that you're the hundredth one that does. But I don't know any algebraic problem in which I'm equal to career plus money. But I do know one thing," he said warmly. "If the situation were reversed . . . if *I* had the choice . . . you against everything else . . . I'd take you . . . my youth and health and you. Everything else could go in the discard. The *earning* of the money would be the pleasure,--not having it thrown at you in a wad. What's a bunch of money, if you're capable of earning it? That's the game,--the *working.*"

"You're purposely putting it so it sounds cold-blooded and greedy, Allen. You know you are. It's *not* just the money. I've tried to make that clear, and you're purposely distorting it. Let me tell you something, Allen. I've been around now, enough to know there are some bigger things in the world than marriage and a prosaic settling down under one roof."

"Now, I'll tell *you* something." He sat up straighter under the wheel. "There *isn't,*--not a thing--when it's two people who really care, and, and settling down under one roof, as you say, is the beginning of a real home. There's *nothing* finer. And now that I've convinced myself those are your real sentiments, and not just a temporary illusion, as I've been dunce enough to think,--I wouldn't want to marry you. . . ."

"Thanks for the chivalry, Allen."

"Don't mention it."

Laura tried to laugh, but the effort was slightly pointless. Always before, she could bring out that cheerful grin of Allen's, but apparently not to-night.

"And while we're talking," he went on . . . "as long as our friendship is so beautiful . . . it might be a good time to tell you that I'm not only through . . . I'm going to be married."

The pulsing blood seemed beating loudly against Laura's throat, and pounding on her forehead. She was disgusted with herself that she felt so disturbed. "Who . . . is she, Allen? No,--let me guess." She found herself sparring for time, wanting to put off the answer. "Not . . . Dolores Thaxter?"

There was rolling thunder in the distance but neither noticed it.

"No."

"Not . . . oh, Allen, not . . . Verna Conden?"

"No."

"Who?"

"I don't know."

At any other time Laura would have dimpled with sudden infectious laughter, and Allen would have grinned his wholesome grin. But they did neither.

"I've thought it all out. I did plenty of it last night and to-day." He went on hotly. "And I'm going to marry--soon. That isn't any spectacular spite affair, either. It's just a plain sensible procedure. There are other nice girls in the world. Because I haven't had eyes or thought for anybody but you, is no sign there aren't any. And before you leave, it isn't going to hurt you to know that I've pulled out of the mood I've been in all this time, and am going to hunt up one and marry her. I'm going to build . . . as fine a home as I can. Maybe you think fellows don't have any domestic side like that, to them. Of course, plenty don't. And then again, plenty of them do. And I'm one of them with a soft spot like that. I'm a little cuckoo on having a nice home of my own. I've loved you--deeply and sincerely. I still do-- Heaven save the mark--I won't lie to you--but I can get over it, and I'm going to. Up to now, you've been the only girl I ever wanted to think of in a home of mine. But even though that's all over now, life is all before me, and I'll be darned if I'll let you and your theories about what's best in life spoil it."

When he paused, it seemed there ought to be something said, so Laura emitted:

"I'll be anxious to hear from you, Allen, . . . how things are going."

"Sorry. But you won't hear. Not from me."

"You're not writing?"

"Assuredly not. When we're through, we're through."

"This looks like a complete fade-out."

"It certainly is."

Could they have overheard, a long array of ancestral feminine Deals and Mackenzies and Wentworths of the nineteenth century would have swooned at the blunt and unromantic dialogue. But they could not overhear. And twentieth century maidens swoon at nothing.

So Laura managed a steady, "It'll seem awfully queer . . . without you, Allen . . . coming back to visit . . ." She broke off.

They were both silent for a moment. The air was stifling and the dusk was descending. In a moment she went on: "That'll be kind of an odd affair, though, Allen,--just going out and hunting up a girl and bestowing your affections on her . . . sort of like going gunning for a pheasant."

"You don't need to worry about that part," he said shortly.

"I expect not," Laura said dryly, and was silent.

Allen cleared his throat carefully. "I decided . . . definitely, last night, or rather this morning, about the time the raincrows began to call . . . to take your decision like a good sport. If money and a so-called career mean everything in the world to you . . . if those are your true ideas of life,--well, it's not my place to talk back to the referee. I'll take the decision, and stop mooning around as though you were the only girl in the world. It'll probably be a stiff game at first . . . but I've made up my mind . . . and so . . . you're free to go your way, now, with no more interference from me. I thought it only right that you should know."

Laura put her hand on Allen's arm. "It will seem . . . *awfully* queer, Allen . . . to think of all those times we've had together . . . never again to . . ." Her voice broke.

"Don't talk like that," Allen said grimly. "And take your hand off of my arm," he added.

Laura drew the offending member away as though it were scorched.

"Well, I hope you'll be happy, Allen . . . with her, whoever she is. I'll wish you that, just as I want you to wish me well in my undertaking. I'll have to admit though, it isn't my idea of love."

"No," Allen said quickly, "it isn't your idea of love. Your idea of love is a *hot* one. *Your* idea of love is to strangle it by the throat. *Your* idea of love is . . ."

A great whirling cloud of dust rolled up the road toward the car and chokingly enveloped them. Simultaneously, a crimson flash of lightning laid open the sky, and crashing thunder rattled the windows of the station. Allen hurriedly backed away from the platform and started down the graveled road toward Cedartown.

The green roadster shot steadily over the miles, into the face of the storm.

CHAPTER 26

Old Oscar Lutz, coming out of the underbrush by the creek bed, was confronted with the sight of great tan and bilious-green low-scudding clouds tumbling over each other, as they rolled in from the southwest.

Wind, that was going to be--the way the sickly green showed under the yellow. He must get back to Marthy. Pshaw,--how old thoughts and habits clung to people. Marthy had been gone for a quarter of a century; and here for a minute, he was thinking of her being afraid in the face of the oncoming storm. It was only of himself he had to think. He must get back before he got soaked and have to pay the price with a good old attack of rheumatism.

He stood for a moment leaning on the cane, trying to decide the better and quicker way,--through the cornfield and then the cemetery to the south, or to retrace his steps along the creek bed and by the old cottonwood to the west. Back by the creek bed again,--that was better. If a downpour came and he should be caught in Allen's recently cultivated cornfield, he'd be mired down in the rich black mud.

He turned back to the underbrush and working his way through to the creek bed, started to the west. It was stifling under the thick growth of wild plums and grapevines and sumac.

Lightning! But far away. He could probably make the journey home before the storm struck. Better take it easy now. Wasn't any use trying to pelt along fast and get all winded,--just a good steady gait with his cane to help him. Couldn't go quite the same pace he used to when he could run up this draw toward home as fast as an Indian.

Another fork of lightning cut across the sky. How scared Marthy would be if she were still up there in the old home. He pictured the house looking small and frail in the face of the oncoming storm, the vines over the door, still and lifeless, in the awesome hush of those moments preceding the wind. If it were back in the old days, Marthy would be lighting the lamps now, setting them in the two little kitchen windows, and then standing, frightened, in the middle of the floor and waiting to hear him halloo from the hilltop.

Queer, how much harder it seemed to go back through the undergrowth than the coming had been. It grew darker and more stifling. Hands clutched at him and held him back,--wild crab-apple hands. Feet were pushed out to trip him,--grapevine feet. His hat was knocked backward on his head and hawthorn branches scratched his forehead. A sharp spear of broken scrub oak was thrust into his side. His mouth brushed against a cluster of choke cherries, so that the taste for a moment was bitter. Some One Else had once known thorn pricks and a spear thrust and the taste of myrrh on the lips. He felt sorry for The Man.

Quite suddenly he emerged from the tangled undergrowth into the open space of the meadow. He felt a sense of relief and stopped to fill his closing lungs with the fresher air.

The wind was beginning now. The first gust came across the meadow grass like a trumpeter sent on to announce the approach of a powerful and evil thing. Old Oscar, leaning on his cane, could see the cottonwood bend before its portentous message. It seemed nodding and beckoning him,--the only old comrade left now from the early days. Queer, to think the little whip he had put in the ground over half a century ago was acting like a human to-night calling to him from the hill top. He started toward the hill. Beat all, how his legs would scarcely respond.

Quite suddenly, it grew darker, with swift descending blackness. Gone were the mellow twilight and the after-glow of the sunset. Gone were the peace of the meadows and the calm of the eventide. And in their place, darkness,--thick, black, warning. The dark alone could not worry him, though. He knew every stick and stone of the hillside. By feeling with his cane and seeing by the lightning flashes, he knew he could retrace his steps to the cottonwood. The rain would be coming along pretty soon now, following in the wake of the wind. Lightning again. The old plainsman's thoughts turned to his own safety. Better stay away from the cottonwood in the lightning. Trees were the settlers' best friends, but in a storm they went back on you,--in a big wind they turned traitors. The old cottonwood was beckoning, all right, but it couldn't fool him. No, sir, not in a storm, it couldn't.

He struck off diagonally, so that when he reached the top of the hill he would not be too close to the old monarch. The wind was coming harder now, so that he crushed his old black hat more securely on his head, and clung to his white scarf and cane the more tightly. It caught and held him at intervals so that he could only sway, his feeble old form making no progress whatever. A great gust took his hat, and wisps of his long white hair streamed out behind. He stood bewildered, as though part of himself had gone away on the wings of the wind. With his cane he felt around in the flattening grass, but the hat must have gone far before the onslaught and he gave up the futile search. He plodded on with a feeling of distinct loss. That was a good hat. He hadn't had it quite twelve years.

The rain came now,--great sheets of it that threw themselves onto the meadow, not steadily, but in gusts as though the rain and the wind were dancing a jazz tune. It cut across his cheeks and forehead like the sting of a hundred whips. His white scarf was soggy and disagreeable to his throat. The long slope toward the hill was getting slippery. He had to dig his cane into the ground to pull himself along. Once he started to fall in the sodden grass, but recovered himself before he was completely down. With each step he waited for the return of his waning breath and the steadying of his swaying body.

Lightning! Not just ordinary flashes, but great enveloping sheets of it. If Marthy were up there in the house now, she would be just about frightened to death. Good thing she was safe.

The darkness was a thick, black, impenetrable thing. Only when the great flashes came, could he see to get his bearings. Always he looked for the cottonwood and steered his course by it. How it turned and twisted and writhed in agony,--like an old man up there on the hilltop it twitched and moaned and cried out in its torment.

And now the rain was hurling itself at him again, madly, so that involuntarily he threw his arms over his bare head. It lashed him in a frenzy, and he made no progress in the face of its violence. He wanted to cry out against its madness. But he could not, for he was choking in a sea of it. His lungs were closed air-tight things that would not function,--a pair of blacksmith's bellows that had collapsed. His mind, too, seemed unsteady, wavering. The wind and the rain were getting the best of him. He was too exhausted to go on. For a long time he stood swaying, holding himself upright only by the pressure of his weight on the cane sunk into the moist earth. For a moment he felt his consciousness slipping, as though he were drifting into some eternal oblivion. But by a superhuman effort he roused his waning forces and focused on one thought: He must pull himself together, and go on. It was just a little way farther to the top of the slope. He must go on. From there he could see . . . from there he could see . . . the lights of home.

He pulled his cane slowly out of the hole it had made in the turf. Cautiously and with supreme concentration on the effort, he started, as one might carefully start an old and disabled piece of machinery to working, so that no false movement would shatter the results of the attempt. Every step was an exertion, every motion painful. But he must not heed such notions. Selfish, that was. Selfish . . . thinking of himself when Marthy was there alone in the house . . . scared . . . waiting for his halloo from the top of the hill. Maybe couldn't even hear him . . . but he'd keep his promise . . . try to let her know he was coming. Must get off his wet things as soon as he could get to the house . . . soaking wet . . . awful tired . . . but . . . keep going . . . and soon there'd be . . . two lights in the kitchen . . .

Lightning! More severe than any previous flash,--red lightning that hung leeringly over the hillside while the thunder crashed simultaneously.

Poor girl . . . Marthy . . . just about . . . scared . . . to death. . . .

He was stopped again. There was a long wait this time, while the wind snarled and the rain hurled itself upon him and the bellows of his lungs closed painfully. His mind was as beaten upon as his body. He wanted to go home. Everybody wanted to go home. When they got old, they knew. They understood. Sometime in their lives everybody wanted to get home. He wanted to get there now. He didn't know it was so far . . . home. It was *too* far. He wanted to whimper . . . to cry out. Would he ever see the lights? "God," he prayed, "all I ask is this . . . two lights . . . at home . . ."

He was nearly to the top now. There was a brief cessation in the crushing force of the rain. One more effort and he would make it. He dug his cane into the sogginess of the grass, and with supreme concentration of his waning powers, pulled himself to the crest of the hill.

God! There they were! The lights of home! Right over the brow of the slope,--shining in the wind and the rain and the darkness. The two lights in the kitchen window. Blurred a little by the mad dashes of rain they were-- but shining steadily. The sight of them brought back clarity to his beaten mind. He felt able to think straight again. Back there in the draw he had been befogged, confused,--now everything was clear. He was seeing life as from a mountain top. Queer how in moments of seeing life like this, everything fell away from one but its essentials . . . all the petty ills . . . arguments . . . quarrels . . . bickerings . . . envy . . . striving . . . scrambling . . . the mad dash for supremacy . . . everything fell out of one's consciousness but the lights of home and all they stood for. And he was home. He had conquered. He felt triumphant. Unconsciously he pointed to the lights with his cane. "Yoo-hoo . . ." he called. Queer, he was experiencing a rare moment of superb strength. The walk hadn't done him up after all. He felt strong. He stood tall and straight near the cottonwood, looking victoriously down on the two blinking lights. "Yoo-hoo," he called, more loudly than he could have expected. "Yoo-hoo, Marthy . . . comin'. . . ."

Lightning! A great wide sheet of fierce red flame that enveloped and blinded and stung him, even as the earth and skies crashed together, and the lights of home . . . were . . . blotted out. . . .

CHAPTER 27

For a few miles Allen drove rapidly, slowing only when great gusts of wind whipped up long clouds of dirt from the fields and dust from the highway. They came rolling across the country together, the low rolling clouds and the high flung dirt, so that one could not tell where the loose soil ended and vapor forms began.

Neither spoke. Allen drove grimly, silently, his eyes on the road. Laura watched the angry clouds, her thoughts as tumultuous as they. Quite suddenly it grew darker with swift descending blackness. Gone were the mellow twilight and the afterglow of the sunset. Gone were the peace of the meadows and the calm of eventide.

"Maybe I should have taken you in to McCullough's," Allen was frowning.

"We'll make it," was Laura's only comment.

"We're in for it now. It's as far back as it is on into town." Allen's own broad acres now lay between them and the cemetery.

The rain came. Great sheets of it that threw themselves onto the roadster, not evenly, but in gusts as though the rain and the wind were dancing a jazz tune. The two windshield wipers worked steadily, but they were no match for the downpour. The lamps shone brightly enough, but their glare seemed too feeble to pierce the density of the rain, and the brown trail of the highway was distorted. Driving was precarious business. Allen was barely crawling. Sometimes he stopped altogether.

Lightning! Not just ordinary flashes, but great enveloping sheets of it.

At each red glare and simultaneous crack of the thunder, Laura shuddered involuntarily. Once, with no volition of her own, she clutched Allen's arm, remembered her rebuff in the earlier evening and withdrew it hastily. Sensing it, and without taking his eyes from the gravel, Allen said: "Nervous?"

"Not especially." Every nerve was taut, every muscle strained. "I'm glad though I'm. . ." She was on the verge of saying, "with you," but stopped herself in time.

"Glad you're what?"

". . . on rubber tires." She finished lamely.

Allen fell grimly silent again.

It was worse now if anything. No sign of the highway was visible. They might have been poised in mid-air with the open sea beneath them. For a few moments they stopped again while the fury of the storm lashed them. Then it ceased and there was a distinct lull so that Allen started on.

Once more the flood gates were opened, and the fury of the wind-blown water stopped progress altogether. Then another interval of rain, less furious, while the lightning quivered without ceasing.

Suddenly there seemed then a definite lurching of the car. "A flat," Allen's tone registered supreme disgust. "As a matter of fact, I've been suspicioning it for some time, but thought I'd give it mental treatment."

He had stopped again. For the first time a glimmer of his old self returned. "Will you kindly sing a verse from 'A Night Like This'? Well . . ." he peered out into the blackness. "I don't like to run on in and have it ruined. We're either near my west pasture or the cemetery . . . at the next flash, I can tell."

The next flash was an immediate reality.

Allen took advantage of it to get his bearings. "We're opposite the pasture. If I can see to get across . . . there's a rough culvert across the ditch into the meadow . . . I don't care to stand here in the road and run the risk of being hit . . . not that traffic's going to be dense. . . ." He was driving slowly, waiting for a flash to show him the cattle-crossing. When he had located it, he turned on to the meadow crossing. But he was not satisfied. "I'll open the pasture gate," he told Laura, "and drive on in. I'm not keen about this long car protruding out into the highway. Nobody would be going north but the doctor or bank robbers, but I don't intend to be hit by either."

He opened the car door and the cold wind rushed in so that Laura shivered from the sudden change. From under the rumble seat he unearthed a raincoat and sweater, slipped into the coat and helped Laura pull the big sweater with its football insignia over her head. The simple act brought a quick mist to her eyes--she could not have told why.

"Allen, I hate to have you," she was saying, "out that way on the wet ground . . . with so much electricity."

If anything happened to Allen . . . ! But she caught herself up at that. Something already had happened to Allen. She and Allen were through with their friendship.

He was opening the gate now, as the rain abated for a moment. Then he was back at the wheel and driving into the edge of the meadow.

What Hand guided them into the green pasture? Who led them by the still waters of the creek bed? What Purpose was achieved? What Destiny fulfilled? For how could Allen and Laura know that they were bringing peace to a tired old man in the storm? How could they know that to a weary old man on the hilltop, the lights of the car were the lights of home?

Allen, out in the rain which sometimes slackened and sometimes poured, jacked the car and changed the wheel, with Laura over on the driver's side holding the flash, and cringing at every glare of lightning. How queer that she and Allen should spend their last evening like this. The odors of the pasture were penetrating,--cold wet loam, clean crushed leaves, and the poignant moist smell of the meadow grass.

She watched Allen at his task, his supple fingers working nimbly in the rain. When he had finished he wiped his hands on a handkerchief, and dripping with moisture came to the running board.

Laura, still on the wheel side, suddenly caught his arm. "Listen, Allen, what was that?"

"Nothing. The wind in the cottonwood."

"No, Allen . . . it sounded human . . . something . . . sort of weird. . . ."

Allen, head up, was listening too.

"Yoo-hoo . . . Marthy . . . comin'!" It came out of the storm with eerie faintness,--the cry of a bittern for its companion, a loon for its mate.

Laura was out and shaking nervously against Allen's arm, so that he slipped it about her shivering body.

"Allen--did you hear--what I heard?"

"Don't worry--just some boys . . ."

"Yoo-hoo . . . Marthy . . . comin' . . ."

Simultaneously, a great sheet of lightning in one terrific wave of yellow light swept and enveloped the whole hillside. For a few seconds the hill was bathed in the brilliant reddish glare, so that every object was distinct. The cottonwood was so well defined that it seemed but a few feet away. Nothing was hidden--every grass blade, every stone, every leaf, was magnified as though by gigantic binoculars.

For an instant, the hillside was a great scarlet etching, without a line missing,--a monstrous picture painted by a huge brush with the red blood of the gods.

And in that brief second, so ghastly and terrible, they saw him. Silhouetted against the great red painting, he stood on the hilltop. Tall, gnarled, drawn to his full height he stood, his grizzled gray beard sweeping back in the wind. Something white fluttered back with his beard--it looked like a mantle. Something was in his outstretched arm. It looked like a staff. For that brief moment, there on the highest point of the rolling hill . . . not far from the cottonwood . . . he stood with outstretched arms like one of the prophets. Elijah, he might have been,--or Moses, who having led his people into a new country, was leaving them with his benediction. Already the cottonwood struck through its heart was dividing, the half tottering for the fall. With wrenching, twisting contortions the last old monarch of the hilltop was swaying toward the last old man of the prairie. Allen shouted, but his voice was drowned in the crash of the thunder. Whether the old man saw it . . . or was unheeding . . . they could not know. He only stood there with outstretched arm, looking toward them, and made no move.

As the tree toppled--protecting, shielding her, Allen with swift tender movement swept Laura into his arms and turned her away from the red glare of the hillside.

CHAPTER 28

For what seemed like long moments, Allen held Laura tightly while the cottonwood twisted and toppled and crashed toward them with a great crackling, swishing sound of rain-soaked branches. Leaves and sticks and water showered them, and the thunder died away into some cavern between the worlds.

Then Allen was releasing her and saying shortly: "Get back in the car, Laura." And Laura was slipping her hand into his and answering: "No--I'm going to stay with you, Allen," half wondering even then if it had a double meaning.

Hand in hand they ran through the pasture and up the slippery, sloping hillside, the rain beating in their faces, and the soaked grass and weeds clutching at them with long clammy fingers. A sharp stick turned under Laura's foot and penetrated the flesh of the other ankle, but at the pain she only caught her lips in her teeth and made no outcry. Her white dress of the afternoon was a rag of mud and water and her hair a sodden thing.

The prostrate half of the tree looked immeasurably larger than when it had been standing on the hillside. The huge branches seemed coming to meet them before they were halfway to the top of the hill where it had grown.

"Stay here, Laura," Allen was telling her, and with the flashlight was working his way in through the mass of splintered branches.

She watched his light flicker here and there through the dim picture, for strangely enough, the lightning was no longer illuminating. It only flashed occasionally far away to the northeast, as though having vented its anger on the one community, it had gone on to find some other place for its wild orgy of sport. It took an immeasurably long time for Allen to return. The light kept flickering low to the ground far away. At times she could see a bit of Allen's figure silhouetted against the feeble glow. And then it was coming back, now high, now low, its light dancing up and down like a weird will-o'-the-wisp.

"How . . . ? What . . . ?" Laura began, her throat aching with the question.

"He's dead," Allen said quietly, and slipped his arm around her.

It was then that she remembered. *I want to go quick . . . like a tree in the wind.*

"Oh, Allen . . ." She could say nothing more. It was such a terrible thing--death, at any time. But out here, alone, in the wind and the rain!

"I can't do anything without help," Allen said. "He's pinned . . . underneath."

Allen's arm still around her, they went silently back down the slope of the hill through the sodden grass. There were the same odors of the night,--cold wet loam, clean crushed leaves and the poignant moist smell of the meadow grass.

Near the car she said, "Oh, Allen, life is so terrible! Such a mixture."

"The big things are simple," he answered briefly, and they got into the car.

There was the short ride into town for help, with the thunder dying entirely away and the wind calm after its mad fury--with Laura wet and bedraggled, winking back nervous tears in her corner of the car, hungry for a comforting word from Allen,--with Allen stiff and stern at the wheel, longing to take her again in his arms as he had done in the storm, but knowing what folly it would be,--and with old Oscar Lutz lying peacefully back there on the hillside after having looked on the lights of home.

A dozen people were ready to go out to the fallen cottonwood and old Oscar. Many hands were willing to perform the last tender ministrations. It is characteristic of the small town and rural districts. Sympathy there takes concrete form. It becomes cakes and cinnamon rolls and sitting up nights, husking corn and washing dishes and closing the eyes of the neighboring dead.

Allen took Laura up to the door of her home after he had notified those nearest the catastrophe and directed the men. People were moving about in old Oscar Lutz's house next door. There were lights in many rooms, for old Oscar was coming home.

"Come on in, Allen, and get dry."

Strangely unnerved by the scene on the hill, confused mentally, shaken physically, intuitively homesick because she was leaving under this combination of circumstances, Laura felt the need of Allen. This whole year he had always had the faculty of helping her set things straight in her mind when she was disturbed. His dependability, his substantial philosophy and his sense of humor,--ever since she had known him well, she had always been able to count on them all to steady her when she was bewildered. And to-night, she was more bewildered than she had ever been.

"No," Allen was saying, "I'll not come in. I'll go on over to the house and see if there's anything more I can do. Change your clothes right away."

"Oh . . . your sweater!" She began tugging at the big soggy woolen thing and Allen helped her pull it off. The simple little act made her feel like crying.

"I can't go to-morrow now." There was temporary relief in her mind. "I couldn't . . . not now . . . after good old Uncle Oscar has gone this way. I'll stay until after the services . . . until Friday at least, I suppose."

"I'll say 'good-by' now just the same." Allen held out his hand.

"Now?" Laura repeated stupidly. "Why . . . I thought . . . maybe . . . staying over . . . this way."

"Yes, now," Allen said. "It's better. After the decision, it's much the best way."

Oh, not now! Some other time, Laura's heart cried out. But not now. Why *"now"* was right this minute. Allen was holding out his hand.

Laura put her hand in his mechanically. Allen held it lightly for only the fraction of a minute. Then he dropped it quickly and slipped his hands into his raincoat pockets. "Well . . ." he tried to grin, "Happy landing."

Oh, what could you say? What could you do? This couldn't be the end of everything. A year of close friendship, and a handshake to end it. Dozens of intimate talks and only a stupid "good-by" at the finish. This wasn't the way life was meant to be. Life was meant to be a sweet unhampered thing, joyful and gay. It should have everything in it,--wealth and travel and happiness and a career and friends and Allen. And if it couldn't have them all . . . oh, it ought to have Allen. It ought, anyway, to have Allen. With the rapidity in which the human mind can travel, her thoughts went back to that moment when Allen had swept her into his arms to protect her from the sight of the tragedy on the hillside . . . even then, the impending disaster to the old man had been momentarily lost in a greater emotion. It had been as though in that one brief bitter-sweet moment, she had been swept again into some haven, had become the center of some great plan.

"Good-by . . ." It was Allen's voice, strange and far away. He had the old sweater over his arm and his hat in his hand. He was turning. He was going. She must say something. Life was stopping. Life was standing still. After Allen would go down the steps for the last time . . . there would be nothing left.

"Allen . . ." Her throat was dry and the words were hard to frame. "When I come back Christmas . . . we'll . . . couldn't we?"

He was down the wet steps with the street lights shining across a mat of glistening, soggy leaves. He turned, his hat still in his hand. The light shone across his blond head with the three waves in his hair . . . and his blue eyes. His chin was up and he lifted his hat high . . .

". . . and good luck."

Laura turned and went fumbling into the house. She climbed the stairs to her room blindly and went in to its comforting darkness. Her dress crackled stiffly about her wet limbs and she felt numb from its moist coldness. Her ankle hurt and, stooping, she felt blood on her stocking. Through the window she could see the lights in the old mansion. There were cars in front of the house and a sound of many feet going up the front walk, tramping rhythmically as though in unison. She remembered again that old Oscar Lutz was dead.

She ought to feel sad about old Oscar. But she couldn't,--not a bit. What did it matter that old Oscar Lutz was dead? What did anything matter? She walked aimlessly about in her crackling skirt and water-soaked shoes. Her mind too went about, but not aimlessly. It was groping desperately, clutching for something upon which to steady itself. She tried to drive it to think of a white bird flying,--to call up visions of silver wings in the distance. But it would not obey. There was no white bird and no sheen of silver wings. Nothing but blackness and loss and deep despair.

She sat down by the window, her wet things clinging clammily to the chintz of the chair. Only once before in her life had she suffered so, and that once by comparison seemed a frail and fragile experience. Once when she had come to the full realization that never again could she read her things to Grandma Deal, she had sensed this same feeling that she was her real self,--not that imaginative person who looked on at other people. And to-night she was her real self. She was down to the very core of her being.

Her mother came down the hall and turned on the light in front of her door.

"You here? Why are you in the dark? Isn't it awful about old Oscar? I came to change my dress before going over there. They say you and Allen saw him struck. Well, poor old Uncle Oscar,--that was a hard way to go. Now where do you suppose his money will land? I think your father knows, but he wouldn't deign to tell *me,* of course. That's one thing about Uncle Harry Wentworth. He doesn't keep people guessing. Just came right out and told that you would be his heir. Just think, Laura, do you ever try to comprehend what that is going to mean to you? I wish I knew how much it is. It's plenty though--*good* and plenty. You'll never have to worry about finances . . . and I can tell you one thing, Laura, if I could have eliminated all the worry about finances from my life . . . I'd have been far happier. It seems as though every one of the relatives has been better fixed than we. Your Uncle Mack . . . of course his big start was through Emma's money from her father's estate, but he had the faculty of knowing how to invest and increase it--something your father didn't seem to have. Your Aunt Margaret and Doctor, too . . . but your father just never had that way of making big money . . . always working hard for small fees . . . always helping the underdog and doing things for nothing. Well, the day I had you go and visit Uncle Harry and Aunt Carolyn was a great day for you, I must say, Laura. And don't ever forget your mother made it possible. You can thank your mother for putting you in a position where you can do *big things."*

Suddenly, Laura burst into unaccustomed nervous tears. To which her mother, with the same degree of understanding she had always shown for her daughter's moods, returned: "My soul! Don't take that old man's death so hard. Why, he's been ready to go for years. Tomorrow you'll be away from it all, and headed straight for what will be a far easier, pleasanter life than I ever dreamed you could have, Laura."

Laura sobbed uncontrollably in the depths of her confusion and misery. How could she tell her? How could she say that she had been on a long emotional journey and back again? How could this ambitious mother see that a young woman, with a head full of fancies and a heart full of longing, had come to the bend in the road? How could she know that one's mind said to go one way and one's heart another?

"It's not of old Oscar Lutz that I'm thinking."

How could she understand there was no sheen of silver wings and no white bird flying?

And so a greater share of the night, Laura shed tears into her soft white pillow. Some of them were for old Oscar Lutz dying on the hillside all alone in the wind and the rain. Some of them were for the general sad fact that hours fly and flowers die. But most of them were shed because of her own sudden and definite realization that even though there come new days and new ways,--love stays.

CHAPTER 29

Eloise thought it ridiculously unnecessary that Laura postpone her trip for the services of an old man who was not even a relative. "That's twice you've put it off, and if I were superstitious at all, it would worry me," she volunteered.

But Laura was stubborn. "I'm not going--not until Saturday. I always liked old Oscar." It was a worthy excuse.

Characteristically, Eloise took charge of everything over at the old man's house. She baked and cleaned and met people at the door. She took care that the flowers were all credited to their rightful donors,--"the sheaf of lilies from Mack and Emma," "the red carnations from Margaret and Doctor Baker," "the pink roses from our family, Laura, and put them right there at the front where they can be seen." A queer mixture was Eloise.

Laura arranged the flowers mechanically, without much thought of what she was doing. Death,--what was it? Life,--what was that, too? It seems a warm lovely thing,--and then suddenly it becomes a cold and dull thing,--a mere matter of packing and taking a train and going about with a noisy old Uncle and a stupid old Aunt. In the meantime there was one more day at home near--one more day at home, for old Oscar was dead.

And then, to add to the confusion and the work, Isabelle and Harrison Rhodes drove in unexpectedly from Chicago on their annual pilgrimage. Laura's Aunt Isabelle and Uncle Harrison were two of those souls who live in a rarefied atmosphere so musical that mere matters of food and dishwashing do not disturb them. They had intended to go to Mack's first, in Omaha, as indeed they had written him, but with the same ease they employed in transposing keys for a song, suddenly decided to try the new Waubonsie bridge at Nebraska City. Inasmuch as the new bridge had held up under the strain of their light coupé, they had come on to Cedartown. And here they were, smiling happily, pleased that no one expected them, and very, very hungry.

With that capacity for handling situations, Eloise rose to the occasion and added a big company dinner to her tasks over at the old Lutz house. Eloise was a mixture of traits, good and bad, but never indifferent.

The services for old Oscar were on Friday afternoon. Humans are queer. A man, living and well, is ignored or criticized. Dying or dead, he is noticed and praised. Death sheds a temporary glamour over the poorest soul. It is as though in dying, he has accomplished something which life never gave him. The sound of old Oscar Lutz's cane thump-thumping on the sidewalks of Cedartown had often brought boredom, impatience, and annoyance to its citizens. It had set women to closing doors quietly so that old Oscar would think there was no one at home. It had reminded men suddenly that they had business elsewhere. Only the children had remained interested and unannoyed. And now that the sound was no longer heard and the cane hung idly on its hook in the decaying Lutz mansion, women missed the friendly tap-tap and the gifts of radishes or carrots or beets. Men recalled the active mind and the stability of the kind old man. Only the children ceased to remember.

The afternoon was lovely. Nebraska's skies were never more fair. Long rippling white clouds slipped lazily across the blue, billowing out like the canvases of phantom covered-wagons seeking homes in some far new country. Since the big rain there had been two cool days and now a fresh little breeze came across the prairie and brought with it the scent of the loam and the fields, and the honey sweetness of newly cut red clover. Yellowing fields of corn rippled sinuously in the breeze with faint rustling sounds of the long tan-colored leaves. Tall feathery spikes of goldenrod laced together Nature's gown of tans and greens. Dark green were the fields of alfalfa and lavender dotted with their perfumed blossoms. Dark green were the pastures and still were the waters. Nebraska was bidding its old settler farewell.

Cars came over the long graveled highways from every direction. The sons of the pioneers, and their sons, and their sons' sons came to see old Oscar Lutz returned to the sod which he had broken when the state was young. Country communities have not yet ceased to pause in their work long enough to pay respect to the dead.

Laura, in a state of mental tumult, went to the services with her mother. Her father was a pallbearer with some of the Rinemillers, sons of the men with whom old Oscar had neighbored in that early day of which he was so fond. Uncle Mack and Aunt Emma, Stanley and his wife, Jimmie and Kathie came into the church together as the nearest relatives. It seemed queer to see Kathie in the role of mourner. She had on a modish dark tailored suit and chic little hat. She looked lovely and solemn, but ready to break into high rippling laughter. Laura, sitting over at the side of the church with Eloise, envied Kathie that infinite capacity to be light and airy and unconcerned the moment a difficult incident was closed. She herself was too serious, too introspective. She thought things out coolly. Kathie took whatever came her way without question. She used her head,--Kathie her heart. She had a multitude of standards and ideals up to which she tried to measure,--Kathie had one unfailing rule: to get all the happiness she could out of life.

The church was flower-scented. People spoke to each other in whispers in that hushed way they employ when in the presence of the dead. As though the dead knew or cared. Before the sermon a quartette sang "The Beautiful City" and afterward "A City Foursquare." How unsuitable, Laura thought. Singing of cities for old Oscar Lutz, who did not like any kind of pavement,--who would not want to go tap-tapping on the golden streets of which they sang,--Old Oscar, who wanted to be in the prairie wind and a part of the prairie sod, and to hear the sound of the wild geese honking.

At the cemetery, the narrow house was ready for old Oscar. Sod houses in the beginning of the pioneer days,--and sod houses at the end. Next to it was Martha's grave, sunken level to the grass line with the snows of many winters--old Oscar's Marthy, whose love had not died at her death.

Laura looked on at the proceedings in a numb unfeeling way. She saw the people and the cars, but they meant nothing. She felt calloused, hard, as though heart and mind were paralyzed. Nothing touched her. Nothing would ever touch her again. A few days ago and the scene would have aroused her emotions, brought the ready mist to her eyes. She would have wanted to write it, would have loved putting down on paper the feel of the atmosphere. She felt she would never write again.

Suddenly she saw Allen through the crowd. He stood beside his mother, hat in hand. Laura's heart throbbed dully in actual pain. He looked big and fine standing there beside his plump little mother. Gone were the ready smile and the gay carefree expression. He looked grave and serious--manly, capable. The girl that Allen married would be in strong, efficient hands. Laura thought she could not stand it to think of her, whoever she would be. The words of the minister came with vibrant tones across the distance: "Here in the same spot where he first turned the virgin prairie . . ."

She ought to be thinking of kind old Uncle Oscar, but she could not bring her errant thoughts into subjection.

"Ashes to ashes: dust unto dust."

Allen would marry,--and she would be East. Allen would build a lovely home,--and she would be dancing attendance on fat old Aunt Carolyn. Allen would bring some nice girl to that home,--and she would be listening to foppish old Uncle Harry's vapid remarks.

There was no question about her love for Allen, now. The previous two long nights had shown her that. She went over the facts for the hundredth time. She had made her decision, and it was not the right one. Only three days ago she had said, "Surely there's something more for me than life gave my Grandmother!" To-day her whole heart was crying out: "What is there to life if you do not follow me?"

She looked across at Allen far on the other side of the groups of people. What if she would just walk across the grass and the graveled paths and say to him simply, "I'm going to stay with you, Allen?" Why, how terrible! *How terrible!* She felt suddenly fearful of herself, as though she might do that crazy thing with no volition of her own. She pressed her lips together and clenched her hands in tense rigidity. People didn't do things like that,--civilized people. That was what civilization was,--covering up elemental emotions.

The sweet weird sound of a bugle came from the trees beyond the grave. Taps over the grave of old Oscar. And taps over the grave of Laura's love for Allen.

Good-night . . . good-night.

Sweet dreams . . . and good-night.

CHAPTER 30

The group about the Lutz lot was breaking up now. People were visiting happily and volubly. There were no close relatives to mourn, and now that respect had been paid to the old man, the affair was turned into something of a social event.

Katherine was asking Dr. Fred Baker and her Aunt Margaret and Aunt Grace to come over to the house to a pick-up supper. Her father and mother and Uncle Harrison and Aunt Isabelle were going to be there. "You come, too, Aunt Eloise, you and Uncle John and Laura and The Tribulation. We're all here, and it will be a nice way for Laura to see everybody before she leaves."

"There are so many of us, Kathie." Aunt Margaret was saying, "When the Deals get together it looks like the old settlers' picnic. Are you sure you can feed us all?"

"Well, I can't just say there will be twelve baskets of Parker house rolls and canned salmon, or whatever it was that John the Baptist or somebody had left over," Kathie was a little vague in her Biblical reference, "but we'll make it go as far as it will. And if Aunt Eloise here has any cold turkey or angel food cake concealed about her person, she can bring it along."

"Certainly." Eloise stepped into the managership. "I have plenty of bread and two pounds of Mrs. Miller's nice fresh butter, some cold meat, and half a cake, a fruit salad and three dozen cookies." Eloise could take an inventory of her possessions, even when far from them.

So it turned out that all the visiting Deals went over to the lovely little English cottage that was Katherine's. Laura at her own home helped her mother pack three baskets, although there is some room for argument about the quality of her assistance, for she put things in and took them out and was impractical and indefinite in what she was doing. Life, like a swift river, seemed sweeping her along to the brink of some deep chasm and she could not stay it. When later, they went over to Kathie's, the friendly familiar faces of all the relatives gathered there seemed looking on at her unsympathetically, with no offer of aid or compassion. She looked at them all,--the fat florid face of Uncle Mack, the calm unruffled one of Aunt Margaret, the prim one of Aunt Grace--and the others,--and wondered dully why they would not help her.

She wanted to scream out, "Oh, stop,--listen! Help me, some one. Don't be so complacent. Can't you see I'm suffering? Can't you see I'm getting near the falls?"

But what could you do, now? There was nothing to do. Everything was settled. She had chosen. She was going back to Uncle Harry Wentworth and Aunt Carolyn. They expected her. But she didn't want to. O God, she didn't want to. Not now. Not now, when she loved Allen.

The house was full of relatives. Patty was downstairs,--the center of attention. Every one was chattering. There was laughter. Sometimes, they referred to Laura's leaving. "Well, Laura, I suppose you'll soon be skylarking around doing big things." *Big things!* What were the big things of life? Once she would have said they were leaving Cedartown and going in for a career. Now the leaving seemed inconsequential, the career merely hypothetical.

Her mother and Aunt Margaret, Aunt Emma and Katherine were all in the kitchen, making sandwiches, cutting cake, opening bottles of olives. Aunt Isabelle was playing softly on Kathie's baby grand. Aunt Grace was wiping trays. Stanley's wife was entertaining Patty and her own two youngest children with a tale of some sort. The men--all the Uncles and her father and Stanley and Jimmie were talking together in groups while waiting for the food. Trib was covertly eating purloined cookies. It was a typical clan gathering with almost every one there,--every one but Grandma. And yet, she seemed as much there in the crowd as any one of these whose presence was visible. After all the years it still seemed that way. She had always felt it,--the presence of Grandma when the clan came together. She could almost hear her comments on whatever subject was under discussion. "Mack, turn around. You're getting balder every day. That's because you used to make fun of old man Johnson." "No, Grace, I can't agree with you. I don't care if it *is* in a scientific book." Grandma had always known her own mind, had stood her own ground even to her eightieth year.

And now, she felt the presence of Grandmother Deal, as always--that same unexplainable presence of the woman who had mothered them all, whose love for her children and her children's children was so deep that after all the years it still seemed a tangible thing, delicate and rare, like the faint subtle odor of a fine perfume.

Could such things be, she wondered vaguely, standing there in the hall doorway and looking on? Could the loved dead come back? At a time like this, was the memory of them so keen to one sensitive like herself, that they only seemed to return and mingle with those to whom they had been devoted? Or was there in some way unknown to humans, a definite magical blending of these imperishable spirits with the mortal spirits of those they had so deeply loved? If it were possible--if Grandmother could return and slip cheerily into the circle, how easy and natural it would be to go to her, now, and pour into her listening ear the confession of this terrible aching in her heart. Out of them all, Grandmother would be the one she would choose to whom to talk. She could say to her quite easily: "Grandma--what shall I do? I've come to the forks of the road . . . the same crossroads that you told me about long ago. I've made my decision, and I've found it's all wrong. I know now--if love is one way and the kingdoms of the earth the other, there is only one way to take. But it's too late, now. I can't seem to talk to one of these. You are the only one who will understand. I'm going tomorrow. And I won't see Allen again. I thought I was wise, but I was ignorant. I thought I knew more than you, but I didn't. I thought you could master love, but it masters you. You, with your limited schooling, how wise you were. I, with my education, how little I have known. See, I kneel at your feet to confess this, for my heart is breaking. All my life I've mixed realities with dreaming,--and now, it's too late. The thing I dreamed about and wanted, Grandma, may become real. And Allen, who was real, will always remain a memory. You chose, once, between two roads. You said it was the right way. How did you know? How did you choose? *Why* did you choose?"

"I saw Will Deal coming down the lane."

It came into her mind as readily and distinctly as though her Grandmother had said it. It came gently, soothingly, as surcease for her troubled thinking. Standing there in the doorway, looking at the noisy, talkative relatives getting their plates and their napkins for the buffet supper, it seemed to Laura that Grandma had spoken, that the very aura of her presence was near, the very tones of her voice familiar.

"Just coming down the lane, Grandma? Was that all?"

"Just coming down the lane."

She could almost hear the gentle cadence of the words, the finality of the tones, as though there could have been no other answer. Grandma had faced life that way always.

Quite suddenly, and almost miraculously, the thing seemed simple. Why had she hesitated when there was only one solution possible? It was as easy as that. She felt calm and content, and something infinitely stronger than either--something unmistakably firm and resolute.

Eloise thrust a tray into her hands. "Here, Laura." She was worried and agitated. "Let's have some order here, folks." She raised her voice, "Get right in line. My goodness,--the only way to do anything right is to have it systematized." As one might as well have tried to systematize the water in Stove Creek as a laughing, garrulous crowd of Deal relatives, there was very little result to Eloise's attempt to bring order out of chaos.

Laura broke away from her mother with, "Not now, Mother, thanks,--later," and ran to the kitchen, bumping into Katherine bringing in a quivering gelatine concoction.

"Horrors, Laura,"--as a miniature seismic disturbance shook the mound--"training for the track team?" But Laura paid no attention to her excepting to say, "Kathie, may I take your car two minutes?"

"Sure--but what do you want?" She called to the fleeing girl. "We have everything we need."

"No--not everything," Laura shot back, and was immediately out the door and in the car.

For a frantic moment she could not get the car started. Then the engine responded, and she was down the driveway and out on the street turning east. She felt gay, light-hearted, intoxicated with her sudden decision. The top of the convertible coupé was down, and she waved cordial greetings to children playing on sidewalks. She drove fast so that a night watchman on his way to work, recognizing only the car, decided he would report that harum-scarum Mrs. Jimmie Buchanan to headquarters.

August sunshine lay over the low rolling hills and the meadows. There was in the air that late summer odor peculiar to the Midwest--a mingling of the smells of roadside weeds and drying hay, of ripening apples and rustling corn, of honey-sweet alfalfa and the lovely dainty scent from a field of clover bloom. The six o'clock whistle blew. She increased her speed. "The ride to the rescue," she said to herself, and laughed at the humor of it. She passed her grandmother's old farm house at the edge of town, dingy and empty now, passed the cedars and the orchard and part of the Rinemiller corn lands and came nearer to the square white house set back in the wide green lawn. She could see Allen's mother dressed as she had been at the services, going in the side door, could see old Tom Dickson, the hired man, and young Tom, his son, carrying milk pails to the kitchen door. She could see Allen stepping out of the garage and closing the long doors behind him. She turned into the long driveway. *Allen was coming down the lane.*

He looked amazed, incredulous. "Laura?" he said as though it were a question, and came hurriedly toward her.

Laura was breathless as though she, herself, had been the motor power by which the hurried trip had been made. Although she was having a difficult time with her respiration, she was smiling gayly, as though she knew a great piece of news. "Allen," she called out, almost before he had reached the car, "have you shot that pheasant . . . I mean, have you picked out that girl yet?"

"Nit-wit!" he said, grinning.

"Get in here," she spoke commandingly, "get in and ask no questions."

He swung agilely over the door. "Where are you going?"

"And ask no questions," she repeated briefly.

Allen's mother came out on the side porch.

"May I take your son away for a little while?" Laura called gayly.

"You can *have* him," she shrugged her plump shoulders in mock disgust: "He's a sullen little boy."

Laura turned the car without a word and they swung out of the driveway and turned toward town.

"What's the big idea?" Allen wanted to know.

"So you think Russia is riding for a fall, do you? But then, there are others who feel the same way." She was as gay and light-hearted as Kathie in her gayest moods.

"It must be terribly clever, whatever it is," Allen said dryly; "do you, yourself, know what you're doing?"

"I realize, of course, that some people think the next war will be between capital and labor, some between the drys and the wets,--myself, I think it will be between those who eat spinach and those who don't."

They passed the old Deal house standing forlornly behind the cedars, came to pavement and turned to the south fine residential portion of town.

"Let me see," Allen said meditatively, "when they're bad, you humor them until you can get a good jiu-jitsu hold. See the birdie?" he asked pleasantly, and pointed to the Jacksons' police dog nosing along the road. Then, with one hand on the wheel, he suddenly closed his other arm tightly around Laura's arms and pinned them down.

"Don't you touch me . . . don't you dare!" She was laughing and frightened, gay and worried.

They turned the corner of the street, then, that led to Katherine's home, and Allen could see all the cars around the curb and in the driveway.

"Lord . . . what *is* this, . . . really, Laura . . . no fooling?" He was serious and disturbed.

"Get out," Laura said shortly, "get out and follow me." At the porch she said tensely, "It's the Deals . . . *all* of them . . . *every one* . . . but if *I* can face the music, you can too. Buck up." They were at the door now. "It's a horribly bad dose, Allen. I'm sorry for you, but it won't last long."

They stepped in, Laura, flushed and starry-eyed and a bit disheveled,--Allen, big and clean-cut and a bit dubious.

All the Deals were, indeed, there. It looked like a convention of the Parent Teachers Association. With trays on their laps, on end tables, on card tables, on the piano bench, the big crowd of relatives sat. The rooms were full of them,--the Mackenzie Deals and the Stanley Deals and the John Deals, the Bakers and the Rhodeses and the Buchanans. As one man they looked up, and seeing the two young people, flushed and breathless, all activities, both of a conversational and gastronomic nature, immediately ceased. Sandwiches were poised in mid-air. Forks ceased their perpendicular traveling. Somebody dropped an olive and in the stillness it bounced on the hardwood floor like a billiard ball.

Laura had a swift vision of a composite picture of Deals--her mother's serious eyes fixed alarmingly upon her, her father's look of blank concern, Uncle Mack's fat red jaws slowing down on their chewing, a little like a startled cow, Aunt Grace setting down a cake plate as though she had suddenly gone weak, Katherine's nostrils quivering excitedly.

"Folks," Laura said, and her voice in the sudden hush sounded as squeaky as a worn-out phonograph record. "I want you all to know I've changed my mind about going East." She looked up at Allen's astonished face above her. "Meet the newest applicant for admission to the clan."

CHAPTER 31

Save for the fact that a bomb would have made a splintered mess of the baby grand and torn unmendable cavities in the floor and ceiling, the effect could not have been more devastating. The clan all sat or stood for a moment in motionless attitudes, like figures dug from some ancient lava-covered ruins. Then their minds began to function and they were no longer archaeologic specimens. There was much talk and there was much laughter, for the Deals chronically ran true to form.

The reaction affected them all in various ways. Aunt Grace looked a little sheepish, as though having killed the canary, she was trying to draw attention away from the feathers by saying, "Why, Laura!" in her most didactic tone.

The men shook Allen's hand, told him how surprised they were, and made trite jokes about running his head into the noose. To which Allen was gentleman enough to withhold the information that he was more surprised than they, and that the noose had been dangling quite out of reach until a few moments before. Laura's father was frankly pleased. Trib, usually voluble, had no words for what seemed to him a horribly embarrassing situation, but with no noticeable delay made elaborate plans for a golf course in Allen's west pasture. The Aunts kissed Laura and asked her multitudinous questions, to which she gave unintelligent answers. Kathie made clever and impudent remarks and laughed gayly at the whole affair.

Eloise stood for a few moments as though stunned. Life was tumbling about her ears with a tumultuous cracking and breaking of well constructed plans. She loved her little daughter, and had tried to save her from all future hardships. She wanted her to be happy, had worked diplomatically many years for Uncle Harry Wentworth and Aunt Carolyn to be the prime contributors to that happiness. By adroit planning, the scheme had worked out exactly as she desired. And now it was crashing about her, all the intricate framework of suggestion and sacrifice--her painstaking work of years--blown down by a puff of romance no stronger than the glance of an eye or the touch of a hand. Romance,--how useless it was! Love,--how impractical! And yet, so strong they were, you could not argue against them, nor battle them nor defeat them.

In the space of a few moments, Eloise had met her Waterloo and her Yorktown, her Richmond and her Marne. But Eloise was no ordinary general handing over her sword while the crowd looked pityingly on. The war department missed something when Eloise Wentworth was born a girl.

She lifted her head in victorious gesture, and smiled at the Deal clan: "Does it surprise you?" She asked sturdily. "I'm glad, Laura, we took this way to tell them while they're all here together. Trib," she turned to her son, "you take the car and go over home and get Laura's picture off my dresser,--the one in the pink formal. If we hurry, I think we can get the announcement in the office for the Sunday edition of the paper."

And so it came about, that although every one of the relatives had talked to Laura and Allen, the star of the day's performance and the leading man had not so much as uttered a syllable to each other. Laura sat with her tray at the edge of the dining room with one group, and Allen sat with his tray at the end of the living room with another. Sometimes, across the crowd Laura caught Allen's challenging eye, but she evaded it adroitly and went on dipping olives into the salt and spreading potato salad on bits of bread. But something told her to beware the Ides of March.

She could hear Allen telling some of the men of his plans to raze the old tumble-down Deal house behind the cedars and build on the same site. She could hear her mother informing the women that there would be lots to do, now; that she intended Laura to have at least eighteen sheets, a dozen pair of pillow cases, four tablecloths, eight lunch cloths, two dozen Turkish towels and four dozen tea towels. Her voice sounded cheerful and energetic. Laura sincerely admired her mother's spirit. What a good sport she was. She felt closer to her than she had for many months.

The impromptu buffet supper was over and the clan broke up. The Mack Deals and the Stanley Deals left for Omaha, accompanied by Harrison and Isabelle Rhodes. Doctor and Margaret Baker left for Lincoln. Kathie, Eloise and Grace Deal cleaned trays in the kitchen. Laura whisked steadily back and forth carrying dishes, with one eye cannily cocked for signs of the approach of any friendly enemy. But Allen seemed busily talking with her father and Trib. Later, when she looked cautiously into the living room and saw it was empty, with a disheveled crumby sort of appearance, she went over to get some crumpled paper napkins in the east end of the room. Quite suddenly, Allen rose up like some huge jack-in-the-box from a big overstuffed chair turned toward the fireplace. Laura whirled abruptly to leave, but he reached out an athletic arm and caught her. "No . . . you don't, young lady. I've been lying in wait for you."

"Don't, Allen--not now. Some one will come in."

"You should worry,--a bold forward woman who kidnaps a man and hauls him to the altar."

"Oh, Allen--wasn't it *terrible*--after you said you were through? I think I . . . was a little crazy . . . I'll probably never be able to look you in the eye again." And she hid her scarlet face under the lapel of Allen's coat, until the statement began to seem fairly true.

Arms around her, Allen's banter and his lightness died. He cupped Laura's chin in the palm of his hand, and turned her flushed face up to him.

"It was great," he said, . . . "and natural and right. I'm more happy and proud that you came for me than you can ever know or understand. But it would have turned out just this same way if you hadn't."

Laura raised startled eyes. "What do you mean . . . just the same?"

"Because," he kissed her sweet fresh mouth, . . . "because I couldn't have let you go, and was coming back to-night to argue it all over with you again."

Suddenly, over the top of Allen's broad shoulder, Laura caught a glimpse of some one looking down at her. From above the fireplace a lovely lady in velvet draperies with pearls at her throat, and reddish-brown hair curling over her shoulder, gazed down from heavy-lidded eyes, her cupid's-bow lips smiling mysteriously as though she possessed the concentrated wisdom of all the ages. One could not conscientiously say that she seemed pleased but neither could one justly contend that she was annoyed and distressed. She merely smiled that puzzling smile as though, sphinx-like, she knew the secret of deep mysteries.

CHAPTER 32

And so Laura chose Allen as women have done from time immemorial. The steamer trunk and the bags were unpacked and Laura wrote a lengthy letter to Uncle Harry and Aunt Carolyn, full of explanations and excuses, which she suddenly tore up and substituted a brief thanks for the kind offer they had made her, and "what seemed to me like freedom to follow a career, seems now not half so important as freedom to follow my heart." After which, she started to embroider fat initials on towels, every stitch a thought, every thought a bit of happiness.

The wheat all in and the corn not ready for the husking, Allen began preparation for tearing down the old Deal house behind the cedars.

And so the old Deal home was to come down. After a half century of standing there in the rain and the sun and the wind, it was to come down to make way for Allen's fine new brick home. For more than fifty years it had sheltered humans, and now it was through, its usefulness over.

The carpenters began their task on the first Wednesday morning in September. Allen was anxious to get the work started so that it could be inclosed before the snows came. He was working with the men, and Laura went over for a while in the afternoon to watch the demolishing of that which had once been dear to them all.

She sat down on an old tumble-down seat under the cedars, where she had often sat years before with her childish writing. Her lap was full of plan books, for Allen had begun the dismantling of the old, even before they had definitely decided on the new. For a long time she watched the wreckers. Sometimes she thought of her grandmother, and the joy that must have been hers at the building of the old house. Sometimes she thought of the half century of living under the gray old roof that had been the Deal family's. But most of all, she thought of her own future pleasure in seeing the new home go up. Occasionally she felt a sense of sadness, that depressing emotion which always came to her when anything in the way of change was to be made. Change! That everything eventually changes was the saddest thing in the world. And the pleasantest.

One of the men was tearing off the shingles with a ripping sound of breaking wood. One was pulling out a rafter with a rending sound of creaking nails.

Yank the shingles! And the joy that had been Abbie Deal's when the old roof was completed. *Creak! Creak! Tear into the rafters.* And the happiness that had been the Deal children's when they saw the rafters go up.

But it could not be torn down completely, Laura was thinking. As long as there was any one left who had lived there or who remembered it--the old house still lived in their memories.

"As long as I live,--you live, too . . ." the words sung themselves through her mind. She wished she had brought paper with her, but had only the plan books. So she turned over a page and began writing verses in scraggling formation along the border. As she wrote her pulse quickened to the pleasure of forming the phrases,--her blood warmed to the joy of the working. She was experiencing a return of the familiar sensation of happiness on constructing. Quite suddenly, in fancy she caught in the far distance a glimpse of silver wings. It gave her a warm thrill of gratification too deep for words. Immediately she knew through some inner consciousness, that no matter what the future would hold,--joy or sorrow, happiness or grief,--that no matter where life's paths would lead her,--through sharp and stony ways or beside still waters,--buried deep within her was an indestructible capacity to visualize a white bird flying. She might never get close to the way of its winging, but always there would be joy in lifting her eyes to the glory of its distant flight.

It was then that Allen coming from the back of the building, saw her for the first time.

"Going to assist?" he called to her across the grassy yard, and as he came nearer: "It's a tough job. Strong--you never saw anything like it. The sturdiest old timbers . . ."

"Like the people who built it, Allen,--sturdy and strong."

He sat down on the old bench which gave a warning sound of its decrepitude under the extra weight. "Not sorry?" he asked.

"Not sorry," Laura answered.

"Not even about the career?"

Laura laughed and then she sobered. "Allen,--do you know, I've stopped kidding myself about that. If I can't see stories in the lives of the people around me,--I just couldn't see them anywhere. If I can't see drama in humanity near me, I guess I couldn't detect it in humans far away."

They both turned at the sound of a car driving into the yard. It was Aunt Margaret Baker from Lincoln, who stepped out and came across the grass, her fine gray head erect.

"Why, Aunt Margaret," Laura was up and across the yard to meet her. "How did you happen to come?"

"I didn't want to," she said. "It's like going to a funeral, but the more I thought about it, the more it fascinated me and I couldn't stay away."

Allen remained for a few moments and then went back to his work. The two sat down on the bench, and together watched the disruption. The creaking of nails and the splintering of wood were the only sounds in the sleepy summer afternoon.

"I wanted Grace to come," Margaret laughed, "but she wouldn't. Your Aunt Grace doesn't like to have her emotions disturbed."

"I know it . . . knowledge, facts, law, order, and discipline make up Aunt Grace's mind," Laura said, and was conscience-smitten at the words. "She can't bear to have it all cluttered up with tag-ends of sentiment."

"Just think, Laura," Margaret Baker went on, "what the old house has seen . . . our childish plays and quarrels and sicknesses . . . Mother dragged in half dead by Christine Reinmueller in the big blizzard of '88 . . . Grace born a few hours afterward . . . your Uncle Mack, a raw country boy, leaving to try his fortune in Omaha . . . I, leaving for the Academy with my ironed-out hair and my cotton stockings . . ."

Splinter! Splinter! Yank the shingles.

"My wedding . . . it seems like yesterday . . . and it's over forty years ago . . . the lane road full of wagons and buggies . . . Doctor and I coming downstairs . . . the ceremony . . . the young folks dancing on the new carpet . . . driving away afterward with Doctor in the June moonlight behind a livery team . . ."

Creak! Creak! Tear into the rafters.

"Father laughing and joking with me as he went out into the yard . . . being brought in dead a few minutes afterward. Old Grandma Deal coming out from Iowa to live with Mother . . . Isabelle's delight over getting a piano."

Crash! Crash! Throw down the timbers.

"Christmas, with every one home . . . the long table . . . and the excitement over getting to sleep, with the packages all around . . . Christmases and birthdays and Thanksgivings. Your father leaving to get married without telling Mother . . . Isabelle getting married, too, in war times just before Harrison went to the Philippines . . . Grace going away . . ."

Crumble! Crumble! Drop the chunks of old plaster.

"Mother living alone, sturdy and brave and unselfish, putting every one's interest before her own . . . hearing that your father had gone to the Spanish-American war . . . saying good-by to Fred Jr. and Stanley going over seas . . . pottering around feebly with the old things she loved . . . dying all alone . . . not one of us here . . . only the old house of us all to shelter her that last day . . . only the old rooms to know whether she suffered or called for us. Just think, Laura, how *human* it seems . . . knowing everything about us . . . the hopes and the joys . . . the disappointments and sorrows . . . the griefs and the happiness . . . just *one* of us, it seems."

Splinter! Splinter! Tear at the shingles.

Creak! Creak! Jerk the rafters.

Laura winked back the suspicious moisture. "And yet, Aunt Margaret, *my* new house goes up right there on the very spot."

"Of course," Margaret Baker put a well kept hand on Laura's, "that was pretty thoughtless of me. Well, I guess that's a sign I'm getting along in years, myself,--trying to live over the buried past. And the new house will contain it all, Laura. You can't evade a thing. Those who try to get around it are weak. Those who meet it gallantly are strong. So many women try to dodge life. They don't economize because it's inconvenient. They don't work because it's tiring. They don't have a child because it's painful. They don't look at the dead because it's saddening. Face them all, Laura. Face them squarely and meet them gallantly . . . as your grandmother did. For every one of the old experiences will be there . . . birth . . . marriage . . . death . . . disappointment . . . grief . . . little joys . . . little sorrows. You'll have to meet them all. It's part of the story . . ."

"I know it . . ." Laura stood up. "Well . . . I'm ready." She threw out her hands in a little gesture of surrender. "I'm ready for them all . . . with Allen."

Pound! Pound! Put up bright rafters.

Scrape! Scrape! Lay the brick and tile.

A new home goes up.

CHAPTER 33

There are those who will say that the love story of Laura Deal and Allen Rinemiller ends here. But they who say it do not define love correctly. For though love has been ridiculed and disgraced, exchanged and bartered, dragged through the courts, and sold for thirty pieces of silver, the bright, steady glow of its fire still shines on the hearth-stones of countless homes,--the homes of which no one reads. For of what news value is the home from which there comes no tale of crime or breath of scandal? And of what dramatic importance is the average decent family going about its daily business?

In time the new house was finished on the site of the old, and any comparison is unfair to the old one which had been considered spacious and comfortable in an early day. The new farm home was of brick and tile. Its heat came up from the cellar, its lights came in from Omaha, its water came in through many pipes. Ice was frozen in its kitchen, food was cooked there without sign of match or fuel, dust from its floor was sucked up into bags and burned. Its coffee was percolated from a plug in the wall, its corn was popped by the same unseen force, its bells rung and its water heated. Laura sat at her desk and talked with friends in their homes. Machines in her immaculate basement helped her wash and iron. Heat regulators kept her warm in winter. Fans cooled her in summer. And symphony orchestras played for her while she worked. Allen touched a button at the house and flooded the barns with light. Blooded cattle were in his pastures. Two automobiles were in his garage. Auto trucks were under their shed. His fields were furrowed by a giant's plow, and cultivated with the latest type machine. A great combine, with a few turns of its iron hands, did the work of a dozen men. And there was much talk of farm relief.

In the years that followed, children were born to Allen and Laura, so that Laura knew the price of motherhood to be pain and responsibility; the reward, love and pride.

And then, after profitable years, there came a summer when a drouth was upon the land. Every so often Nature strikes a blow of some kind at each section of the country. It is as though she grows tired of being unnoticed by a neglectful people, craves adulation, precipitates a forceful shock upon a prosperous community, so that the old primitive order of nature worship shall be restored.

Such a summer came to many of the agricultural states. Nature slipped back, for a time, into the parsimonious ways of pioneer times. Day after day the sky kept its hard blue glare. Only thin lines of moistureless clouds slipped across the sky. The creek waters went down. The grass in the pastures dried. Corn curled brown on the stalk. Berries were hard knots on the stems. Nature had turned traitor, was apparently in league with the eastern markets. Depression, like the rippling of a huge circle of water into which a stone had been flung, sent its out-bound waves through the agricultural country. Land was not moving. Cash renters had nothing with which to pay. Crop renters had little to divide with the owners. If a man could not meet his obligations at the bank, suddenly he found he could not hold his land. Farm products went for bed-rock prices. Wheat was so low, many farmers ground it for feed. Hogs sold for a song. Everything,--the last war, the tariff, the administration, extravagance, the eighteenth amendment, a fallen meteor,--was blamed.

Nebraska did not suffer to any dangerous extent; was, in truth, the least hard hit of the agricultural states, but still there was much talk of depression. Men owed Allen money which he could not collect. He grew worried and silent. Ready cash was scarce in the Rinemiller household. Laura bought sparingly or not at all, in order to help tide affairs over the crisis. She turned and mended the children's clothes. She cared faithfully for her chickens, and saw eggs drop to ten cents a dozen, as her grandmother had experienced.

It was all they could discuss,--the cloud under which they lived. Something hung over them. Something out of which they wanted to emerge.

"After all, there *are* other subjects," Allen would say.

"If you dare to quote 'The man worth while is the man who can smile, when everything goes dead wrong,' I'll throw something at you," Laura would laugh. It took all their common sense and philosophy to face life these days. The two are synonymous.

"Allen, here's a queer thing," Laura said once. "I've written a few stories and sold them . . . when I didn't need money . . . and now, that I want cash so badly . . . genius won't burn. I'm nervous and tense, and thinking about the money all the time I write . . ."

"Which goes to prove, you can't buy off the Muse," Allen returned.

"I'll be so glad when we can get hold of some good hard cash, again,--money that's actually available and not all tied up in land. We're simply land poor, Allen. I want a dozen things. A new dining-room rug for one . . . bedroom curtains for another, and I *could* make use of a new dress. I'm so sick of my same hat that I've a notion to trim it with zinnia blossoms from the garden. They're so hardy I think they wouldn't wilt until I got home from club."

Aunt Carolyn Wentworth had died the previous year, and now in the midst of the depression, word came that Uncle Harry Wentworth had been killed in an auto accident. "Allen," Laura was excited, "maybe he has left me some money. Oh, Allen, he would! He liked me. Just *imagine!"* Her cheeks were pink and her eyes were starry. "I feel it. Something tells me he wouldn't go back on me entirely."

"Don't count on it," Allen advised. But she could see that, in spite of himself, he had brightened visibly. Everything was going to be all right in a year or so, but in the meantime, some of Uncle Harry Wentworth's money, even a sum not large, could be used in a dozen ways.

And then, a few days later, came a report of Uncle Harry Wentworth's will--a long official envelope. Laura had a pair of Billy's coveralls in her lap, and as Allen brought in the mail, was finishing the application of a hexagonal-looking patch to the place which Billy invariably wore out from sliding down the roofs of the farm buildings. Allen held the letter gingerly between a thumb and forefinger, as he crossed to the low rocking-chair where Laura sat. Neither spoke. Laura's heart was in her throat, and she felt almost faint. So much hung on the moment. Uncle Harry would have remembered her. Out of all that money, he surely would have given her a share. In the years that had passed she had seldom thought of it, so absorbed had she been in her family life. But now, it seemed an almost probable gift.

Allen put the letter in her lap. She did not touch it for a moment. Her throat felt dry, and her fingers were without feeling. Just a few thousand dollars out of his wealth at this time of depression,--and there were a dozen things she could do.

She pulled herself together and tore open the envelope. Even then, she had a swift vision of Uncle Harry flashing his brown eyes at the stenographer who had taken the original dictation of the will.

The words of the letter stood out clear and black in the morning sunlight. Uncle Harry Wentworth had kept his word. He had meant what he said. That there should be no legal controversy over any omission of her name, she was mentioned. "To my grandniece, Laura Deal Rinemiller, I give and bequeath the sum of one dollar."

The flush slipped away from her cheek and for a moment she felt sick with disappointment. Suddenly, she laughed, a little unsteadily to be sure, but she laughed and handed the letter to Allen.

Allen read the formal statement.

"Well, that's that," Laura said.

"I'm not sorry," Allen said stoutly. "It wouldn't have been good for us. Money coming that way does something to people. It weakens something inside them."

"There goes our last chance for immense wealth, Allen. After this, it's just the same old story, 'What's the price of corn to-day?' 'How is the Omaha cattle market?' and 'What are you paying for eggs, Mr. Porter?'"

"Yes--and you'll see, corn's going up and so are cattle, and the egg money isn't such a punk amount at any time. Just wait until agriculture comes into its own again." Allen was off on a favorite topic. The eternal hope! Three-quarters of a century before, the settlers had said: "You'll see, some day we'll be raising more corn than we can use ourselves."

The check for the dollar came, as portentous looking with its executor's signature as though there had been a half-dozen naughts after the "one." Laura endorsed it and told Allen to cash it for her. "I want silver, Allen, a big round silver dollar."

"Why so particular?"

"I want to have a hole drilled in it and wear it around my neck to remind me what a heavy burden you've been to me." Allen grinned at her. They understood each other's various moods, and each knew that the other did not care deeply about the disappointment. It was an incident, closed now, with life going on as before.

At noon of that day, Allen brought the silver dollar home and presented it very formally to its owner.

The day was soft and balmy, with a little breeze in the elms and poplars and great banks of cloud snow drifting across the sky's blue highway. In the late afternoon Laura called to the children and asked them if they would like to go down to the pasture with her and play, while she mended in the shade. Talking volubly, skipping and running, they all went with her down through the garden, past the four o'clocks and the cosmos, past the turnips and the fat cabbages, through the red raspberry patch, and came then to the edge of the pasture, where Laura spread out an old blanket and settled herself for the weekly sewing of buttons and the filling of large and unexpected cavities. But she did not work. She sat idly under the tree and thought of many things,--of her full life, of the hopes she and Allen had for the children's futures, and of her own plans for further writing. For never in the midst of her busy life had she lost sight of the distant sheen of silver wings.

For a long time, the three larger children romped and played by the creek bed, where the low water moved sluggishly, and shadows lay thick under the trees--Billy and Phyllis and Jane. And the baby tumbled about on fat uncertain legs.

After a time, Laura called out to them: "I've a new game for you, children. Do you want to try it?"

"Sure," they all called, and the baby who did not even know what they were talking about, kept repeating, "Soor--soor," with moist pink mouth.

"All right. You are to lie down on the grass over there--face downward--and eyes shut tight--until I say, ready."

The three threw themselves on the grass with excited chuckling, and the baby tripped happily over all their plump legs.

Laura reached in the pocket of her pink house dress and took out Uncle Harry Wentworth's dollar. She looked at it a little ruefully for a moment, lying there in the palm of her hand, and then she threw it far out into the pasture. For an instant she saw the bright flash of its circling, and then it settled into the brown streaked grass curing for the hay barn.

"All right," she called, "game's ready."

They hopped up and came for instructions.

"Out in the pasture," she told them, "is one of the most valuable things in the whole world. You're to look all around the pasture and find what you think is the most valuable thing out there, and then come to tell us when I call."

For a long time they ran around the pasture in search of this most important thing, shouting to each other in the excitement of the hunt.

"Hoo--hoo . . . time's up," Laura called.

They all came racing in.

"I'm ready . . ."

"So'm I . . ."

"So'm I . . ."

"Well, who goes first . . . the oldest or the ladies?" Laura asked. And because they were very normal youngsters, they all crowded around with vociferous:

"Me first! . . ."

"No--me!"

"Me!"

"We'll begin at the top then, Billy . . . what do *you* think . . . What did you find, that was the most valuable thing out there in the pasture?"

"The tree . . ." Billy said unhesitatingly, "the big cottonwood tree that sits in the middle where the cows come for shade and where we play. Dad told me your Grandfather Deal planted a whole row for a windbreak . . . and it's the last one from a seedling of that old windbreak. It stands there so old and nice and shady . . . it made me think of the verses you made us learn, about:

"Poems are made by fools like me,
But only God can make a tree.

I'll bet it's the tree, Mother. Is it?"

"Maybe," Laura smiled. "And Phyllis?"

"Mine's a meadow lark, Mother. There's a nest down in the grass right by a post. I *love* meadow larks. It must be that . . . Mother, for can you think how it would be, to never, *never* hear a meadow lark sing again, when it's all nice in the morning and summer? It's the meadow lark, isn't it, Mother?"

"Maybe. And what's yours, Jane?"

Jane, who had one hand over her mouth and was jumping up and down with smothered glee, said through her fingers, "You never could guess . . ." and then removing her hand, shouted at the top of her voice: *"The Baby.* It's true . . . Mother, he *was* out there. . . . He ran out once, and when I saw him toddling toward me, I knew right away it was the baby."

The baby, seeing he was the center of all admiration, suddenly became shy and ran to his mother and hid his face in her neck.

There were tears in Laura's eyes. "Well, well," she said. "Trees, birds, babies . . . what lovely, valuable things you found. You were *all* right. Now we must go up to the house and get Father's supper . . . How do muffins sound to you?"

"With raisins, Mother?"

"Yes, with raisins, Mother."

"Just stuffed with 'em, Mother."

They all crowded around her, while the baby rode up on her arm.

Allen came up from the field swinging along in his giant stride. "Where's the parade going?" he called, and came up to them and took the baby.

They all went into the house, and ate muffins. And night came and other days. And the sun shone and the rain fell. The hay was cut and hauled to the barn and the pasture plowed. And Uncle Harry Wentworth's dollar was turned deep under the sod. But though the sun shone on it and the rain fell, nothing ever came from it,--*not a green thing nor a singing thing nor a human soul.*

www.ingramcontent.com/pod-product-compliance
Lightning Source LLC
Chambersburg PA
CBHW051431130726
47987CB00005B/1997